A RAMAZ DONA.

CW00392591

NO WAY
BACK

AJ LIDDLE

ISBN: 978-1-8381911-3-9

For Kirsty and Ross

Victory to your power, look down on them.
They are small, those whom you make suffer.

— Iavnana (Lullaby) Anonymous

ALSO BY AJ LIDDLE

No Harm Done (A Ramaz Donadze Thriller)

PROLOGUE

How long had she been here? Three days in Tbilisi, four or five in Georgia? She'd lost track of time but knew she had to get out. The other two girls wouldn't listen, still choosing to believe the lies. Veronika had stopped believing the first time she'd been raped.

She lay on the narrow bed, feigning sleep. Streetlights shone through thin, badly fitted curtains, throwing faint light on the other girls lying huddled under foul blankets. She eased herself off the grubby mattress, its worn springs protesting as she stood. She held her breath, listening to the man who had raped her the second time—the guard. Later, he had made her bring him food and wine as he lay, slumped on the sofa, gaping at an English television programme, the excitable presenters gushing about fast cars in dubbed Georgian. He was snoring now, deep in an alcohol-induced stupor.

'What are you doing?' Anzhela, woken from shallow sleep, whispered from the other side of the room.

Veronika held her finger to her lips, urging silence, then crossed to her bed and knelt beside her. She glanced across the room. The Georgian girl lay still and silent. 'I told you—I'm leaving. Come with me,' she spoke into Anzhela's ear.

'I can't. What would we do? Where would we go? Stay—it'll get better.'

'You know it won't,' Veronika said, watching Anzhela's face in the dim light as a single tear rolled down her cheek.

'I can't...'

'Then tell them you didn't hear me leaving—they might believe you.'

Veronika knew that she'd be punished if caught. She stood and walked out of the bedroom and into the hall, pausing at the open lounge door to watch the guard. His shaved, sweaty head had fallen onto his barrel chest and drool trickled from his open mouth. Half-eaten food, a rank overflowing ashtray, empty wine bottles and a glass tumbler littered the area around him. *Pig*, she thought, fantasising about lifting a bottle and smashing it over his head.

She moved to the apartment door and drew back the security bolts. She told herself that the metal-on-metal squeal wasn't as shrill as it sounded to her. The door key had been left in the lock and that, thankfully, clicked open. She left the apartment and eased the door shut, trying to control her breathing, her heart pounding.

A man stepped from the shadows as she reached the foot of the stairs. He was tall and heavily built, his hands deep in his hoodie pockets, his face and head obscured by the hood. He must have been waiting for her as she crossed the hallway. She stumbled backwards as he moved towards her, his hands coming out of his pockets.

'Please, don't,' she whispered.

A second man said something in Georgian. He stayed in the shadows, watching her for a moment before speaking again, this time in accented Russian, 'Go home. Go home now.'

The first man returned his hands to his pockets and took a half-step back. Veronika ran for the exit, brushing by him—his form solid, immoveable and terrifying. She turned as she rounded the door and saw two figures climbing the stairs. She thought of the girls still in the apartment, crossed herself and fled into the night.

ONE

Lieutenant Ramaz Donadze nodded his thanks to the uniformed cop who moved the control barrier to let him through. He paused inside and looked up and down Gali Street, taking in the mix of run-down and modern low-rise apartment blocks which crowded the narrow road. Faded graffiti sullied the red-brick and cement-washed structures and detracted from what could, at a stretch, be described as the street's charm. The police presence had restricted the road to single file traffic and the driver of an SUV scowled as he manoeuvred his vehicle around the obstruction. Donadze raised a finger to his forehead in mock salute and the driver responded by accelerating away in a cloud of blue smoke. 'Thank you for your patience, sir,' he muttered as he watched the car speed off.

The apartment block was on two levels and in poor condition. A large structural crack ran diagonally from the first to the second level. Render had crumbled and fallen off the walls in several places, exposing brickwork to the weather.

Donadze walked up the worn stairs, avoiding touching the rickety handrail, showed his ID to the cop guarding the apartment door and stepped into the hall. The late autumn warmth had accelerated decomposition and the smell of death was both familiar and shocking. The forensic examiners had completed their work and black magnetic fingerprint powder clung to handles and surfaces. He heard voices and walked into a room where the body of a heavy set man sprawled on a sofa. A narrow stream of dried blood had trickled from the blackened hole in his forehead and his head rested on a halo of blood, grey matter and fragmented bone. Two detectives were standing over the body and they looked up as he entered.

'*Gamarjoba*, Lieutenant. Have you been assigned to this case?' Detective Soso Chichua asked as he hitched his trousers. Chichua was a big man and found it difficult to find clothes that fitted properly.

'Major Gloveli asked me to look. He said you weren't able to speak to him.'

Chichua seemed embarrassed. 'I was going to call him after I got out of here. Captain Nakani had stopped by and I wasn't sure how he would have reacted, what with the Major being retired…'

'That's okay, Soso. To be honest, I thought you might have given me a heads-up as well. Captain Nakani wouldn't have minded that and I'd rather have heard about this first-hand.'

Chichua shrugged. 'Sorry, Ramaz. I would have called, but it was early and you have the baby now—'

'Let *me* worry about my family, Soso.' Donadze turned

to the woman standing beside Chichua. 'Hey, Irina.'

Detective Irina Jaqeli had transferred to the Crime Police from the uniformed branch about a month ago. Donadze hadn't worked with her yet but had heard some grudging praise from his male colleagues. The Crime Police had made a determined effort to recruit more female officers but the gender structure remained predominantly and defiantly male. 'Is this your first murder investigation?'

'Yes, I suppose it is. But I've seen plenty of bodies, of course. Uniform cops have to deal with the dead more than detectives do.'

'Well, you're not in uniform now, Irina—but point taken. Can you talk me through what happened here?' he said.

Jaqeli glanced at Chichua, who shrugged. 'Of course,' she said. 'Soso and I think it's a turf war.' She pointed at the corpse. 'This good looking gentleman was David Glonti, a low level enforcer working for the Kaldani gang.' She seemed to appraise Donadze. 'Soso told me about Dato Kaldani, how he and you took him down last year.'

Donadze glanced at Chichua who coloured, embarrassed to have been caught trying to impress the young female detective. 'Well, it was a team effort but it wouldn't have happened without Soso. You received a commendation for that work, didn't you, Soso?' he added, smiling.

Chichua cleared his throat. 'Thanks Ramaz. The point is, Irina, there was a power vacuum after Kaldani was killed and it took a while and some bloodshed before his cousin, Otar Basilia established control of the gang. Probably shouldn't call it the Kaldani gang now but it's mostly the same players, the same scams.'

'And now someone wants a piece of that action?' Donadze asked.

'We think so. This seems to have been a safe house for girls in transit. There's two in the bedroom—both dead,' Chichua said.

'Not so safe then. You think they were being trafficked?'

'Come and take a look.'

Donadze followed Chichua and Jaqeli through a short hallway into a large, bare room. The frame of the single window was rotted, its glass cracked and greasy. The walls had once been papered but the patterns were now lost, the colours bleached by years of sunlight and neglect. A threadbare rug covered the middle of the room and a bare light bulb hung by a twisted brown cable from a yellowed ceiling rose. Single, cot-like beds were pushed against each of the four walls.

He looked at the bodies. The women had been killed by shots to the head; one was lying on a bed and the other lay splayed beside a cupboard door.

'Have you identified these girls?' Donadze asked.

'We think so,' Jaqeli said. 'We found their ID cards along with fake Georgian passports. IDs for three girls, not two. There's no sign of a Ukrainian called Veronika Boyko, eighteen years old. We think she was in this apartment until quite recently.'

'What about these two?' Donadze said.

Jaqeli pointed to the body by the cupboard. 'Anzhela Bakay. Ukrainian. Nineteen years old.' She turned to the body on the bed. 'Mariam—'

'Alasania. Georgian. Eighteen years old,' Donadze interrupted.

'What's going on, Ramaz?' Chichua snapped.

'She's from Shindisi. Major Gloveli knows her family.'

'So, he didn't trust us to do our jobs properly. Sent you to check on us?'

'He didn't *send* me to do anything. And it's got nothing to do with you. He wants me on this case. He wanted me to see this for myself.'

'Why would he want that, Lieutenant?' Jaqeli asked.

'He knows me, knows how I would react. This was his way of motivating me.'

'So you *will* be assigned to this case,' Chichua said.

'Unless I'm mistaken, I'm already on it. I'll see you back at the station.'

Donadze crossed to the bedroom doorway and looked back into the room, fixing the scene in his memory. Two young women killed—efficiently and dispassionately—before their lives had truly begun. He made them the promise he made to all his murder victims, 'Anzhela, Mariam. I'll find whoever who did this to you.' He nodded his head in affirmation then turned to leave the apartment.

'It looks like you have friends in high places, Ramaz,' Captain Bagrat Nakani said, smiling but with an edge to his voice. He and Donadze were in the commander's office in Mtatsminda Station. Nakani was short with an overdeveloped upper body, the latter a result of heavy gym work and protein supplements and probably compensation for the former, Donadze thought. He had tightened station discipline since being appointed a year ago. Police dress code was enforced and he had made it clear that officers could no longer accept the *courtesies* offered by local businesses such as free meals and coffee. This move was overdue but insufficient by Donadze's estimation. He knew that the station's former commander had been inherently corrupt and suspected that several colleagues continued to accept kickbacks and bribes from the criminals they were hired to police.

At thirty-three, Nakani was a year older than Donadze but both had gone through the Police Academy at the same time. Donadze knew that he had been passed over for promotion in favour of Nakani as punishment for his conduct during a recent murder investigation.

'I doubt if they're friends of mine, Captain,' Donadze said. 'But it certainly looks like Major Gloveli is still well connected.'

Nakani straightened in his chair, the material of his tightly-fitting shirt straining against his shoulders and upper arms. 'I told you to call me Bagrat when we're on our own, Ramaz. You're right. I never served with Gloveli but Colonel Meskhi seems to hold him in high regard.' He paused. 'The Colonel called me this morning and I agreed that you will lead the Gali Street investigation.'

Donadze suppressed a smile at Nakani's insinuation that he had any choice but to agree. 'Yes, sir,' he said, observing Nakani preen while being addressed respectfully. *So much for calling you Bagrat*, he thought.

'And I want Detective Jaqeli to partner with you. It'll be good experience for her.'

'Sir.'

'Do you agree with Chichua? Someone's muscling in on the Kaldani family's empire? The Kutaisi Clan maybe?'

Nakani was referring to one of the two major criminal organisations which made up the Georgian Mafia—the Kutaisi and the Tbilisi Clans. The Kaldani family was affiliated to the Tbilisi Clan. Both clans had developed during Stalin's era and had flourished across the former USSR and into Western Europe, Israel and North America. They were bitter rivals and often resorted to extreme violence to defend and extend their territories. Leaders, such as Otar Basilia, were highly respected within their criminal fraternities and honoured as *thieves-in-law*.

'It looks that way. There was a lot of infighting before Basilia took control and that's left the family weak. So it's a good time to make a move against him. And he's also not fully established authority within his own organisation yet—maybe some don't think he's the man Dato Kaldani was and are looking to switch allegiances. Add all that up and Basilia looks vulnerable.'

'So we can expect him to react.'

'Yes. He'll have to. There's blood in the water and the sharks are circling.'

Nakani smiled. 'Good metaphor.' He paused for a moment, 'But why kill these girls? Why not just run them off?'

'It sends a message of intent and a warning to Basilia's people, lets them see that they could be next. And, of course, the girls in Gali Street were worth money to Basilia. Killing them has hurt him financially—if only a little.'

Nakani shook his head 'What a world we live in.'

Donadze didn't comment and Nakani continued, 'All the girls had fake Georgian passports, even the Ukrainians?'

'Yes, they were probably heading for the EU—one of

the Schengen countries. No entry visas required for Georgians of course.'

'Prostitution?'

'That's where the money is so, probably, yes.'

Nakani looked at Donadze closely. 'I wasn't sure about allowing you to lead this investigation, Ramaz. I know what you're like with certain case types and I don't want you to embarrass me or this station—understood?'

Donadze felt himself colour, surprised to be given such an abrupt and unprovoked warning. 'Yes, understood,' he said.

'Good. This is a great opportunity for you. Run the case by the book, get a result and you could be looking at the promotion you missed. I suggest you find Jaqeli and get started.'

Donadze stood. 'Thanks, *Bagrat*,' he said, watching the Captain's face darken as he stood to leave the office.

'We'll take my car, Irina. See you outside,' Donadze said.

'We're going somewhere?' Jaqeli asked.

'Yes, Shindisi.'

Donadze walked to the station car park, got into his aging BMW and called Major Levan Gloveli. 'You played me, Major,' he said.

Gloveli let out a long sigh. There was a catch in his voice as he spoke. 'I've known that girl all her life. I was at her baptism. Her family are good people, they don't deserve this. I need you to find the men who killed these girls.'

'Just the girls? How about Basilia's thug—Glonti?'

'Is that his name? I don't care about him. The world's a better place without him.'

'I'll have to speak to Mariam's parents. How are they coping?'

'How do you think? Telling them about her was one of the worst things I've ever done. But they believe in God's will—maybe that will give them comfort of sorts.'

'Religion—the opiate of the masses,' Donadze said, paraphrasing Karl Marx.

'Don't knock it, Donadze, not if it helps them cope.'

'Any siblings?'

'A brother, Luca. He's fifteen.'

Donadze paused. 'Major, you know I'll do my best to find the killers. But when I do find them, they'll go to trial. There can't be any vigilante action—not this time.'

There was silence for a long moment. 'Did you really have to say that, Donadze?' Gloveli eventually replied, his voice tight.

'I hope not.'

Gloveli said nothing and Donadze continued, 'What did Colonel Meskhi say when you asked him to assign me to this case?'

'It wasn't difficult. He wants a result and he knows you're his best chance of getting it.'

'Really? I thought he was going to sack me the last time we spoke.'

'He should have sacked you—I would have. I warned you, didn't I?'

'Yes, but I'd probably do the same again.'

'And you accuse me of being a vigilante? Listen, Ramaz, I know I've pulled strings to get you to lead this investigation but I don't want you to become damaged by it. Do your best but don't take any of it home with you.'

Donadze noticed Jaqeli scanning the car park, trying to find him, and he bleeped his horn to attract her attention. 'I need to go,' he said.

'Come and see me after you've spoken to the parents.'

'Yes, okay.'

Jaqeli opened the passenger door and got into the car. 'So, we're going to Shindisi,' she said.

'Yes, we need as much background on Mariam as we can get. Who she mixed with, places she went, anything odd her parents might have noticed.'

'So we're partners on this case?'

'Yes, weren't you told?'

'No, I wasn't. What about Soso? I've been partnered with him since I got out of uniform.'

'I assumed everyone was in the loop. I'll speak to Soso later today. He'll be okay.'

She pushed her seat back and stretched her legs as Donadze manoeuvred out of the car park.

'Since we're going to be working together, why don't you tell me something about yourself,' he said.

'Good idea—but you go first.'

Donadze refrained from reminding her of their relative seniorities. 'There's not much to tell.'

'Well, I know you have a baby,' she said, using her thumb to indicate the baby seat installed behind her.

'I'm amazed that you picked up such a subtle clue, Irina.'

'Yes, I thought that would impress you. So you're married?'

'Not yet. Eka is six months old. Tamuna's her mum.'

'You're not from Tbilisi,' she stated.

Donadze paused. 'No, Abkhazia…'

'Sorry, I knew that already. I'd heard about your family…'

'It's okay. I was luckier than some.'

'It's not something you like to talk about?'

'Not usually. Anyway, it's your turn. Where are *you* from? And why join the police?'

Jaqeli shrugged. 'Born and brought up in the city, bachelor's degree from TSU. The police were targeting recruitment of female officers and I thought I'd help smash their glass ceiling. Trained at the Academy then a couple of years in uniform.'

'And has the glass ceiling been smashed yet?'

'It's completely intact and well protected by most of your colleagues.'

'Your colleagues as well, Irina. What did you study at TSU?'

Jaqeli turned in her seat. 'Psychology,' she said, smiling.

Donadze raised his eyebrows. 'Glad I asked,' he said.

'Don't worry, I always get that reaction.'

The traffic was light and they quickly cleared the city streets to take the steep, winding road leading to the high hills above Tbilisi. 'We'll be there soon,' Donadze said.

TWO

❖

Donadze bumped his car onto the rough ground beside the property's outer wall and he and Jaqeli took the dirt path to the front door, scattering hens and chasing off a friendly goat as they went. The house was typical of the traditional build found in many rural areas and it reminded Donadze of his childhood home in Abkhazia. Set in about a hectare of fertile land, he knew that the Alasania family would be self-sufficient in fruit, vegetables, milk, cheese, eggs, chicken and goat meat. The vines growing over the door arch and in the south-facing borders would ensure that the family had sufficient wine for everyday consumption and for the *supras* celebrating special events. Repairs had been made to the property over a period of many years with materials which were mis-matched and not in keeping with any colour scheme. Donadze thought the general effect was patchy and a little dilapidated—but not without charm. The contrast with apartment living in Tbilisi was stark and he inhaled the clean, cool air gratefully.

Nodar Alasania opened the front door before Donadze could knock. '*Gamarjoba*,' he said. 'Levan told me you'd be coming.' He shook hands with Donadze, nodded to Jaqeli then led the detectives into the sitting room. 'My wife,' he said needlessly, gesturing towards a woman in her late thirties or early forties who was dressed in a faded black dress, her hair covered by a silk scarf. She was laying out food and drinks for her guests as traditions of hospitality required, her head bowed. She wiped her hands on the apron tied around her waist and took Donadze's hand briefly, her touch like that of a fragile bird's, he thought. Her eyes were red and swollen as she looked at Jaqeli.

'I'm Irina Jaqeli, Mrs Alasania—we're so sorry for your loss.'

'Thank you, please sit down,' she whispered, indicating the chairs placed around a large dining table.

Donadze and Jaqeli sat facing Alasania, his wife standing nervously behind him, wringing her apron.

Jaqeli smiled at the woman. 'Please take a seat, Mrs Alasania,' she said.

Donadze nodded his thanks as he was passed plates of bread and cheese. 'Your son, Luca?' he asked.

'At school. He didn't want to go but we thought it was for the best,' Alasania said.

'Yes, I understand but we will want to speak to him.' He took out his phone and opened the memo app. 'I'm going to record this interview if that's okay?' he said, noting Alasania's shrug of agreement. 'When did you last see Mariam?'

'Last Friday, about six in the evening. Just before she left to take the bus,' Alasania said.

'To go to Tbilisi?'

'Yes.'

'On her own?'

'Yes, she said she was meeting friends there, was going for a meal and would be home by eleven.'

'She *said* she was meeting friends?'

'Yes, our daughter lied to us,' Alasania said.

'Don't say that,' his wife pleaded. 'She's a good girl, never gave us any trouble. She must have had her reasons for telling us that.'

Donadze looked away as a tear ran down Alasania's face. 'I know she's a good girl,' he said, pulling his hand away when Jaqeli touched it.

Jaqeli glanced at Donadze and picked up the questioning. 'How do you know Mariam wasn't meeting friends?' she asked.

'We spoke to them.' Alasania got up and crossed the room to a dresser where he picked up a book. He placed it in front of Jaqeli. 'And we found this. It was under her mattress. We weren't meant to see it.'

The book cover was pink and diamante. Jaqeli opened it by its edges, revealing pages covered in handwritten text and multi-coloured doodles.

'Her journal,' Alasania said. 'It looks like she had a boyfriend and was meeting him in Tbilisi.'

'Can we take this?' Jaqeli asked.

'Yes, why not?'

'But we'll get it back?' Mrs Alasania blurted.

'Yes, of course… Mariam mentions her boyfriend in the journal?' Jaqeli said.

'Yes, he's called Beso.'

'No family name?'

'Just Beso.'

'And you don't know him?'

'No,' he said as his wife shook her head.

'How did Mariam behave recently. Did you notice any changes?'

'No, nothing,' Alasania said.

'Yes,' his wife contradicted. She glanced at her husband before continuing. 'Not something a father would notice, but I did. She was always a quiet girl, respectful. Helped me in the house and with the animals. But she became moody, dressed differently, wore more makeup than usual. It worried me a bit but I put it down to her age. I did think that there might be a boy in the picture but she denied that when I asked.'

Alasania was staring at his wife. 'You didn't say anything to me…'

'There was nothing *to* say. I thought it was just something girls go through…'

'None of this was your fault,' Donadze said. He paused before continuing, 'We'll have to speak to Mariam's friends. You have their names and contact details?'

Alasania crossed the room, came back with a small address book and read out two names and phone numbers. 'Girls she was at school with. They're in Tbilisi now.'

'Is there anything else you think we should know?' Donadze said. 'Anything that—'

'What was my daughter doing in that apartment, Lieutenant?' Alasania interrupted. 'What happened to her? Did someone hurt her, you know what I mean, was she…'

Donadze glanced at Jaqeli before speaking, 'We think that—'

'Mr Alasania, Mariam did not want to be in that apartment,' Jaqeli interrupted. 'She was tricked into going there. She wasn't there for long and, in the end, she didn't suffer.'

Alasania stared into Jaqeli's face then nodded and dropped his head into his hands. 'Please God,' he mumbled.

Donadze stopped the recording and put his phone back into his pocket. 'I think that's enough for now,' he said.

'You *will* find who did this to my daughter,' Mrs Alasania demanded.

Jaqeli reached across the table and took the distressed woman's hand. 'Mrs Alasania, I promise we'll do our very—'

'Yes, we *will* find them,' Donadze said.

Donadze and Jaqeli left the house and walked to the garden gate. 'Let's speak to Major Gloveli,' he said. 'It's not far, we can leave the car.'

'I'm sorry for interrupting you back there. It's just—'

'Don't apologise. These people are devastated and they needed to hear you say that Mariam hadn't suffered.'

'Even though, in their hearts, they know that she had…'

'Whatever helps them cope.'

They walked down a dusty street past small shops and a bakery, Donadze's mouth watering from the aroma of freshly baked bread. Gloveli's house was smaller and more dilapidated than the Alasania's. He was in his garden digging up potatoes with a fork as Donadze opened the gate, the hinges squealing and causing him to look up. '*Gamarjoba*, Major. Your hinges could use some oil,' Donadze said.

Gloveli was in his mid-sixties but looked older, Donadze thought. As a senior police officer, he had always maintained a smart appearance but now, retired and with his wife dead, he seemed happy to dress for work in his garden and saw no need to keep his white stubble or bushy eyebrows in check.

'You've come to advise me on home maintenance, Donadze? No need, I like to hear people coming.' Gloveli had been attacked in his home a year ago by the Kaldani gang. Observing the older man walking stiffly towards them, Donadze felt guilty, knowing that the assault had left lasting damage. 'You must be Detective Jaqeli. Sorry, I can't shake your hand,' he said, smiling and holding his soil encrusted hands up for inspection.

Jaqeli strode forward and took his hand in both of hers. 'Irina Jaqeli. It's an honour to meet you, Major. We didn't serve together but you're remembered with great affection and respect at Mtatsminda Station.'

The old policeman blinked. 'Well, that's kind of you to say so, Irina. I'm not sure it's warranted…'

'It's not,' Donadze said. 'Can we go inside, Major?'

'No chance of becoming conceited with Donadze around, eh, Irina? What did you do wrong to end up being partnered with him?'

Jaqeli smiled but made no comment.

'Let's go in. Donadze, bring my potatoes.'

Donadze picked up the basket and followed Gloveli and Jaqeli into the house.

'Give me a minute to wash my hands,' Gloveli said, running the single, cold water tap in the small cooking area. 'Take a seat. Donadze, pour the wine.'

Donadze picked up three glasses from a cabinet and

selected a plastic bottle from the collection on the stone floor. He sat beside Jaqeli and poured the wine as Gloveli joined them, placing a bowl of hazelnuts on the table.

Gloveli raised his glass and saluted his guests, '*Gaumarjos*.' He sniffed the wine before taking a generous sip. 'Ah, that's good, best harvest I've had for years.' He put his glass down. 'You've spoken to the Alasanias?' he said.

'Yes, they couldn't tell us very much. It looks like Mariam was meeting with a boy or man called Beso. We'll try to track him down, maybe her friends know who he is, but we don't have a family name yet. What's your take on this, Major?'

'It's exactly what it seems,' Gloveli said angrily. 'Mariam and the Ukrainian girls were caught up in a trafficking scheme, held in Gali Street to be made drug-dependent and desensitised to providing sex-on-demand. They were going to be shipped to the EU as prostitutes to make money for the Kaldani gang. Except, someone didn't want that to happen and they were put down like dogs!'

'Sorry, Major. I know this is hard for you.'

'Don't patronise me, Donadze. It doesn't matter how *I* feel,' Gloveli snapped. He sat back, sighed and took a sip of wine. 'Sorry Ramaz. You didn't deserve that—I'm spending too much time on my own, getting grumpy…'

'That's okay, Major but, for the record, you've always been grumpy,' Donadze said, straight-faced.

Gloveli shook his head. 'Maybe, but I had plenty of provocation, don't you think? Anyway, what's your plan?'

'What do you think, Irina?' Donadze asked.

Jaqeli paused for a moment as she gathered her thoughts. 'Well, we have some leads we'll follow up. We'll speak to

Mariam's friends, see if they know anything. We'll try to track down the boyfriend, if that's really what he was. Try to find the Ukrainian girl who got away—Veronika Boyko. Check who owned the Gali Street property, ask neighbours if they saw anything. We'll apply pressure where we can, see if we can get anyone to open up. Apart from that…'

'Do you have any thoughts, Major?' Donadze asked.

'Yes, but it's not something you'll find palatable. Speak to Otar Basilia. He's an animal— but try to see things from his warped perspective. The Kaldani gang is under attack and he can use all the help he can get. As a supposed *thief-in-law* he can't be seen to be openly helping the police. But I know these rodents. If he thinks that'll give him an edge, he'll tell you what he knows.'

'Thanks, Major, good advice.'

'I still have my moments. How's my goddaughter and Tamuna?'

'Both well, I'll bring them to see you soon.'

'Do that.' Gloveli stood and lifted the wine glasses and bottle. 'When I was in charge, my detectives didn't sit around drinking wine all day. I suggest you two get back to work,' he said, turning his back and limping to the sink.

Donadze stood. 'Let's go Irina,' he said.

'Are you here for Mariam?'

Donadze and Jaqeli were returning to his car and stopped as the boy stepped out of the doorway. He was slim and slightly taller than Donadze. His hair was unusually fair and long and fell lankly over his forehead. He had delicate features and his upper lip and cheeks sported a light adolescent growth. A branded sports bag was slung over his shoulder and he appeared to be dressed for school.

'Luca?' Donadze said.

'You're the detectives who came about Mariam?'

'Yes. I'm Ramaz, this is Irina. Do you want to go back to your house to talk?'

'No, there's a playing field at the end of the road. Could you bring your car and meet me there?'

'You're fifteen, aren't you Luca? Your parents should be with you,' Jaqeli said.

'We'll see you in ten minutes, Luca,' Donadze said.

The detectives watched the boy tug the hood of his uniform sweatshirt over his head and shuffle away, stooped and scuffing the pavement with his dusty trainers. 'Let's get the car,' Donadze said, continuing to walk.

'What about his parents?' Jaqeli said as she caught up with him.

'It's obvious that he doesn't want to talk in front of them.'

'But even so…'

'Let's see what he has to say.'

Luca was waiting at the playing field entrance as Donadze pulled up. Jaqeli had taken a seat in the back and he lowered the passenger window. 'Get in,' he said.

Luca opened the door. 'Could you drive out of the village, please,' he said, slumping in his seat and pulling his hood further over his face.

They drove for a few hundred metres. 'Up ahead. Stop there.'

Donadze pulled into a cut in the road. It was large

enough to contain two cars if parked with consideration, shaded and, judging by the litter which was strewn around, used by motorists taking a break on their journeys.

Donadze applied the brake, stopped the engine and turned to face the boy. 'We're very sorry for what happened to your sister, Luca. Can you help us to find who did it?'

Luca continued to stare ahead, remaining silent.

'Could you look at me, please,' Donadze said.

The boy paused a moment, then turned in his seat.

'Your hood please, Luca.'

'Okay, okay,' he snapped as he tugged the hood clear of his head. He glanced at Donadze then looked away. 'Sorry…' he said.

'Nothing to be sorry about, Luca,' Jaqeli spoke from the back. 'Why didn't you want to speak in front of your parents?'

'There's things they don't know about Mariam, things they don't need to know. There's no point in making it worse for them.'

'What sort of things?' Jaqeli asked, her voice low, even and empathetic.

'She was meeting someone, doing things they wouldn't have liked. She was going to leave home to be with him.'

'She told you that?'

'Yes.'

'Who was she meeting?'

'Someone in Tbilisi.'

'A man? What was his name?'

'Beso. He worked in a bar in Tbilisi.'

'What was she doing that your parents wouldn't have liked?'

Donadze watched as the boy coloured. 'Was she sleeping with Beso?' he asked.

He didn't answer.

'It's okay, Luca, you can tell us,' Jaqeli said.

'Yes, she was sleeping with him,' Luca blurted. 'She told me that she loved him. That they were going to get married. He told her that she would be a model, that he would take her to Europe—she wanted to go to Germany.'

'What did *you* think about that,' she asked.

'I didn't believe it. She's pretty enough but she could never be a model. Not tall enough, not thin enough. I tried to get her to see sense, but she wouldn't listen, just got angry. Angry with *me*.' He paused. 'I just wanted her to be safe, not to do anything stupid. I thought about telling Mum and Dad—but I couldn't. They wouldn't have understood, they might even have gone to the priest.'

'Did you ever meet this Beso?'

'No, she always saw him in Tbilisi. But she had pictures on her phone.'

Donadze glanced at Jaqeli and she shook her head—no phone was recovered from the crime scene.

'Can you describe him?' Jaqeli asked.

Luca shrugged. 'He looked okay, I suppose. About twenty, probably. Seemed to be a little bit taller than Mariam, so kind of short I suppose. And thin. I remember he had dark hair, quite long,' he said, putting a hand to his shoulder before continuing, 'And he was wearing a suit, so he probably likes clothes.'

'Thanks Luca, that's very useful. We'll get you to help us make a facial composite. It's a drawing done by computer and will let us see what Beso looks like.'

'You think *Beso* killed Mariam?'

'At this stage, we just need to find this man and ask him some questions,' Jaqeli said.

'Did Mariam say which bar Beso worked in?' Donadze asked.

'No, it was just a bar. I need to go now, my dad will be wondering where I am.'

Donadze looked at Jaqeli. She shook her head, she had nothing else to ask. 'Take my card. Call me if there's anything else you think we should know,' he said.

Luca blinked back more tears. 'I could have stopped this. Could have told my dad what was happening…'

Donadze put his hand on the boy's shoulder. 'No, Luca—you're not to blame.'

'How would you know?' Luca snapped and turned in his seat to push the door open, pulling his hood over his head as he scuffed his way home.

Jaqeli took the vacated seat. 'Are you okay, Ramaz?'

'Let's get back to Tbilisi,' he said.

THREE

Donadze was tired. Eka's first tooth was coming through and she was letting everyone know about it. His mother had, of course, heard the baby crying and had wanted, really wanted, to take her. She had traditional views on the roles of the sexes and Donadze knew that she didn't approve of fathers being hands on with their children, although she had the good manners not to say as much. It had taken all Donadze's willpower to refuse—it wouldn't have sat well with Tamuna but, in any event, being awake and soothing your baby at five in the morning was, in its own way, special. Or so Donadze had told himself. It was after seven now. Eka had been fed by Tamuna and was now back in her cot, oblivious to the devastation she was wreaking.

'You should have let me take her, *Ramazi*,' his mother said as she walked into the kitchen area. 'Let me get you something to eat.'

Donadze knew better than to refuse. 'Thanks, *Deda*,'

he said, topping up his coffee mug and adding extra sugar for energy.

She laid bread, cheese and cooked meats on the breakfast bar. 'Come here and eat.'

Donadze put his mug down and perched on one of the tall stools.

'How are things with you and Tamuna, Ramaz?' she said. The early morning light was shining on her face, accentuating the lines which Donadze hadn't noticed until her heart attack just over a year ago.

'Fine, *Deda*, why do you ask?'

'No reason, really.'

'Okay,' he said, knowing she had more to say.

She busied herself wiping down surfaces before finally blurting, 'Ramaz, I want you to tell me the truth. Are you and Tamuna still happy for me to live here?' Tamuna and Donadze had worried about her being on her own after her heart attack and had persuaded her to move in with them.

'Of course we are. I told you, it was Tamuna's idea, but I want you here as well. And anyway, you're helping *us*— who could take better care of Eka when Tamuna is back at work?'

'The baby's only six months old, Ramaz. She's too young not have her mother around. You know, I've got some money put aside if Tamuna wants to stay off work a little longer…'

'It's her choice, *Deda*. And it's not about money.'

'What's not about money?' Tamuna said as she came into the living room.

'I've just been telling my mother that it's time she went home.'

28

'You're not that brave, Donadze,' Tamuna said, smiling.

'You don't have to be brave when you carry a gun,' he said, winking at his mother.

Donadze's phone vibrated in his pocket. Jaqeli was calling. 'Irina?' he said.

'Can you come to the station—now?'

'What's happening?'

'Our missing girl—Veronika Boyko. She's here.'

'On my way.' He ended the call and returned the phone to his pocket. 'Got to go,' he said.

'Who's Irina, *Ramazi*?' his mother asked with studied lack of guile.

'My other girlfriend,' Donadze replied, then caught the piece of bread that Tamuna threw at him. He kissed her and his mother, walked to the bedroom and stood over Eka for a moment, watching the slow rise and fall of her tiny chest and listening to her almost inaudible breathing. He felt his heart swell. 'What have you done to me?' he whispered, then turned and left the apartment.

Donadze manoeuvred his car out of the apartment block's basement car park, its clutch slipping on the steep ramp taking him to surface level, noxious blue smoke belching from the worn and over-revved engine. He resolved once again to replace the aging BMW, its odometer being well passed the two-hundred thousand kilometres mark. He eased onto Kandelaki Street, trying not to think about how congested the roads would be. He considered using the car's blue lights and siren but decided against it, judging that they would make little difference to his journey time but would, nevertheless, add to the chaos and the cacophony that constituted driving in Tbilisi.

He arrived at Mtatsminda Station and hurried into the building, feeling the early-morning chill bite through his thin jacket. Jaqeli was in the detectives' bureau speaking to Misha Arziani. He had been promoted to lieutenant recently, a well-deserved recognition of his performance, Donadze thought, but resented by many as he was still only in his late twenties. A keen sportsman, Arziani was, unusually for Georgian men, teetotal and a non-smoker. He was always smartly dressed and carefully groomed and Donadze had noticed he had many female admirers.

'Misha, Irina,' Donadze nodded to the two detectives, observing them self-consciously separate and wondering if their relationship was strictly professional.

'Hey, Ramaz. Not too early for you, is it?' Arziani joked.

'Where's the girl? Did she come in by herself?'

'Interview Room One. Yes, she came in by herself,' Jaqeli said. 'Asked at Reception for the "big policeman from Gali Street." The desk officer guessed she meant Soso and he called us both.'

'Have you spoken to her yet?'

Jaqeli shrugged. 'Just to introduce myself. Will we need an interpreter? She only speaks Ukrainian and Russian.'

'Your Russian isn't good enough?' Donadze asked. Russian was the official second language when Georgia was a Soviet republic but younger people were now more likely to speak English.

'It's reasonable. How about you?'

'I think we'll be okay.'

'I'll see you later,' Arziani said, smiling at Jaqeli, who smiled back before averting her eyes, her cheeks colouring.

Donadze looked at both his colleagues in turn. 'Okay, Irina,' he said. 'Let's see what Veronika can tell us.'

Donadze knocked on the interview room door and entered, followed by Jaqeli.

Veronika was sitting by the black, metallic table. She was dressed in blue denims with a white cotton shirt and a short black leather jacket. Her shoulder-length, dark brown hair was dishevelled and she looked tired and anxious. A mug of coffee and a plate with biscuits had been placed in front of her. She flashed a tight smile as Donadze spoke to her in Russian. 'Hello, Veronika. I'm Lieutenant Ramaz Donadze. You've met my colleague, Irina Jaqeli?'

'Yes,' she said, offering Jaqeli another tight smile.

Donadze and Jaqeli sat on the opposite side of the table. 'Before we begin, do you need to see a doctor?' he asked.

'No, I'm okay.'

'Well, depending on what you tell us today, we may ask a doctor to look at you, possibly take some photos. Would that be okay?'

She shrugged, 'I don't know, maybe.'

'All right. Let's see how we get on. Are you happy to speak to us now?'

'Let's just get this over with.'

Donadze used a remote control to switch on the recording equipment and opened the interview, noting the people present. 'Please state your name, age and date of birth.'

She cleared her throat before speaking, 'Veronika

Boyko, I'm eighteen, I was born on the second of June, two-thousand and three.'

'You are a Ukrainian national?'

'Yes. We live in Mykolaiv.'

'You have family there?'

'Mother and sister. Dad died, three years ago now—shipyard accident.'

'I'm sorry.' Veronika didn't respond and Donadze continued. 'You asked to speak to the detectives who attended a crime scene at twelve, Gali Street?'

'Yes, I saw your friend there,' she said, nodding at Jaqeli.

'Had you been staying at that apartment?'

'Yes, for a few days. After I arrived in Georgia.'

'When did you leave?'

'You know when—yesterday morning.'

'But then you went back?'

'Yes, to check on Anzhela and the Georgian girl.'

'Anzhela Bakay?'

Veronika nodded. 'She should have left with me…'

'I'm sorry. Was she a friend?'

'Not really, we only met in Georgia. Turned out we had the same *boyfriend* though.'

'Tell us about him.'

Veronika looked down, her hair falling over her face. 'His name was Antin…'

'Antin…?' Donadze said.

'Antin Honchar. Or at least, that's what he told me. And I believed *everything* he told me. I really thought he loved me. He was the first boy I had ever been with, you know?'

'Yes, we understand,' Jaqeli said. 'Please continue, Veronika.'

'He was sweet at first, brought me flowers, presents, we had lovely romantic meals… But, that changed, he changed…' Veronika paused then lifted her head, fixing her gaze on Jaqeli and avoiding eye contact with Donadze. 'He wasn't as kind as before—asked me to do things I didn't like. Sometimes he was rough. He warned me not to speak to anyone, not even Mum. He said she would stop us seeing each other, that he'd have to go away. He said he had to protect me so he took my phone, deleted my texts, contacts, all my social media…'

'You said he was rough?' Jaqeli said.

Veronika looked down, her eyes fixed on the tabletop. Jaqeli took a packet of paper tissues from her pocket, leaned over and passed them to the girl. 'Take your time,' she said.

She dabbed her eyes and nose, putting the used tissue into her jacket pocket. 'Yes, sometimes, when we made love. Other times, he'd get angry and hit me—but never my face. He'd apologise, promise it would never happen again—but it did. He said that it was living in Ukraine that made him behave that way, that there was no future for us there, that we should get out, go somewhere in Europe. He said we'd get good jobs, make enough money to get married… And I believed him, couldn't see what was happening…'

'You were trusting, Veronika. It's a lot more common than you would think,' Jaqeli said.

'I know, but I didn't think it would happen to me. I thought he loved me.'

'So what *did* happen?'

Veronika shook her head. 'One day, he was very

excited, said he'd talked to someone who could get us into Europe. He said it would be expensive but that he'd find the money because it was the only way we could be together... The thought of running off scared me but, to be honest, there wasn't a lot of reason to stay. Mum had changed after Dad died, lost interest in most things. I'm close to my sister but Antin said we'd send for her once we'd settled, that it would be good for her as well.'

'So you agreed to go?' Jaqeli asked.

'Yes, I loved him, trusted him. He said it was the only way for us.'

'How did you get to Georgia?'

'I was hidden on a truck, ferry from Chornomorsk to Poti then driven to Tbilisi.'

'Just you?'

'Yes, Antin said we had to travel separately, that he'd meet me in Tbilisi.'

'And you were taken to Gali Street?'

'Yes, Anzhela and the Georgian girl were already there.'

'What happened at the apartment?'

Veronika took another tissue and dabbed her eyes and nose again. 'There was a man in the apartment, he was there to stop us leaving, I think. I asked him when Antin would arrive. "Soon," he said. "Don't worry." But then he laughed. I thought that was strange but told myself everything would be okay once Antin came for me. But, of course, he never did come. He'll still be in Ukraine, lying and tricking other stupid girls like me...'

'Tell us more about the apartment,' Jaqeli said.

'It was horrible... The first night there, the man who was guarding us took a phone call. He got nervous, shouted a lot. We were told to dress up. Put on makeup. Someone came over, his boss, I think. We were lined up in the lounge. He took the Georgian girl into a bedroom, hit her when she wouldn't go with him—we could hear them. I never knew her name…'

'Her name was Mariam Alasania. What did this man look like?'

'Ugly. Older than you, I think, maybe about forty. About your height, but fat. Big shoulders—strong.'

'Anything else?'

She hesitated. 'It was his nose I noticed most, bigger than it should be, you know, swollen and red —horrible looking.'

Donadze looked across to Jaqeli. She nodded— Veronika had described Otar Basilia. 'We'll take a full description later. So this man came to the apartment, chose Mariam then raped her, is that correct?'

'Yes.'

'What happened next?'

'It happened to all of us after that, twice for me, different men, one was the guard. I don't know how often it happened to Anzhela and Mariam.'

'You were raped twice?'

'There was nothing I could do, no one who could help…'

'How did you escape?'

'The guard got drunk, fell asleep.'

Donadze paused, observing the distressed girl. 'You've been very brave, Veronika,' he said. 'But you've been through a lot. I'd like to get a doctor to—'

'You said you went back to Gali Street to check on the

other girls,' Jaqeli interrupted. 'Why did you do that?'

'Because of the men.'

'What men?'

'The men who stopped me on the stairs then let me go…'

'You saw these men as you were leaving the apartment?' Donadze asked.

'Yes, two of them, waiting. They were going to kill me, I knew it.'

'But they let you go?'

'Yes, one was in charge. I think he told the other one to leave me then he told me to go home.'

'Why would he do that, Veronika?'

'It sounds crazy, but I can still hear his voice. It seemed kind, somehow. Like he felt sorry for me, that he didn't want me to die…'

FOUR

'So, Lieutenant, Detective, what have you learned so far?' Captain Nakani was leaning back in his chair, his hands behind his head and flexing his impressive biceps—almost certainly for Jaqeli's benefit, Donadze thought.

'Early days, sir,' Donadze said. 'These girls were certainly being trafficked to the EU, all tricked by supposed boyfriends and, we think, all being groomed for prostitution.'

'And you spoke to one of the girls?'

'Yes, Veronika Boyko. She realised what was happening and got out of the apartment. We think she saw the killers. Not a great description but better than nothing.'

'What is it with these women?' Nakani said, shaking his head.

'Sir?' Jaqeli said.

'I mean, why do they fall for these fairy tales. Whisked away by the love of their lives to live happily ever after in the land of plenty? Come on, you must be asking yourself the same thing, Detective. How can they be so naive?'

'If you're asking *my* opinion, sir, these women are carefully selected, their insecurities exploited. They're manipulated, controlled, isolated. By the time they know or suspect what's happening to them, they have nothing, nobody. They clearly think we, the police, won't help and that's something we should put right.'

Nakani's hands were now in his lap and his lips were tight. 'You seem well informed on the subject, Detective.'

'There's a training module available, sir—human trafficking—it's very informative.'

'Training—wish I had the time,' Nakani said, forcing a smile. He looked at his watch. 'Speaking of time, I've a meeting with Colonel Meskhi at HQ. I'll tell him you have a lead and you're confident you'll be bringing charges soon. Okay?'

'We certainly hope so, sir,' Donadze said.

'Let's try for something a bit more positive than that, please.' He looked at his watch again. 'You'd better get back to work. Lieutenant, a word before you go.'

Nakani waited until Jaqeli had left his office. 'I'm sorry if working with Jaqeli is going to create problems for you, Ramaz,' he said.

'Problems, sir?'

'This may be the wrong case for her, she seems to be using it to promote something of a feminist agenda. I wouldn't want it to get in the way of your investigation. And *you* need to get this one right if you're going to salvage your career.'

'Some things are more important than our careers, don't you think, sir?'

'Yes, of course. Anyway, let me know if you *do* have any problems with her.'

'Thank you, sir.'

Donadze left Nakani's office and walked to Jaqeli's desk. Her head was down and she was venting her anger on her keyboard. 'Let's get out of here,' he said.

She pushed the keyboard away but didn't reply.

He waited until she had collected her jacket then followed her as she strode out of the station and through the car park. They got into his car and he started the engine.

'What did Nakani want to talk to you about?' she demanded.

'You—he's worried because he thinks you're a feminist.'

'He should be—because I am.'

'Good. We all need to take a stand sometimes. But my advice? Don't let that define who you are. No one can tell you what to think but try to keep what you say and do under control.'

'Yes, I've heard you're good at that.'

'Well, don't follow my example.' He manoeuvred his car into the congested Tbilisi traffic. 'You didn't ask where we're going,' he said.

'I know where we're going—Shindisi.'

'Psychology, eh? Why did you give it up?'

'Who said I did?' She sat back in the seat and stretched her legs. 'Thanks, Ramaz,' she said after a few minutes.

'Lieutenant, Detective. We weren't expecting you,' Nodar Alasania said.

'Sorry, we should have called ahead. But we won't take up too much of your time.'

'It's not a problem, just that our priest is here.'

Alasania held the door as the detectives walked into the lounge. Mrs Alasania and Luca were sitting on one side of the dining table, the priest on the other. He looked about thirty and was slim, with shoulder length hair, his traditional beard trimmed and tidy. He stood and straightened his cassock, then walked around the table, smiling at the detectives.

'Bless, Father,' Jaqeli said, holding her hands together to receive a blessing.

'May the Lord bless you,' the priest responded, making the sign of the cross and placing his right hand in Jaqeli's for her to kiss. He looked expectantly at Donadze.

'*Gamarjoba*, Father,' Donadze said.

'These are the detectives I was telling you about, Father,' Alasania said.

'I'm Lieutenant Ramaz Donadze. This is Detective Irina Jaqeli.'

'And I'm Zurab Chanturia. I should let you get on with your business.'

'There's no need for Father Chanturia to leave, is there, Lieutenant?' Alasania asked.

'It's your home so your decision,' Donadze said.

'Please stay, Father.'

Mrs Alasania placed additional plates and glasses on the table and gestured for Donadze and Jaqeli to sit.

Alasania took a chair beside the priest. 'How can we help?' he asked.

'We have an update for you and something we'd like to discuss.' Donadze said. He smiled at Luca. 'Could you give us some time alone with your mum and dad? We won't be long.'

'I'm staying,' Luca snapped, throwing himself back in his chair and locking his arms across his chest, his head down and his hair falling over his eyes like a veil.

Alasania shrugged. 'Please go ahead, Lieutenant.'

'Irina?' Donadze said, inviting Jaqeli to speak.

She looked to each family member in turn. 'Well, I want you to know that we are doing everything we can to find the men responsible for what happened to Mariam. And I'm pleased to say that we have made progress. We now know why Mariam was taken to Gali Street.' She paused and looked around the family again. 'I'm sure you've heard of human trafficking, sometimes called modern-day slavery?'

'Slavery?' Mrs Alasania said, her voice small and strained. 'My Mariam was a *slave*?'

'Well, you see—'

'For sex?' Alasania interrupted.

'I'm sorry, yes, we think so...'

'No, she would never have gone along with that, she couldn't—'

'Mr Alasania, it didn't happen,' Jaqeli interrupted.

'Because she died first?'

'Yes, she died before she could be forced into it. I really am sorry.'

Mrs Alasania dropped her head into her hands, her shoulders heaving. Chanturia leaned across the table to rub her arm. 'Be brave, child, no one can hurt your girl now.'

Jaqeli looked at Donadze and he nodded for her to continue. 'Mariam was held in an apartment with two other girls, both Ukrainian, both tricked into coming to Georgia.

One was killed at the same time as Mariam and the other escaped. We talked to her this morning. She gave us a partial description of the men we think are responsible and we will be doing our best to locate them.'

'The Lord will guide you,' Chanturia said.

'Let's hope so, Father. In the meantime, we also want to find this man,' Donadze said, taking a sheet of printed paper from a folder and handing it to Alasania.

'Who's this?' Alasania asked.

'Beso, the man in Mariam's journal.'

'Her boyfriend?'

'He's not what Marian thought he was,' Jaqeli said.

'How do you know that's him?' Mrs Alasania asked.

'We got a good description—from Luca—he's been a great help.'

'Luca!'

'She had pictures on her phone, she showed them to me!' Luca cried, his arms wrapped tightly around his chest again.

'It's thanks to Luca that we'll find this man,' Donadze said. 'Do you recognise him?'

Alasania held the facial composite close, turning it through different angles and holding it to the light, scowling in concentration. 'No,' he said. He handed it to his wife.

'Sorry, no,' she said, returning it to Donadze.

'May I see it?' Chanturia asked.

Donadze handed the composite to the priest. 'Do *you* know this man?'

'No,' he said after a moment. 'But may I keep it? I can ask around, someone in the village might know him.'

'That's not a good idea. If Beso hears that you're

42

making inquiries about him, he'll make the connection and run.'

'Well, it's your choice, Lieutenant. But, if there's one thing we priests understand, it's discretion.'

Donadze hesitated then passed him a business card. 'Keep the composite. Call me if you have any information,' he said.

'Of course,' Chanturia replied with a smile.

'We'll go now,' Donadze said to Alasania. 'Thank you for your help. Father, may I have a word outside?'

'I'll walk with you.'

The priest stood and walked behind the detectives to Donadze's car. 'Yes, Lieutenant?'

'I'm worried about Luca. He's blaming himself for what happened to his sister. Could you speak to him?'

'That's very perceptive of you. Thank you. I'll do what I can.'

'You have my card, call me any time,' Donadze said. 'Let's go, Irina.'

He bumped his car off the rough ground and took the road back to Tbilisi. Jaqeli looked out of her window at the passing houses and shops. 'It's like a different world,' she said. 'Nothing like the city.'

'Yes, it's easy to see the attraction.'

They left the village, the landscape opening to show Tbilisi nestling in haze at the foot of the hills they were descending.

'You didn't like the priest,' Jaqeli stated.

'Why do you think that?'

'You were quite abrupt. He just wanted to help.'

'Yes, and I'm happy for him to do so.'

'Okay,' Jaqeli said.

They drove in silence for several minutes and Jaqeli shut her eyes, lulled by the movement of the old car's worn suspension.

'You know my family had to leave Abkhazia?' Donadze said.

'Yes, it must have been awful.'

'Thirty thousand dead, two hundred and fifty thousand displaced…'

Jaqeli didn't reply and Donadze continued driving in expectant silence, finally saying, 'I had a sister, Ana. She was one of the thirty thousand.'

Jaqeli turned in her seat to look at Donadze. 'I'm sorry, Ramaz. Please don't talk about it if you'd rather not…'

'It's okay, talking helps, sometimes… It happened in our home. It was our neighbours, our friends—or that's what we thought they were, anyway. Ana was raped and killed. There was nothing we could do, nothing *I* could do.'

'Of course there wasn't. You must have just been a young boy.'

'Our priest was there…'

'He tried to stop them?'

'No. He was with them; he was one of the men who killed Ana…'

There was a long pause before Jaqeli spoke, 'Ramaz, I can't imagine what you went through. But you can't hold *all* priests responsible for the actions of one evil man.'

'I don't, I just treat them the way I treat everyone else.' Donadze adjusted his rear-view mirror to protect his eyes from the setting sun. 'Thanks for being a good listener,' he said.

'Anytime.' She yawned. 'How long till we get back to Tbilisi?'

'Thirty minutes.'

'Wake me when we get there, would you?' she said, sitting back and shutting her eyes.

'I'll see you tomorrow, Irina,' Donadze said.

Jaqeli looked at her watch. 'Is that it for the day?'

'It is for you, we'll pick things up again tomorrow.'

'Are *you* going home now?'

'Not yet, I want to keep the momentum going.'

'Well, so do I.'

Donadze shrugged. 'Your choice. Do you want to call Misha and let him know you'll be late?' he said, his face deadpan.

'I don't know what you're talking about. But how about *you* calling Tamuna and letting her know *you'll* be late. I'll be five minutes,' she said, getting out of the car and walking towards the station building.

Donadze picked up his phone and called Tamuna.

His mother answered. 'Tamuna's feeding the baby,' she said.

'That's okay, could you tell her I'll be a little late getting home.'

Her tone hardened, 'How late, Ramaz?'

Donadze looked at the clock on his car's dash. It was six-thirty. 'I'll be home by nine-thirty.'

She sighed. 'I'll tell her…'

'Thanks, *Deda*,' he said, hanging up. He went into his

call history and dialled another number.

'Dream Casino, how may I help you?' a professionally friendly female voice answered.

'Is Otar Basilia in this evening?'

'I'm not sure, who may I say is calling?'

'Tell him Lieutenant Donadze wants to talk to him— thirty minutes,' he said, hanging up.

He started the car when he saw Jaqeli hurrying out of the station building. 'Where are we going?' she said.

'Taking Major Gloveli's advice—we're going to speak to Basilia.'

'Really, what about?'

'Let's play it by ear.'

They arrived outside the casino and Donadze parked by the main entrance, ignoring the car park which was only half full. A slim, athletic-looking man intercepted them as they went through the gilt doors, his hands held high and wide, blocking their way. He was wearing a badge identifying himself as Tengo Sakhokia, the casino's security manager. 'Lieutenant Donadze?' he asked, smiling.

Donadze stepped close. 'Get out of our way, Tengo,' he replied loudly enough to attract attention from the customers in the lobby.

Sakhokia dropped his hands, looking confused. 'But Mr Basilia asked me to meet you and show you to his office.'

'We know the way, step aside unless you want to be charged with obstruction.'

'Just trying to help,' the man muttered, reaching for his radio.

'This way,' Donadze said to Jaqeli, walking past columns of flashing, clanging slot machines, their blank-faced acolytes dipping into plastic buckets to feed them with the tokens they had purchased with real money.

Jaqeli caught up with him. 'This is fun,' she said. 'You've been here before?'

'This way,' he said again, turning left at the top of the central stairway.

They reached the office which Donadze had visited during a previous murder investigation. He banged on the door and pushed it open. It was the same as Donadze remembered—small and functional. Basilia was sitting behind his desk, a few papers and a glass containing a pale-gold liquid in front of him.

'Mr Basilia,' Donadze said from the doorway. 'We've not met. I'm Lieutenant Donadze, this is my colleague, Detective Jaqeli. May we come in?'

'I know who you are,' Basilia said. The Kaldani crime family had been founded by Basilia's uncle in the breakaway region of South Ossetia and Basilia spoke with a thick Ossetian accent. He attempted a smile. 'Do I need my lawyer?'

'That's your prerogative, sir.'

'I think we should be okay, come in, Detectives.' Basilia stood and motioned for Donadze and Jaqeli to join him at his desk. He was about one metre seventy tall, with thick legs, massive shoulders and an expansive belly bursting out of his tailored black cotton shirt. His head and face had been shaved to a black shadow and his eyes were dark and narrow. He smiled through full lips and his nose was swollen, lumpy and red. He looked like a rugby player gone to seed Donadze thought.

'Join me?' Basilia pointed to his glass. 'Eighteen year-old Macallan. Water, no ice, the way it should be drunk.'

'We're on duty, unfortunately,' Donadze said.

Basilia took a sip from his glass, darting his tongue over his lips and smiling at Jaqeli. 'What can I do for you, Detectives?' he said.

Donadze shook his head in mock disappointment. 'This wouldn't have happened if Dato were still in charge.'

Basilia frowned. 'What wouldn't have happened?'

'Gali Street, of course. The Kutaisi Clan—they wouldn't have had the balls to take on Dato like that, would they?'

Basilia's frown deepened. 'I saw something on television about killings in Gali Street—but what's that got to do with me or Dato?'

'This conversation is off the record so let's drop the bullshit,' Donadze said. He reached over the desk and lifted Basilia's glass, placing it slightly out of his reach, watching as the gangster's face tightened. 'How much trouble are you in?'

Basilia placed his hands palms-down on the table and leaned towards Donadze. 'Off the record or on the record, I'm in no fucking trouble at all. So why don't you and Miss Georgia stop wasting my time and tell me what it is you want.'

Donadze turned to Jaqeli. 'Did you hear that, Detective? Mr Basilia mistook you for a beauty queen.'

'Yes, I did hear that, Lieutenant, very flattering.'

'Last chance,' Basilia said with menace.

'All right,' Donadze said. 'We don't want to be here any longer than we have to. Of course you're in trouble. Gali Street wouldn't have happened under Dato and you know it. But that's only the start. The Kutaisi Clan is coming after you. You'll hit back of course, take out some of their operations, kill some of their people. But your family isn't what it was. Your people are nervous, some are probably thinking of changing sides, some have probably done so already and you just don't know it yet. It's only a matter of time before you're out of business—and you have to know how that will end for you.'

Donadze watched as Basilia's eyes narrowed in calculation. 'You may have been watching too many gangster movies, *Ramaz*. But even if any of what you said was true, why would you care?'

'About you? We don't care at all. But we do want to find the men who killed these girls.'

'If I did have business interests in Gali Street, don't you think I would want to find these men as well.'

'I'm sure you would. So, help us and help yourself at the same time.'

'Ah, the enemy of my enemy is my friend?'

'We both know we'll never be friends, but right now, we do have a common enemy.'

Basilia smiled. 'A common enemy?' He reached over the desk and took his glass back. He drained it and placed it on the desk. 'You know, Lieutenant, Dato and I were more like brothers than cousins. I was upset when I lost him—I still am. You and I, we're not too different, we both know what it's like to lose someone we love. How did you feel? Didn't you want to hit back, take your revenge?'

'Who ordered the hits at Gali Street? Was it Anzor Kalmikov?' Donadze demanded.

The Kalmikov family was affiliated to the Kutaisi Clan

and Anzor, the head of the family, was known to be ambitious. The gangster's face flickered in recognition and he appeared to come to a decision. 'Maybe it was. What do you want from me?'

'From *you*? Tell me, when was *your* last visit to Gali Street?'

Basilia's face hardened. 'Never been there, why would I?'

'Oh, I don't know. To have a look at the new girls coming in, perhaps. Make sure you got to them first. I mean, you're the boss, right? You were entitled.'

'Get out of my fucking office, Donadze.'

Donadze stood, 'Let's go, Detective,' he said and walked to the door to hold it open for Jaqeli.

Basilia watched her stand and follow Donadze out. 'You're sure you're not a beauty queen, darling?' he said, pouring more whisky into his glass.

Jaqeli turned at the door. 'I'd ease up on that stuff if I were you, Otar,' she said, tapping her nose. 'You wouldn't want it to ruin your good looks.' Donadze looked at Basilia and winked then caught up with Jaqeli. The detectives walked down the stairway and through the lobby together, watched from a distance by the security manager.

'That really *was* fun,' Jaqeli said. 'I think I'm going to enjoy working with you, Ramaz.'

'Of course you are,' Donadze said. 'Everyone does.'

FIVE

Donadze returned home thirty minutes earlier than he'd promised.

'*Ramazi*,' his mother said, standing. She kissed him and hustled into the cooking area to extract a small ceramic pot of *lobio* from the oven, the delicious aroma from the bubbling beans and herbs reminding him that he hadn't eaten in more than eight hours.

'Thanks, *Deda*,' he said, pulling Tamuna in close to kiss her.

'Is everything okay, Ramaz?' she said and he realised that he had held her a little tighter and a little longer than was appropriate.

'It's just been a long day. How has our baby been?'

He watched her face brighten. 'Wonderful—her first tooth came through today.'

'Well, that's good, just about what we expected, wasn't it?'

'Yes, six months is about right.'

'And how have you been?'

'Okay, a bit tired, I suppose.'

Donadze's mother finished laying out his meal and poured him a glass of *Mukuzani* from an open bottle. 'Well, I'm certainly tired,' she said, kissing them both. 'I'll leave you to talk.'

'*Dzli nebisa*,' Donadze said, watching his mother walk stiffly to her room. He turned to Tamuna. 'That's usually an ominous sign…'

'She's just giving us a bit of space.'

'Yes, she's good that way, I suppose. Give me a minute, I'll just look in on Eka while my *lobio* is cooling.'

'Okay, but *don't* wake her.'

The blackout curtains shut out nearly all light and it took a moment for Donadze's eyes to adjust. He followed the dim glow of the baby monitor and looked down into the cot. His daughter was lying on her back; fastened safely into her sleeping bag, her breath soft and precious. He leaned into the cot and inhaled sweet baby smells deep into his lungs—soft cotton, milk and shampoo. He straightened and placed his hand on her chest, feeling her warmth and sensing all that lay ahead of her and all that lay ahead of him, also. He stood by the cot for a moment longer, then took a deep breath and left the bedroom, blinking in the bright light as he returned.

'The proud father…' Tamuna said, grinning.

'Is it that obvious?'

'You should see your face.'

'That's why I don't play poker.'

Donadze sat on one of the tall stools placed around the breakfast bar and tore a piece of bread to dip into his *lobio*.

Tamuna joined him on the adjoining stool and he poured sparkling water into a glass and placed it in front of her. 'You said you were tired today?'

'A little, but I'm fine now.'

'Are you looking forward to going back to work.'

'Not really, I know Eka will be perfectly okay with your mother, but it doesn't feel right, somehow.'

'Goes against your instincts, I suppose… But you know Tamuna, we've talked about this. You don't have to return to work yet, if you don't want to, if you'd rather be around for Eka. I earn enough, we'd get by…'

'I know, but *I'm* not ready for that yet. I don't think *we're* ready for it either.'

'Well, I think I am.'

'Let's not discuss this tonight, Ramaz. It's late and we're both tired. Oh, I nearly forgot—you're taking me out for dinner tomorrow evening.'

'Really?

'Yes, I have a table booked for the King David. Taxi from here at seven—please don't be late.'

Major Gloveli limped to his garden gate as Donadze and Jaqeli pulled up outside his house. 'What's going on, Ramaz?' he said.

'Misha Arziani is on his way. He's bringing a young woman I want you to meet. Her name's Veronika Boyko and she needs your help.'

'What are you talking about, Donadze? What help? Why me?'

'Here they are now.'

Arziani parked behind Donadze's car and he and Veronika got out. 'Hey, Ramaz, Irina. Do you want me to stay?' he asked, smiling at Jaqeli.

Donadze turned to observe Jaqeli return his smile before dropping her eyes, her hand reaching to push a stray strand of hair behind her ear. 'I suppose you'd better,' he said.

'Always happy to help, Ramaz.'

'Will you please tell me what's going on, Donadze,' the Major demanded.

'Let's go inside…'

'This had better be good.' He held the garden gate open for Veronika and Jaqeli. 'After you, ladies,' he said before pointedly walking ahead of the other men into the house. 'Arziani, bring these chairs over. Donadze, get the wine,' he ordered. 'Are you hungry, ladies?' he asked.

'Please allow me, Major,' Jaqeli said, crossing to the kitchen area.

They sat round Gloveli's small table. 'Major Levan Gloveli, this is Veronika Boyko,' Donadze said, speaking in Russian.

Gloveli looked at the girl then reached to offer his hand.

She took his hand and immediately released it, offering him a quick, nervous smile but not speaking.

'Veronika,' Donadze continued. 'Major Gloveli was my commanding officer. He is also a good friend. I would trust him with my life and the lives of my family. You can trust him too.'

Veronika lifted her head to meet Gloveli's gaze. She

held it for a moment then nodded.

'Major, Veronika needs your help. She was trafficked out of Ukraine and held in that Gali Street apartment. She described someone who fits Otar Basilia's description raping Mariam. Her testimony could take Basilia down.'

'I understand, Ramaz, but—'

'There's more. Veronika was able to escape. She got out just before the two other girls in the apartment were killed. She saw the killers…'

There was a long, tense silence before Gloveli spoke, resorting to Georgian. 'It won't work, Donadze. I'm an old man. I can't protect this girl...'

'I think you can and you should. No one gets into this village without you knowing about it. You have *friends* here that I don't even want to think about. And I haven't forgotten what happened when Kaldani's thugs came for you.' Donadze was referring to an attempted hit on Gloveli which had resulted in one of the would-be assassins being killed.

'It's crazy, Ramaz. How could that young girl stay with me? What would people say?'

'I wouldn't flatter yourself too much in that regard, Major,' Donadze replied. He looked at Veronika. 'She needs your help—will you take her in?'

'You know, Donadze, you can be a real pain in the butt sometimes.' He appeared to come to a decision and sighed. 'Okay. If she wants to stay here with me then, yes, I'll take her in.'

'Thank you, Major.' Donadze turned to Veronika and continued in Russian. 'Veronika, I brought you here today because I think you need to be somewhere safe. I would like you to stay with Major Gloveli until we have arrested the men you saw at Gali Street.'

Veronika looked at Gloveli and around the sparse, primitive room. 'Stay here? No, I'm going home, back to Ukraine!'

Donadze shook his head. 'It'll be too dangerous for you there. The men you saw could find you in Ukraine as easily as they could in Tbilisi. You know that. Major Gloveli will keep you safe until you are able to go home again.'

'No, I hate this country. I'm going home now.'

'It's not just you, Veronika,' Jaqeli said. 'You have a mother and a sister, don't you? They'd also be at risk if you go home now.'

Veronika stared at Jaqeli, tears welling in her eyes. 'I should never have spoken to you. Why was I so stupid?'

'You were brave, Veronika, not stupid. Ramaz is right. Stay with Major Gloveli for now. We'll get you home as soon as we can, I promise you.'

Veronika looked at Gloveli. He nodded. 'You'll be safe here. No one will hurt you when you're with me.'

'How well do you know the village priest, Major?'

Gloveli was watching Veronika. She had elected to wash the collection of dirty plates and glasses which he had allowed to build up and was now tidying and cleaning around his cooking area. 'I hope this works out,' he said.

'I'm sure it will.'

Gloveli continued watching. 'Does she—'

'Understand Georgian? No, she doesn't. Father

Chanturia, Major—how well do you know him?'

Gloveli re-filled his glass with wine and poured water for his guests. 'He's been with us for about two years. He's young and some think a bit modern, I've heard. But I'm not religious, I don't go to his church, so I don't know him very well. Why do you ask?'

'There's something about him. It seems that he's always there, everywhere I turn. He was at the Alasania's home yesterday.'

'That's what priests do, Ramaz. They bring solace to people in pain.'

'Yes, but it seems to me that he was a bit too interested in this case. He wanted to see the facial composite Luca gave us and then he asked me if he could keep it.'

'How would that be a problem.'

'Well, Mariam's boyfriend doesn't know we're looking for him yet…'

'Oh, come on, Ramaz! You're surely not thinking Father Chanturia would tip him off?' Arziani said.

'I'm not thinking that—not yet anyway. But he knows the family as well as anyone. He certainly knew Mariam. I'd like to understand how a girl from Shindisi got caught up with international traffickers—maybe Chanturia can help.'

'No, that can't be right, Ramaz,' Jaqeli said. 'Not the priest, he's a man of God. He could never do something like that.'

'I would advise you two to be a bit more open-minded,' Gloveli said. 'Donadze's right. You're too young to remember, Irina, but the Church wasn't always held in the high regard it is now. Your parents probably told you about the *Mkhedrioni*, the things they did following the Civil

War?' Gloveli was referring to the para-military, criminal organisation which had had a reputation for extortion, smuggling, armed robbery and murder. 'What they probably didn't tell you was that, after it was disarmed and banned, several of its members turned—supposedly—legitimate. Some even became priests and some are still in the Church today. Father Chanturia is too young to have been with the *Mkhedrioni*, but don't assume that donning a cassock automatically makes you a good man.' Gloveli shrugged and took a sip of his wine. 'Sorry for the lecture. I'm an old man, things have changed, Georgia's not the country it was,' he said.

Donadze was pleased to see the old policeman so animated. 'Some things never change, Major,' he said.

Gloveli nodded. 'Unfortunately, not.'

Donadze stood and brushed crumbs off his trousers. 'Let's speak to Father Chanturia again,' he said.

The breeze was fresh and cool and Donadze hitched his jacket collar around his neck and dug his hands deep into his pockets as he and Jaqeli walked the short distance from Gloveli's house to the village church. It was perched on a small untidy mound, its stone walls and tiled roof overdue maintenance by fifty years or more. The heavy wooden doors were hung on black, ornate hinges and open to welcome the faithful and assure the doubting. The detectives climbed four worn, stone steps, Jaqeli making the sign of the cross as they entered, her thumb and two fingers touching forehead, sternum and right to left shoulders, beseeching the Father, Son and Holy Spirit to provide Orthodox protection from the ungodly. The aroma of musty, citrus incense was steeped into the fabric and fittings of the old building and Donadze closed his eyes and inhaled deeply, immediately returning to his childhood in Abkhazia and a time when his faith was not questioned.

Father Chanturia was standing in front of the three-door iconostasis. He raised his hand in greeting then crossed the small nave, stopping on the way to speak to an old women stooped in front of a gilt-framed icon, her shaky hand placing a smoky candle in the sand-filled tray which faced it. '*Gamarjoba*, Lieutenant, Detective. You want to speak to me about Mariam,' he said, crossing himself.

'We do, Father,' Donadze said. 'Where can we talk?'

'My wife is expecting me home, let's go there.'

Donadze looked at his watch and Chanturia added, 'It's not far.'

The detectives followed the priest out of the church and along a dusty path. His house was small and modern and built on a single level from red brick. The garden was proportionately small but had been planted with fruit and vegetables to maximise the available growing area. The front door was unlocked and Chanturia pushed it open and stood to the side to allow Donadze and Jaqeli to enter. A young, attractive woman was peeling potatoes in the cooking area. She smiled and looked at Chanturia. 'Keti, this is Lieutenant Ramaz Donadze and Detective Irina Jaqeli. They want to speak to me about poor Mariam. Detectives, this is my wife, Keti,' he said.

She wiped her hands on a towel and smiled again.'

Welcome, please take a seat,' she said, indicating a round wooden table with four chairs. Donadze and Jaqeli sat while she brought food and drinks.

'Let me take this thing off,' Chanturia said, removing a wide leather belt and unbuttoning his cassock. He was wearing blue denim jeans and a light blue shirt underneath, the sleeves folded back off his wrists. He rolled the sleeves down and buttoned the cuffs, smiling at his wife, 'I suspect these officers will want to speak privately,' he said.

'Of course. Sergo will be wakening up soon anyway…'

The priest joined Donadze and Jaqeli at the table.

'Sergo? You have a son?' Jaqeli asked.

'Yes, he's nearly two. A daughter on the way as well, four months to go.'

'Congratulations.'

'Thank you.' He looked at Donadze. 'You suspect that I might, somehow, be involved in Mariam's abduction,' he stated. 'Or maybe you think I had something to do with her death?'

'Why would we think that, Father?'

'Why else would you be speaking to me? Listen, Lieutenant, I want to help. I'm not offended and I've got nothing to hide. What do you want to know?'

Donadze opened the memos app on his phone, started it recording then placed the phone in the middle of the table. 'How old are you, Father?'

'I'm thirty.'

'Is Shindisi your first parish assignment?'

'Yes, I was ordained two years ago and assigned here after that.'

'So you were twenty-eight when ordained. Three years

of theological studies before that?'

'Yes.'

'You have to be a graduate before beginning studies with the Church?'

'Usually. I have a bachelors in business administration from The University of Georgia. Not the normal route for priests. Most of my colleagues studied history or philosophy—but I hadn't received the calling at that point.'

'How old were you when you graduated?'

'Twenty-two.'

'So three years between your bachelors and your theological studies?'

'Yes. And to answer your next question—I drifted. I'd experimented at university: parties, alcohol, drugs, casual relationships. I was lucky to graduate, couldn't keep a job. It was a bad time. But Keti stayed with me, helped me find what I was missing.'

'God?'

'Yes, and more. You might understand this, Lieutenant. The need to serve.'

The priest's unexpected candour had thrown Donadze off guard and he looked to Jaqeli to pick up the questioning.

'Did you speak to Luca after Lieutenant Donadze told you that he was worried about him, Father?' she asked.

'Yes, as you requested.'

'What did you talk about?'

Chanturia smiled at Donadze. 'Your instincts are good, Lieutenant. Luca did blame himself for Mariam being killed. We talked about that. I told him people *should* keep confidences when asked to do so. It can even be a sacred duty—the confessional for example. I told him that he had done nothing wrong, although I don't think that helped much.'

'What else did you talk about?' Donadze said.

'Well, Lieutenant. It appears that Luca was very protective of his sister. Mariam's boyfriend? He knew a bit more about him than he told you. He told *me* where I could find him.'

'Beso?'

'Yes, Beso Eristavi. He works in a bar in Shardeni Street called Shots.'

'You saw this Eristavi?'

'Yesterday evening—at the bar.'

'Why did you go there?'

'I told you—I want to help.'

'Was the facial composite accurate?'

'Yes, it's a good likeness.'

'What did you say to him?'

'Nothing, I just went to have a look, to see if I could find him. I wasn't sure what I would do after that.'

'When were you going to tell us this?'

'I had to speak with Luca first. I told you, keeping confidences is important. Luca allowed me to give you this information. I had your card and would have called you today if you hadn't come to me.'

Donadze stared at the priest for a long moment. 'Tell us about your tattoo.'

'Tattoo?'

'The tattoo on your arm. The one you didn't want us to see when you took your cassock off.'

Chanturia stood and took off his shirt, revealing a toned torso. His right shoulder had a tattoo of an eight-

62

pointed star and his left forearm was tattooed with an inverted spider's web. 'As I said, it was a bad time.'

'So, a gangster turned priest?'

Chanturia raised his hands in surrender. 'Yes.'

'Let's go, Irina,' Donadze said.

SIX

❖

'So, let's arrest this Beso Eristavi and see what he can tell us about Basilia's trafficking operation,' Captain Nakani said.

'We could do that, sir. But I doubt he would tell us much—he'd rather do more jail time than go up against Basilia.'

Nakani frowned. 'You know we have to keep momentum going, Ramaz. Bringing in Eristavi would demonstrate we're doing that. We're being watched, it's important that we get results—it's especially important for you.'

'Yes, but surely not low-value results. Eristavi is a bottom-feeder. Just a cog in the machine.' Donadze paused. 'I've got an idea and would like your approval to proceed.'

Nakani crossed his thick arms across his chest. 'Tell me,' he said.

'Father Chanturia. He said he wants to help and I think we should accept his offer.'

Nakani sighed, closed his eyes and sat back in his chair.

'Help from a priest?' he said. He sighed again. 'Okay, I'm listening.'

Donadze tapped the desk for emphasis. 'The first question is, can we trust this priest? Do we believe that he's put his past behind him, that he's now legitimate? Well, I think we *can* trust him.'

'Do you? And if you're right?'

'We get him inside Basilia's organisation.'

'And how do we do that?'

'He has something of value—information. We get him to offer it to Basilia—for a price.'

'What information?'

'Father Chanturia is the Alasania family's priest. We'll be speaking to the family to let them know how the case is progressing. The family is religious and they'll confide in their priest. They'll pass information to Chanturia and he'll forward it to Basilia—the information that we want him to have.'

'I don't know, Ramaz, it sounds pretty unethical to me. We'd have to lie to the Alasania family.'

'No, we wouldn't lie. Just present the facts in a certain way.'

Nakani shook his head. 'That's lying by my estimation. How would Chanturia even get to speak to Basilia?'

'Through Beso Eristavi. Father Chanturia knows about Mariam's journal and can say he tracked him down through that.'

'And he'll ask Eristavi to set up the meeting with Basilia? Why would Eristavi do that?'

'He'd have to, he couldn't risk upsetting his boss.'

'But if Eristavi knows we can find him from Mariam's journal, he'll run.'

'I don't think so. We don't have evidence to prove that he lured Mariam to Gali Street. He can say that she was just a girl who came to his bar. There's no reason for him to run, especially if Father Chanturia tells him there's nothing in the journal to incriminate him.'

'How do you know that this priest would even agree to help us?'

'I think he will. There's something about him. He's angry and wants justice for Mariam. I think that's why he tracked down Eristavi.'

'Okay, but Basilia would know something was wrong. Priests don't sell information.'

'This one might. Father Chanturia has the right background. He's only been a priest for a few years, maybe he misses the life. He has a family, a baby on the way. He needs money. Or maybe he dresses it up a bit, asks for money for the church or for the village poor. There's lots of ways to play it, Chanturia just has to be credible—and I think he is.'

'What if you're wrong. What if we can't trust Chanturia. What if he hasn't given up the life. How do you know he won't play *you*?'

'I'm not wrong. You'd feel the same way if you met him.'

'Possibly. But let's talk this through. We manage to get Father Chanturia on the inside—how does that help us?'

Donadze shrugged. 'It depends on how well he can penetrate Basilia's organisation, how much he's trusted, who he gets to speak to. But we have a lot to gain and not much to lose.'

'Really? Being responsible for a priest's murder wouldn't create any fall-out?'

'I agree that there's a risk but Chanturia knows that and he's prepared to help. He said it's important for him to serve.'

Nakani appeared to come to a decision. He shook his head. 'No, sorry, Ramaz. I can see you've put a lot of thought into this and I appreciate your efforts—but I can't support it. It's too risky. Let's bring Beso Eristavi in.' He pulled his keyboard towards him, signalling that the meeting was over.

Donadze remained seated. 'I'm sorry, Bagrat. But, with respect, I can't accept that.'

Nakani pushed the keyboard away, his face colouring. 'What do you mean? That's my decision—you'd better accept it, Donadze.'

'No. Using Chanturia is the right thing to do. If you don't believe *me*, then run it past Colonel Meskhi, get his support, make sure you're covered. Tell him it's your idea if you prefer.'

'You think this is about me trying to steal your glory? You really haven't changed at all, have you, Donadze?'

'Forget about me, take this to Colonel Meskhi. He'll know it's the right thing to do.'

'And if I don't?'

'I think it's something the Colonel needs to hear. It would be better coming from you.'

'You'd go behind my back! Tell me, Donadze, how will *you* feel when *you* eventually get a command and your officers conspire against *you*.'

'I'm sorry, Bagrat. I'm not conspiring against you…

It's just the right thing to do.'

'It's Captain Nakani to you, Donadze. You're dismissed. Get out of my office.'

Jaqeli looked up as Donadze left Nakani's office. He shook his head slightly, advising her not to speak. 'Wait five minutes then meet me at my car,' he said as he passed her desk.

He turned before leaving the bureau. Nakani was glaring at him through his office window. Donadze held his gaze for a moment, then left. He got into his car and closed his eyes, playing back their conversation. Nakani's implication that he had conspired to undermine him had wounded. There was no conspiracy but Donadze knew that he had not treated his commander fairly.

There was a knock on the passenger's side window and he opened his eyes to see Jaqeli. He unlocked her door and she got in. 'Didn't go well, then?' she said.

'Not well at all.'

'So we won't be asking Father Chanturia for his help?'

'I think we will. I said I'd go to Colonel Meskhi if the Captain won't agree.'

'What! Why did you do that, Ramaz? Talk about a death wish.' She turned in her seat to confront him. 'Colonel Meskhi is certain to back the Captain and he won't be happy that you've broken the chain of command.'

'I know he won't be happy but I think he *will* back our plan. I've worked with him before and know the way he thinks. He's unconventional but smart and only really interested in results. If he thinks our idea is good, he'll back it.'

'Unconventional but smart and only interested in results—a bit like you then?'

'Not really—very little of what I do is smart.'

Jaqeli laughed and punched him on his shoulder. 'Don't be too tough on yourself, Ramaz,' she said. 'So when do we visit Colonel Meskhi?'

'Let's wait and see what Nakani decides. He may come around.'

'And if he doesn't?'

'I'll speak to Meskhi. But not with you. You don't want to be associated with this. In fact, you probably don't want to be associated with me at all.'

'Who says I don't. We came up with this plan together, didn't we? Why should you get all the credit?'

'You don't want the credit I'll be getting. But there's no point thinking about it anymore tonight. Let's see what happens tomorrow.' He started the car's engine.

'Where are we going?' Jaqeli asked.

'The bar where Beso Eristavi works—Shots. I want to see what he looks like.'

'Good idea, but you're not going. You're taking Tamuna out for dinner this evening, aren't you?'

'Well, I was.'

'No—you *are*. And don't forget to buy flowers. That poor girl certainly deserves them, don't you think?'

Donadze stepped through his front door and into a scene of

domestic bliss. Tamuna was nursing Eka, his mother watching, a contented smile on her face. 'How are my three favourite girls?' he said, holding up the flowers he had bought on Jaqeli's advice.

'Well, at least two of us are hungry,' Tamuna said, smiling and looking up to be kissed. 'The flowers are lovely, thank you. Best get ready though, the taxi's coming in twenty minutes.'

Donadze kissed the top of Eka's head and his mother's cheek and walked to the bedroom. He sat on the bed and kicked off his shoes then, replaying the argument with Captain Nakani, used his fingers and thumb to create an imaginary pistol and held it to his head. *Don't think so*, he thought, putting the imaginary pistol backs in its imaginary holster. He continued sitting for a moment longer then, shaking his head to clear negative thoughts, stripped, showered, dressed and returned to the living room, pushing his damp hair into position with his fingers.

Tamuna had finished feeding the baby. 'Can I take her?' he asked.

'Go to Daddy,' Tamuna said, passing Eka over and standing. 'Five minutes.'

Donadze jostled his baby girl in his arms, watching her eyes grow heavy, her mouth nuzzling his knuckle. His mother smiled approvingly. 'You're blessed, *Ramazi*. I hope you realise that,' she said.

'I do, *Deda*. I know I'm blessed.'

'Buying Tamuna flowers was a nice thing to do…'

He shrugged. 'It wasn't that much.'

'Still, it was a nice thing to do…'

Donadze knew his mother wanted to say more and he

looked at her expectantly.

She shook her head. 'I shouldn't say anything, it's none of my business…'

'What's wrong, *Deda*?'

She sighed. 'Your father, *Ramazi*, he never brought me flowers, never told me he loved me. But that was normal for men of his generation. The thing is, he didn't have to do these things. I knew he would always be there for me and that was enough. Whatever you and Tamuna have, make sure it's enough for her…'

Donadze stared at his mother. He knew she was right. His relationship with Tamuna was fragile. She had still not agreed to marry him, unconvinced that he would be able to maintain the work-life balance he had promised. He knew that losing her would be devastating. And, if he lost her, he would probably lose his daughter as well. He felt that possibility as a dull ache in the pit of his stomach.

'I'll put her down now, *Ramazi*,' his mother said. 'Enjoy your dinner, no need to rush home.' She held out her hands to take the little girl to the bedroom, cradling her gently, her lullaby promising no troubles would ever intrude into her small world.

He heard Tamuna leaving their bedroom and stood, fixing a smile on his face.

'Ready?' she said.

She had brushed her brown hair out so that it lay on her shoulders, applied her usual light make-up and changed into a black, knee-length dress which was complemented by the gold necklace he had given her. He caught a hint of her perfume as he kissed her. 'You look fantastic,' he said with complete sincerity.

'Thank-you. You don't look too bad yourself.'

Their taxi was waiting and took them to the Old Town and the King David, their favourite restaurant. It was quiet, most of the tables which were generously spaced around the ancient, brick-built cellars, empty. They requested and were shown to their favourite table. The flickering candle cast Tamuna in soft focus, her eyes and the gold chain around her neck sparking in its reflected light. Donadze felt his tension ease. 'It's nice to get out together, isn't it?' he said.

'Yes, it is,' she replied.

The waiter arrived. They knew the menu well enough and ordered their favourite dishes without consulting it.

'Would you be okay with wine?' he asked.

'Just a glass for me,' Tamuna said.

'Two glasses of *Tsinandali*, then.'

'Why not get a bottle?'

'Even better.'

They chatted easily over their food, Tamuna eking out her wine with sips of sparkling water. The waiter had just served the restaurant's signature dish, mixed *shashlik*, the skewers of meat, chicken and fish flaming on their stainless steel stand, when she appeared to come to a decision. She put her cutlery down and looked into Donadze's eyes. 'Tell me what's bothering you, Ramaz.'

'Bothering me? Nothing at all. I'm just enjoying being out with you.'

'You're certainly putting on a good show, and I'm not complaining. But there's part of you that's not here. Tell me what's wrong.'

Donadze put down his cutlery and filled his glass. He reached to take Tamuna's hand. 'I'm sorry. I'm probably a bit distracted with the case I'm on. Two girls killed. You know how I get. But I promised you my work won't come between us again and I'm going to keep that promise.'

'Well, okay, but that doesn't mean we can't speak about these things. We're here for each other, aren't we?'

'Yes, we are.'

'I want to be part of everything you do.'

'Yes, that's what I want as well.'

They finished their meal and took a short walk along the riverbank, stopping to appraise the futuristic and controversial Bridge of Peace, agreeing that it was indeed beautiful and that its design and location, spanning the river to the oldest part of the city, worked in ways they couldn't explain.

Donadze called a taxi, the taciturn driver racing at reckless speed to return them to Kandelaki Street. His mother had taken Eka into her own room and Tamuna waited until he had locked the door, then took his hand and led him to their bedroom where they made gentle and familiar love. Afterwards, while Tamuna lay on her side, sleeping, Donadze lay on his back beside her, staring at the ceiling, his mind racing, already thinking about his investigation and plotting his next moves.

SEVEN

Donadze had slept fitfully and risen early. He
skipped breakfast, despite his mother's
protestations, and gulped a large mug of strong,
sweet coffee as he prepared to leave the apartment. He arrived
at Mtatsminda Station and was surprised at the level of early-
morning activity. The Desk Sergeant greeted him
enthusiastically, 'This is sure to stir things up a bit,
Lieutenant.'

'What is?'

'You don't know? I thought you'd been called in.
Colonel Meskhi's already here, speaking with Captain
Nakani in his office. It looks like Basilia's hit back at the
Kutaisi Clan. He bombed Anzor Kalmikov's gym last
night—his gym and narcotics distribution hub, that is. You
know it—LA Fitness in Shroshi Street. Two of Kalmikov's
men are dead.'

Donadze hurried to the detectives' bureau. It had been
over a year since Donadze had last seen Colonel Meskhi and

he hadn't changed in any perceptible way. He was wearing his customary dark suit, his tall, lean frame upright in his chair as he faced Nakani across the small desk. He appeared to notice Donadze but declined to acknowledge his half smile or his hand raised in tentative greeting.

Soso Chichua was sitting at one of the bureau desks, typing a report with two fingers, his dark cotton shirt stained and his face and head sweaty as he struggled to cope with the station's fully-on or fully-off heating system.

'Hey, Soso,' Donadze said.

'Lieutenant,' Chichua replied.

'I hear that Anzor Kalmikov's gym has been bombed?'

'Looks that way.'

'When did this happen?'

'About four this morning.'

'And you were called by the desk?'

'Yes.'

'But you didn't call me? I thought we'd discussed this, Soso? Didn't I say that—'

Chichua pushed his keyboard away, his sweaty face turning a deeper shade of red. 'Listen, Ramaz, leave me out of this, okay? You've got an issue with Captain Nakani or he's got an issue with you. I really don't care. *I* would have called you but *he* told me not to. So why not take that up with him, not with me.'

Donadze looked up to see Nakani staring at him through his office window. He said something to Colonel Meskhi then waved to summon him to his office.

Donadze put his hand on Chichua's warm, moist shoulder. 'Thanks for looking out for me, Soso,' he said.

'That's okay, Lieutenant. Sorry if I got a bit riled…'

'Forget it...'

He walked to Nakani's office, knocked on his door and entered. '*Gamarjoba*, Colonel, Captain,' he said.

'Lieutenant,' Meskhi responded.

'I was about to update Colonel Meskhi on the Gali Street investigation, Lieutenant,' Nakani said. 'We've discussed your idea about using Father Chanturia to infiltrate Basilia's organisation. As you know, I had some reservations about a priest being involved, especially *this* priest with his history. But I have given it some more thought and you may proceed.'

'Thank you, sir.'

'Well, that's it. We'll let you get back—'

'Not yet,' Meskhi interrupted. 'Sit down, Lieutenant.'

Donadze took the last free seat, feeling uncomfortable in the confines of the small office and in being physically close to Meskhi.

'Let's talk this through,' Meskhi said. 'Captain, give me your summary of the case to date.'

'Yes, sir,' Nakani replied. 'It started with the triple murders in Gali Street. Two girls and one of Otar Basilia's men. The girls were being trafficked into the EU by Basilia. We think all three were killed by Anzor Kalmikov as part of his play to force Basilia out of Tbilisi.'

'You think?' the Colonel said. 'Aren't you sure?'

'Lieutenant Donadze interviewed Basilia, sir,' he said. 'Basilia himself believes that Kalmikov's behind the killings.'

'His sincere belief or a story he told Donadze?'

'He must have believed it, otherwise he wouldn't have attacked Kalmikov's gym last night.'

'Basilia has confessed to the bombing?'

'No, of course not. But it's a logical conclusion.'

'So, a straight-forward power play between the Tbilisi and Kutaisi Clans? That may be a logical conclusion and it's certainly the most obvious. But is it the only possibility?'

Colour was rising in Nakani's thick neck and sweat was beading on his forehead. 'Well, of course we aren't discounting other possibilities, sir, but our working assumption, for now, is that this is a feud between Kalmikov and Basilia.'

Meskhi turned to Donadze, inviting his opinion.

'Colonel,' he said. 'I share the Captain's belief that this is probably a struggle between the two clans…'

'But?'

'But we shouldn't exclude other possibilities.'

'Such as?'

'Such as, this could be the work of a third party who would benefit from one or both of the gangs being weakened.'

'Who might that be?'

'An ambitious deputy?' Nakani said.

'Perhaps,' Meskhi replied. 'But let's keep our minds open to *all* possibilities. Continue with your summary, Captain.'

Donadze had previously experienced similar interrogation by Meskhi and he nodded his encouragement to Nakani.

'There was a third girl in the apartment and she got out before the other two were killed,' Nakani continued. 'She came here, to this station and was interviewed. She confirmed that Basilia is trafficking women internationally, using Georgia as a transit location. She described Basilia coming to the apartment and raping one of the girls. And she also saw the girls' killers taking the stairs to the apartment where the murders were committed.'

'So a material witness,' Meskhi said. 'I take it she is now under police protection?'

Nakani looked to Donadze. 'I've placed her under the protection of Major Gloveli, sir,' he said. 'She's staying with the Major at his home in Shindisi.'

'I wasn't aware of that, Lieutenant,' Nakani said. 'Gloveli's retired, that's really not an acceptable—'

'I believe that is an acceptable arrangement,' Meskhi interrupted. 'Please carry on, Captain.'

Dark stains had appeared under Nakani's arms and he used the back of his hand to wipe sweat from his forehead. 'Yes, sir. One of the murdered girls was Georgian, from Shindisi. Her brother, Luca, spoke to Lieutenant Donadze but didn't tell him all that he knew. He was more open with the village priest—Father Chanturia—and we've identified the man who persuaded her into going to Gali Street.'

Meskhi nodded. 'Very well, that's all clear. Anything else?'

'No, sir,' Nakani said.

'Then let's discuss priorities.' Meskhi turned to Donadze. 'Lieutenant, what are your thoughts?'

'Priorities, sir?' He took a moment to consider. 'Well, the bombing has certainly raised the stakes. Five dead within the space of a few days and a business destroyed—a business located in Vake at that.' Donadze was referring to an area of the city which hosted many upmarket bars, restaurants and apartments. 'That's going to attract political interest.'

'Yes, it already has. So what do you suggest we do about it?'

'We should send a message to Basilia and Kalmikov. Warfare on the streets of Tbilisi stops now. We raid their premises, arrest their people, scare off their customers, strangle their revenue streams.'

'I agree and have already given orders to that effect. The raids will begin this morning. What else?'

'We have two innocents dead—the girls in Gali Street. So let's find their killers and get them into court.'

'Yes, of course. But I want more than that. I want this trafficking obscenity stopped. It's an evil trade and I'm ashamed it's still going on in our country.' Meskhi took a notebook from his jacket pocket, wrote something on a page, ripped the page from the book and handed it to Donadze. 'Some time ago I established a unit to tackle this problem. You have the assumed name of one of my undercover officers. He'll contact you. You and he are to share information and, where appropriate, work together. The murders of these girls and the trafficking are connected. I want you to identify their killers and build a case that we can take to the Prosecutor. And I want slavery—modern-day or otherwise—within and through Georgia ended permanently. Is that understood?'

'Yes, sir.'

'You still have my contact details?'

'Sir.'

'Then call me at any time.' He returned his notebook to his pocket. 'Any questions?'

Donadze looked at the name on the paper then folded it and put it in his jacket pocket. 'You said an *assumed* name, sir?'

'Yes, an assumed name, I told you, my officer is undercover, you don't need his real name. Anything else?'

'Detective Jaqeli, sir. I'd like to keep her partnered with me on this case.'

'You may do so but use good judgment about how much you tell her.'

'Thank you, sir.'

'Captain?'

Nakani cleared his throat. 'My role, sir?'

'You are Lieutenant Donadze's commanding officer and he will, of course, keep you appraised. But I'm afraid there will be details which he will not be able to divulge. Anything else?'

Nakani looked unhappy. 'No, sir.'

Meskhi appraised each man in turn. 'Then that brings me to my remaining priority—the professional relationships between my senior officers. Yours, gentlemen, has broken down and I expect you to repair it. You don't have to like each other, but you do have to work together. Understood?'

'Yes, sir,' Donadze and Nakani snapped out together.

'How was your evening, Lieutenant?' Jaqeli said.

She had arrived at the station and appeared to be working at her desk but Donadze thought she was probably more interested in the meeting in Nakani's office. 'Evening?' he frowned.

'Dinner with Tamuna? Yesterday evening? You did go out for dinner, didn't you?'

'Seems like a long time ago. Yes, it was very nice.'

'Very nice? The last of the great romantics!' She sat back in her chair and nodded in the direction of Nakani's office. 'What was that about?'

Donadze put a finger to his lips.

Colonel Meskhi was leaving. He strode to Jaqeli's desk, his head narrowly missing the light fittings set into the suspended ceiling. 'Detective Jaqeli?' he said.

'Yes, Colonel.'

'You're partnered with Lieutenant Donadze on the Gali Street investigation?'

'Yes, sir.'

'Good. I want you to be careful. Follow the Lieutenant's instructions and keep yourself safe.'

'Yes, sir.'

'Good luck,' he said, nodding to Donadze before moving to the exit.

'The great man,' Jaqeli said quietly to his back.

'Yes, I suppose he is,' Donadze replied, without conviction.

'So, your meeting?'

'Just a minute,' Donadze said and returned to Nakani's office. He knocked on the door and went in, closing it behind him. 'Sorry, Captain. I should have warned you,' he said.

Nakani shook his head. 'It feels like I've just gone ten rounds with Wladimir Klitschko but I'll know what to expect next time.'

'It's not personal, just his style. I've had the same treatment in the past.'

'You two have history…'

'Yes, and not all good. Listen, Captain, I wanted to apologise if I've undermined you in any way. I didn't mean to do that and I'm sorry if that's what Colonel Meskhi picked up on.'

Nakani frowned. 'What else could it have been? But we have our orders now. We don't have to like each other but we do have to work together, isn't that right? So, what next? Are you going to see the priest?'

'Yes.'

Nakani nodded and reached for his keyboard. 'Let me know how that goes.'

Donadze remained standing for a moment as Nakani turned his attention to his computer screen. 'Yes, will do,' he said and left the office, returning to Jaqeli's desk.

She looked at him inquisitively.

'Let's talk in the car,' he said.

'Shindisi?'

'Yes.'

As he drove, Donadze briefed Jaqeli on the meeting with Colonel Meskhi but omitted to inform her that he had been instructed to work with an undercover officer.

'So, Nakani has come round to your way of thinking, he's going to let us work with the priest?'

'I'm not sure *Captain* Nakani had much choice, but yes.'

'Ah, it's *Captain* Nakani now. I stand corrected.'

'He's doing the best he can, Irina. We're on the same side, let's try to be supportive.'

They completed the drive to Shindisi without talking. Donadze pulled up outside Chanturia's house. 'All good?' he said.

Jaqeli gave him a huge smile. 'Yes, of course it is, *Lieutenant.*'

Father Chanturia was in his garden, digging potatoes with a garden fork. He was wearing blue jeans and a T-shirt, the inverted spider's web tattoo clearly visible on his muscled arm. He straightened easily and drove the fork into the ground. 'Detectives,' he said, his hands held wide and open in welcome. 'I thought I'd be seeing you again.'

'Can we talk?' Donadze said.

Chanturia picked up the potatoes he had pulled from the rich soil and dropped them into a straw basket. 'Let's go inside,' he said, lifting the basket. He led the way and stood by the door as Donadze and Jaqeli went ahead. 'Keti, we have guests,' he shouted to his wife.

Keti came into the living room with a toddler in her arms. 'Welcome back, Detectives,' she said.

'So, this is little Sergo?' Jaqeli said, smiling at the toddler who turned his face into his mother's protective shoulder.

'Go to Daddy,' Keti said, putting the little boy on the ground and patting his bottom. He looked at Donadze suspiciously then ran to his father who threw him into the air then held him with one arm while his wife began preparing food and drinks for her guests.

'We would like to talk to you, Father,' Donadze said.

'You mean talk to me in private?'

Donadze hesitated, 'It's sensitive.'

'If it's what I think it is, then Keti needs to hear it as well. Please take a seat.'

Chanturia waited until his wife and the detectives had sat at the table then joined them, his son on his knee, refusing to acknowledge Jaqeli's smiles. 'How may I help?' he asked, as his wife poured water into four glasses.

Donadze paused before speaking. 'You hide it well, Father, but I know you're angry.'

Chanturia smiled, 'Okay, Lieutenant, you have my attention…'

'You're angry about Mariam. You think you could have done more to keep her safe. You're angry with yourself.'

Chanturia stopped smiling, his face hardening. 'Yes…'

'Luca told you about Beso Eristavi and you went to see him in Shardeni Street, at the bar he was working in—Shots. You said you only wanted to find him, that you didn't know what you would do after that.' Donadze watched closely as the priest's mouth tightened. 'What did you *want* to do? In your other life, what *would* you have done?' he said.

Chanturia unconsciously rubbed the tattoo on his arm. His voice coarsened as he spoke, 'I wanted to kill him and dump his body in the river. In my other life, he'd be dead already.'

There was a long moment of silence as Donadze looked around the table. The toddler seemed to have picked up on the charged atmosphere and was whimpering in his father's arms. Chanturia rubbed his leg, whispering in his ear to comfort him. His wife sat back in her chair as if recoiling from shock, her hand at her mouth. Jaqeli was staring at the priest, her eyes wide.

Chanturia was the first to speak. He raised his head and smiled. 'A leopard can't change its spots, isn't that—'

'No!' his wife interrupted, putting her hand on her husband's arm to silence him. She turned her attention to Donadze, speaking with quiet fury, 'You're the one who

84

can't change, *Lieutenant*. You made up your mind as soon as you saw my husband's tattoos. But you know nothing about this man. You don't know him the way I do. The things he does for people, for his family, the sacrifices he makes every day. He's not the man you think he is. Why can't you give him a chance?'

The priest spoke calmly, 'It's alright, Keti. I believe that Lieutenant Donadze is about to offer me that chance.'

Donadze gazed at Chanturia, his pregnant wife and his young son, no longer certain that he could ask the priest to put himself and his family at risk.

Chanturia returned Donadze's stare. 'It's alright, Lieutenant. Tell me what I should do.'

Donadze took a deep breath and pushed his concerns aside. 'You want justice for Mariam? Here's how to get it,' he said.

EIGHT

The tourist season was over and the trendy girls and cool, confident boys were working hard to attract customers into the bars and restaurants lining Shardeni Street. Donadze wasn't surprised that their banter stopped when he and Jaqeli walked by, knowing that, by a process which was both familiar and mysterious, they had been identified as police—to be treated with caution and reluctant respect.

The Old Town street was narrow and congested with tables and chairs spilling out from archaic buildings. Donadze was walking a pace behind Jaqeli, leaving room for people travelling in the opposite direction. Cool air was tumbling down the surrounding hills and funnelling through the twisting streets and he savoured the warmth radiated by the space heaters they passed along the way.

Shots was busy—a fashionable place to be seen in, apparently. The row of tables along the outside wall were all occupied, an aroma of tobacco, apple, mint and smouldering charcoal from *shisha* pipes, drifting tantalisingly in the swirling breeze.

'*Gamarjoba*, Officers,' the doorman said, smirking. 'I'm sorry, but we're full. Why not come back later?'

Donadze didn't speak but stepped close to the man. He stood his ground for only a few seconds before opening the door and standing aside.

'Here we go again,' Jaqeli said under her breath as she followed Donadze into the bar.

They paused inside the doorway, their eyes adjusting to the dim light, the background volume dropping as their presence was noted and absorbed. Donadze looked around the bar, narrowing his eyes theatrically to focus on individuals who may or may not have had something to hide from the police. A few decided it was time to leave and squeezed out the door. Donadze strolled to the brightly-polished, white-marble bar, its chromed edging reflecting light from the illuminated glass shelves on the wall behind—from which, he thought, the expensive branded bottles were rarely lifted.

Beso Eristavi was working behind the bar, polishing glasses and charming two heavily made-up young women sitting cross-legged on the stools opposite, clearly thrilled to have attracted his attention. Donadze was sure Eristavi practiced his dazzling smile in front of a mirror. He said something to the women and they glanced at Donadze before easing themselves off the stools, stooping indecorously to lift their bags from the floor and totter away on precarious heels.

Luca had provided an accurate description; Eristavi was slim and shorter than Donadze. He was good looking in a slightly effeminate way, with a clear complexion and light facial growth. His long dark hair had been scraped back and constrained in a loose bun tied at the back of his head. He was wearing designer denim jeans and a tightly-fitting white T-shirt, his outfit probably costing more than the uninitiated would believe.

Donadze invited Jaqeli to take one of the vacated stools then joined her on its neighbour. He swivelled slowly through three-hundred and sixty degrees, making sure they had the bar's full attention. 'What would you like to drink?' he said to Jaqeli while staring at Eristavi.

'White wine, please.'

'Two glasses of *Tsinandali*.'

Eristavi risked a nervous smile then turned to take an open bottle from the fridge behind the bar, his hand shaking slightly as he poured the wine. 'On the house, Detectives.'

Donadze looked at Jaqeli. 'He called us *detectives*. You told me you haven't been here before.'

Jaqeli shook her head, seemingly perplexed. 'I haven't. Maybe he knows *you*, Lieutenant?'

'No, I'd remember him.' He turned to Eristavi, 'How did you know that we're police officers?'

'Look, is there something you two want?' Eristavi said with unconvincing menace.

'I think you've upset the barman,' Donadze said.

'Well, I didn't mean to. Maybe we should go.'

Donadze took a sip from his glass and winced. He stood and smiled at Eristavi. 'We'll talk again, *Beso*,' he said. He slapped a fifty *lari* note on the bar. 'Keep the change.'

They re-traced their route, walking single-file along Shardeni Street to Donadze's car. He started the engine and adjusted the thermostat to generate warm air.

'Well, that was different,' Jaqeli said.

'We got his attention. He'll have told Basilia about our visit by now.'

'And that's going to make Basilia more open to receiving—supposedly—inside information from the priest?'

'Hopefully. That's the idea, anyway.'

'I'll let you know when I've figured it out.'

'Figured what out?'

'You. You might be a genius, but—somehow—I doubt it.'

'If you're in doubt, assume genius, Detective.'

'If you say so, Lieutenant.'

Donadze glanced at the clock on his dash. 'Where do you want dropped off, Irina?' he said, manoeuvring into the traffic flow.

Donadze took Jaqeli to the address she had provided, Misha Arziani's apartment block. It was after ten when he left his car in his own basement parking and walked the short distance to the elevator, his eyes gritty with fatigue. He pressed the call button, irritated that the elevator was at the top level and would take thirty seconds or so to descend. He stood facing the stainless steel door, his eyes closed, trying to be patient.

'Ramaz Donadze?' he heard a man's voice close behind.

Donadze spun, dropping instinctively into a defensive posture.

'Easy, Lieutenant,' the man said, a satisfied smile

playing on his lips. He was around forty, tall, lean and broad shouldered with a narrow face, high cheekbones and two or three days stubbly growth. His salt and pepper hair was buzzed short and he was wearing a black leather jacket, black collarless shirt and blue jeans. His height, build and proximity were, in themselves, intimidating but the scar which ran from below his left ear and across his cheek to his mouth projected menace. Something he probably worked on, Donadze thought.

The elevator chimed its arrival and its doors opened. 'We'll talk in your car,' the man said, turning away.

Donadze waited a moment then followed, reaching for his key to unlock the car's doors. The big man surprised him by sitting in the back, his long legs pressing against the back of the driver's seat. Donadze thought for a moment then sat in the front passenger seat. 'Who are you?' he said.

'You've been told to call me Sandro. What is it that you want?'

Sandro was the name given to Donadze by Colonel Meskhi. 'What do I want? You came to me, didn't you?'

'Yes, as ordered. But that doesn't tell me what you want.'

Donadze shook his head. 'Listen, *Sandro*,' he said. 'I've had orders as well—from our mutual boss. I assume your orders are the same as mine.'

'And what do you *assume* these to be?'

Donadze tipped his head, closed his eyes and exhaled. He waited a moment then locked eyes with Sandro. 'All right,' he said. 'Colonel Meskhi is pissed that women are being trafficked through Georgia. He's pissed that these women are being forced into prostitution and he's really pissed that at least two have been murdered. He formed a unit to put a stop to the trafficking. You're part of that unit and he's ordered us to work together. Does that sound about right?'

Sandro gave a half-smile, 'Yes, about right.'

'So, what does working together look like to you?'

'I don't know yet. Colonel Meskhi vouched for you and I trust his judgement. But what I'm doing—it's dangerous. You say the wrong thing, speak to the wrong person? At best, my cover's blown. At worst, I'm dead.'

Donadze stared at Sandro, the scar on his face red and angry in the dim light. 'All right, I understand, you have to be careful. But if we are to work together, we'll have to share information and I know nothing about you or the work you're doing.'

Sandro paused, seemingly considering how much Donadze could be trusted. 'Anzor Kalmikov,' he said. 'He thinks I'm working for him.'

'So, the bombing at Shroshi Street?'

'That was Otar Basilia, of course.'

'How about the murder of the two girls at Gali Street?'

Sandro took out his phone and pressed buttons. Donadze's phone rang. 'If you have to contact me—do it on that number.' He opened the door. 'And if you do have to contact me—your name is *Dachi*. Otherwise, sit tight and I'll be in touch,' he said, getting out of the car and leaving the door open as he disappeared into the shadows.

NINE

'Where are you, Ramaz?' Jaqeli asked.

'I'm on my way to Shindisi,' Donadze said. 'I couldn't sleep and decided to drive out to see Major Gloveli. I'll be back in the station by ten.'

There was pause before Jaqeli spoke, 'A personal visit?'

'Not really. I want to discuss our investigation with him. It's something we do. It's useful for me to get a different perspective and he likes it—it keeps him connected to the job.' Donadze hesitated for a moment. 'But there's a bit more to it than that. Gloveli's a tough old guy but I like to keep an eye on him, he's let things slip a little since his wife died.'

'I don't mind an early start, Ramaz. I would have been happy to go with you. I thought we were working this case together.'

'We are...' Jaqeli remained silent and he added, 'Something wrong, Irina?'

'I'm fine... Just let me know how it goes.'

'Will do,' Donadze said, ending the call. He arrived at

the village and continued the short distance to Gloveli's house, wondering if Jaqeli was upset with him or if something else was on her mind—a fallout with Arziani perhaps. He'd only had a few romantic relationships before meeting Tamuna, and none with colleagues—a situation he thought could get messy. But he hadn't been entirely truthful with Jaqeli either. He had thought it unwise for her to know about Sandro and was travelling to Shindisi on his own for that reason. He got out of his car, refusing to acknowledge to himself that he shouldn't be discussing Sandro with Gloveli either.

Gloveli was sitting in his garden, his breakfast on a small table beside him. He looked different and it took Donadze a moment to realise that he had cut his hair, trimmed his eyebrows and shaved. He was also wearing smart trousers and an open-necked dark-blue shirt in place of the work clothes he habitually wore to tend his garden. The overall effect made him look at least five years younger.

'*Gamarjoba*, Major,' Donadze said. 'Job interview?'

'You're becoming something of a fixture around here, Ramaz. What can I do for you?'

Donadze sat on the spare chair and pointed at the mug on the table. 'Coffee would be good.'

Gloveli sighed, pulled himself out of his chair and limped into the house. He returned a minute later and reclaimed his seat. 'She'll bring it out,' he said.

'Veronika? How is she?'

Gloveli shook his head, 'I'm glad Tina and I never had a daughter,' he said, referring to his dead wife. 'The sooner you send her back to Ukraine, the better.'

'Yes, I can see how difficult this must be for you,

Major,' Donadze said, deadpan, watching Veronika walking towards him with a mug of coffee and a plate with cheese and bread.

'*Gamarjoba*, Lieutenant,' she said, placing the mug and plate on the table. She was wearing the same denims and leather jacket she had worn in the station but had brushed and pleated her hair. The cool, fresh mountain air had flushed her skin pink and the anxiety Donadze had observed was gone. She looked her true age, a girl of just eighteen.

'You're learning Georgian?' he said, receiving a blank look in return. 'How are you, Veronika?' he continued in Russian.

'I'm okay. How much longer do you think I'll have to stay here?' she said, missing Gloveli's frown.

'We *are* making progress, Veronika. But it'll be a while before it's safe for you to leave.'

She gave a small shrug. 'It's not too bad, I suppose. I've spoken to my mum and my sister and they're okay.'

Donadze glanced at Gloveli and he also shrugged. 'It's not a problem, Ramaz.'

'More coffee, Levan?' Veronika said, smiling at Gloveli.

The old policeman scowled and shook his head. She lifted his empty mug and carried it into the house.

'More coffee, *Levan*?' Donadze said with mock incredulity.

'What can I do for you, Donadze?' Gloveli growled.

'I told Veronika that we're making progress, Major. And we are.'

'Tell me,' Gloveli said, immediately alert and engaged.

Donadze provided an update on his investigation, including the role he had asked Father Chanturia to take and Colonel Meskhi's instructions to work with Sandro.

'Didn't you know Chanturia's history?' Donadze asked.

Gloveli shook his head. 'I must be losing my touch,' he said.

'You haven't seen his tattoos?'

Gloveli paused. 'I'd heard about them.'

'So you *did* know—why didn't you tell me?'

'Listen, Ramaz, when Dato Kaldani sent his thugs here last year, you know what kept me alive? Not you and not the police. It was the people here—in this village—who protected me. Don't you think some of them might have *history*? I have to live here and they have to trust me. You heard me tell Arziani and Jaqeli that wearing a cassock doesn't make you a good person—I knew you'd figure it out for yourself.'

'Your friends in the village might have to trust you, Major—but so do I.'

'If you're in any doubt about that, then you should leave now.'

There was a long pause before Donadze spoke, 'I know I can trust you, Major. But maybe you could trust *me* as well...'

Gloveli cleared his throat and fumbled for the coffee mug which Veronika had removed. 'Yes, you're right. Okay, let's start again. What can I do for you, Ramaz?'

Donadze took a moment to re-focus. 'Let me run this by you. Otar Basilia and Anzor Kalmikov are at each other's throats, both haemorrhaging cash, with not much coming in. We have an opportunity to get people inside both organisations. Sandro's in with Kalmikov already and we'll try to get the priest in with Basilia…'

'So you'll receive information from both sides...'

'Yes, but maybe they can do more than that…'

Gloveli leaned back in his chair. '*Agents provocateurs*?'

'Yes. Get them to feed Basilia and Kalmikov with false information. Stir things up between them.'

'It's a common enough strategy. But what if the war spills onto the streets and innocent people get hurt?'

'We're already trying to stop that happening. You've probably seen the raids that were reported on television news.'

'I did.' Gloveli paused, thinking. 'It's worth thinking about but probably difficult in practice. But regardless, cover yourself, speak with Colonel Meskhi, make sure you have his support.'

Donadze stood. 'Thanks, for looking after Veronika, Major. I suppose it's okay for her to call her mother and sister occasionally, but please don't let her phone anyone else. Especially not her—supposed—boyfriend in Ukraine.'

'Antin Honchar? You don't have to worry about him.'

Donadze sat back down. 'What have you done, Levan?' he said.

'Me personally? Nothing, of course. But you know I still have my contacts across the old Soviet.'

'Is he—'

'Dead? No, but he should be. He just won't be luring young girls away from their homes any time soon.'

'But we talked about this. Didn't I tell you—no vigilante action.'

'You also said we should trust each other. I didn't have

to tell you about Antin Honchar and no one else needs to know. You want trust—this is what it looks like, Donadze.'

Donadze left Major Gloveli's house and walked to the church, taking time to breathe the cool, fresh air deep into his lungs. He made a mental note to bring his family to Shindisi to visit Gloveli and escape the city's smog, if only briefly.

Chanturia was alone in the nave, removing spent candles from their sand-filled trays and smoothing the sand with his fingers. '*Gamarjoba*, Father,' Donadze said.

'*Gamarjoba*, Lieutenant. Welcome.'

'Where can we talk?'

'By the stacidia, I think,' Chanturia said, indicating the single row of high-backed chairs which lined the long walls of the nave to support worshipers as they stood during services.

Leaning against the stacidia with his back to the fresco wall, Donadze closed his eyes and inhaled, imagining the sweet, aromatic incense entering his lungs where it would be absorbed by his blood and carried through arteries to bond with every cell in his body.

'It never leaves you, does it?' Chanturia said.

Donadze's instinct was to deny understanding the priest's meaning—but knew he wouldn't be believed. 'No, I suppose not. What about you, has God always been with you?'

'You mean when I was outside the law? Yes, even then, I think. Although, I had it well suppressed back then.' He paused for a moment. 'Are you here to give me my instructions?'

'I can't *instruct* you to do anything. But, if you're still willing to help, I would like you to return to Shots and contact Beso Eristavi. Irina and I visited him yesterday. He's rattled and knows we're looking at him. But he doesn't know what we have on him—yet. That's where you come in. Get him to set up a meeting with Otar Basilia.'

'So I can sell him information?'

'Yes, but don't appear too keen and make sure you're paid well. Remember, you're a priest—selling your soul shouldn't come cheap.'

'Selling my soul? That sounds about right, I suppose.'

'I'm talking about appearances. We both know that's not what you're doing.'

'I want something from you, Lieutenant. If this goes wrong and something happens to me, I want the Church to know what I was doing, that I was helping the police. I want my family looked after. And I want the Church—and the world—to know that I didn't die a criminal. I need that for Keti, for Sergo and for my daughter when she's born.'

Donadze instinctively knew that vows made in this church would be held sacred. 'I'll make you two promises, Father. Keeping you safe is my top priority, more so than bringing a case against Otar Basilia, Beso Eristavi and their like. I promise I'll do all I can to protect you. But if things do go wrong, I promise I *will* speak for you; the Church will know that its priest died a true Christian warrior.'

Chanturia grinned. 'A true Christian warrior? I doubt you use that kind of language every day, Lieutenant.'

'No, I don't. Do you have any questions?'

'Will I be wearing a wire?'

Donadze shook his head. 'No. We certainly won't be strapping a radio transmitter to your chest. *Wire* is a dated term, anyway. Recording devices are tiny and can go anywhere now: a pen, button, shoes. But it's still too dangerous. Eristavi might not check, but Basilia will. You'll also be on your own. We can't risk putting any officers near you, he'd know we're there.'

'Okay, when should I approach him?'

'This evening—call me after you've met.'

'Yes, okay.' Chanturia paused. 'Is there something I can do for you, Lieutenant?'

'What do you mean?'

'Your ambivalence towards the Church, to God. You drag guilt around like a ball and chain. I know you're in pain—let me hear your confession.'

Donadze felt a sudden and overwhelming need to tell the priest how his sister had died, how he couldn't save her and how that guilt, although irrational, tormented him still. But, at some level, he also understood that it was the torment which gave him his motivation and his edge. 'Not today, Father,' he said, pushing himself up from the stacidia and walking towards the ancient church doors.

Donadze arrived at Mtatsminda Station three hours later than promised to Jaqeli. She was at her desk, staring at her screen as he approached. 'Hey, Irina, sorry I'm late.'

'What?' she said, her eyes still on the screen.

'Never mind. What are you doing?'

'Sit down a minute.' She waited until Donadze had pulled a chair to her desk. 'I've been thinking,' she said. 'About slavery. When Europeans shipped people from Africa and sold them as slaves in sugar and cotton plantations, they called it a trade, didn't they—the slave trade. It was evil but, as far as they were concerned—just business. It spanned three continents, Europe, Africa and America and must have required a fair degree of organisation and communication. But there was no Internet back then, no email. Now, people trafficking, or modern-day slavery is no different from the slave trade out of Africa. Basilia's operation doesn't span three continents but it does span at least three countries: Ukraine, Georgia and Germany. How does he run that operation, communicate with his suppliers and his buyers? How does he move his money around?'

'I've got a feeling you're going to tell me.'

'Right. Basilia has the Internet, email and messaging apps, but he also has a problem the European slavers didn't—his business is illegal. What do you know about the deep web and the dark web?'

'I've heard about them.'

'So, not much then. What most people think of as the *web* consists of all the web sites which can be found by search engines like Google. The *deep web* is everything else. And, because these sites can't be found by Google, that means anyone using the deep web enjoys a level of privacy not available on the web. The deep web is massively bigger than the web and most of its sites are legitimate. Are you with me, so far?'

'Assume I am.'

'Okay. Now, the *dark web* is different. It makes up

about five percent of the deep web and many of its websites *are* still legitimate. As an example, it might be used by dissidents of oppressive regimes to stay anonymous and keep their families safe from reprisal. But it's also an area of the Internet where you can buy and sell illegal goods and services such as drugs, weapons, personal information, child pornography—'

'And people?'

'Yes. You've heard of the Silk Road?'

'Not Marco Polo's Silk Road?'

'No, although I'm sure that's where the name came from. This Silk Road was an infamous online black market. It was big—more than a billion dollars of Bitcoin was seized when the site was eventually shut down.'

'You think Basilia could be trading on something like the Silk Road?'

'Misha thinks so and I agree it's likely.'

'Misha—this is his idea?'

'Yes, we were talking about it this morning and I did some digging while you were in Shindisi. How did you get on by the way?'

'Let's come back to that later. What are you proposing?'

'We go onto the dark web and find Basilia.'

'And that's what you've done?'

'Hardly, but I know where to start. The whole point of the dark web is that its users stay anonymous. Basilia will be using one or more techniques to hide his activities, probably connecting to the Tor network through a VPN if he's smart. Difficult to break into but not impossible.'

Donadze looked at Jaqeli blankly. 'Tell me,' he said.

'Okay. Using a VPN or Virtual Private Network hides your real IP address and encrypts your Internet connection. It's commonly used to access foreign streaming services such as Netflix. Tor is a network which keeps data secure by bouncing it around multiple locations. Its logo incorporates an onion—supposedly representing the multiple layers of protection it gives you.

'And difficult to break into, but not impossible?'

'Exactly. The Silk Road was supposed to be impenetrable—but the FBI found a way in.'

'We're not the FBI.'

'No, but we can request help from INTERPOL. People trafficking is a huge issue right across the world currently and INTERPOL has the expertise to help.'

'You said you know how to start?'

'According to Misha, we go through Georgia's NCB— the National Central Bureau. He's got a contact.'

'Well, this is great, Irina and definitely worth a shot. But I think we need Misha's help—would you be okay if I ask him to join our investigation?'

'Is there any reason I wouldn't be?' she said, colour rising in her cheeks.

TEN

Donadze's phone beeped the arrival of a text from Colonel Meskhi. '*Join me HQ soonest. Notify arrival time.*'

'Love and kisses to you, too,' Donadze muttered as he glanced at his watch. It was two twenty-five and he texted his reply, allowing a generous hour for the journey.

He left his car in the Gulua Street car park and entered the building. His last visit to the Ministry of Internal Affairs' HQ had been about a year ago. He assumed that Meskhi occupied the same office and, after presenting his ID at Reception, took the elevator to the fourth level. He knocked and opened the door. Meskhi was sitting at the small conference table in the corner of the office, reading and annotating a stack of documents. 'Come in, Lieutenant. Help yourself to coffee,' he said, pointing to a tray containing a stainless steel vacuum flask and white ceramic mugs.

Donadze had not been offered hospitality in Meskhi's office before and his mind raced as, adding sugar to his cup, he tried to think why he had been summoned.

'Captain Nakani informed me that you and he are now on better terms.'

Donadze didn't believe that was the case. 'Yes, sir. I apologised to the Captain,' he said.

'Sit down.'

Donadze sat, facing Meskhi across the table.

'I would normally have asked your commanding officer to join us...'

Donadze hesitated, expecting Meskhi to elaborate. 'Yes, sir,' he said, feeling uncomfortable under his appraising gaze.

'You know, Lieutenant,' he said at last. 'I like my job. Most aspects of it, anyway. It's rarely acknowledged, but what we do makes a difference. We protect people and keep them from harm. Our citizens walk safe streets and sleep soundly in their homes—but it wasn't always like that.'

'Of course not, sir. I remember that time very well. It wasn't so long ago.'

'Not even a generation ago. But some of us have short, or possibly, selective memories. So, although I like most aspects of my job, I most certainly do not enjoy managing the politics. Sometimes, it feels like our political masters are working against us.'

Donadze didn't respond, sensing that Meskhi had more to say.

'At best, they're short-sighted. But it may be worse than that—some are probably corrupt.' Meskhi paused. 'But that's not your concern. It seems, Lieutenant, that our dealings with Otar Basilia and Anzor Kalmikov have been heavy-handed and insensitive. The bombing at Shroshi Street and the subsequent raids I initiated on their premises have been widely reported, even internationally. I'm told that CNN will run a story this evening, describing how crime in Georgia has escalated. A return to the bad old days they will say, although it appears that the murder of innocent young people and the continued trafficking of people through Georgia have gone unnoticed. Regardless, our political leaders don't like the attention and I have been ordered to scale back our operations.'

'But, sir, how can we—'

Meskhi raised his hand to interrupt. 'Our leaders worry that adverse publicity will have an impact on business investment and tourism. And, for a politician, that's a legitimate concern.' He paused. 'But it's not for me.'

Donadze was uncertain how Meskhi expected him to respond and he took a moment before asking, 'So, we ignore your orders, carry on as before?'

'Tell me, Lieutenant, when I last summoned you to this office, what did you think would happen?'

'I thought you would dismiss me.'

'Yes, and I had been ordered to do so. To answer your question, *I* will carry on as before. However, if things go wrong, you will be exposed and I may not be able to protect you this time. *You* shouldn't be held responsible for carrying out *my* orders. I will therefore instruct Captain Nakani to re-assign you.'

'No, that won't be necessary, sir.'

'It wasn't a suggestion, Lieutenant.'

'I realise that, sir.' Donadze stood. 'Will that be all, Colonel?'

Meskhi picked up the document he had been reading. 'I believe so. Carry on, Lieutenant.'

It was six thirty when Donadze returned home. An appetising aroma met him as he opened the front door. Music was playing quietly and Tamuna was settled on an easy chair, Eka nestling in her arms and staring adoringly at her mother. 'Daddy's home,' she said.

Donadze leaned over to kiss her and the baby. 'She looks happy enough.'

'Well she is now, lucky you weren't here half an hour ago.'

Donadze chose not to hear the implied reproach. 'Where's my mother?'

'Visiting friends, she thinks she has to give us time on our own.'

'Yes, I know. Is she alright?'

'I think so, she seems to have the same amount of energy as before, no fatigue or shortness of breath. But you know what she's like, she wouldn't let a heart attack slow her down.'

'We'll keep an eye on her.'

'Yes, Ramaz, I'm doing that.'

'Are *you* okay, darling?'

'I'm fine.' She smiled. 'It's time for this girl's bath. Do you want to do it?'

'Yes, but don't tell my mother.'

'My lips are sealed. Take her while I fill the bath.'

Donadze rolled up his shirt sleeves and took the baby from Tamuna. She complained a little then settled her face into his shoulder. He loved her smallness, her tiny feet and hands. He dropped his head onto hers and inhaled deeply—

106

he loved her smell.

Tamuna returned to the living room with the plastic baby-bath, one of the many new, and apparently essential, pieces of equipment that could be found in every room of the apartment. She placed the bath on the floor, a small amount of soapy water splashing over the sides. Donadze sat on the easy chair and undressed the baby, pausing dramatically with his fingers gripping the nappy's sticky tape. 'Is this safe?' he said.

'It is where I'm sitting,' Tamuna said. 'We'll get her off to bed then eat.'

Donadze removed the nappy then transferred Eka into the water, her little legs kicking with excitement as she was lowered in. He knelt by the bath, helping her play with her toys and splashing warm water over her body. She cried when he rinsed her hair but stopped when wrapped in a warm towel and dressed in clean, warm pyjamas.

Tamuna held out her hands to take the baby back. 'I'll feed her in the bedroom,' she said.

Donadze waited until she had taken Eka away before making the call.

'Yes?' he heard when the call connected.

'Sandro? It's Dachi.'

'What do you want?'

'You said you'd be in touch.'

'I also told you to sit tight. What do you want?'

'We need to talk.'

There was a long pause. 'Okay, take your car to the Radisson Hotel's car park. Stay inside—I'll find you.'

'When?'

'One hour.'

Donadze paused. He could hear a lullaby playing over the baby monitor and Tamuna whispering her love to their baby.

'Is that a problem?' Sandro asked.

'No problem,' Donadze said.

Donadze collected a ticket at the barrier and parked as far from the hotel as possible. There was little movement in the car park and he thought that Sandro had chosen a good place to meet. He was ten minutes early and he shut his eyes to focus his thoughts, trying to block the memory of Tamuna's hurt expression when he had told her that he had to go out again.

There was a knock on the side window and Sandro got into the car, dropping quickly onto the passenger's seat and closing the door. Donadze had turned off the courtesy light and they sat in near darkness, the steady rumble of traffic from Rustaveli Avenue, muted. Sandro turned in his seat to face Donadze, his breath sour as he spoke, 'You wanted to talk.'

'You don't like doing this, do you?'

'No, but I follow orders, just like you. Now that that's been established, what is it you want?'

'We're both following orders. Maybe neither of us like it, but since we don't have a choice, we should try to make it work.'

Sandro paused as light from a passing car threw a shadow across his scarred, stubbled face. 'And how do we do that?'

'How close are you to Anzor Kalmikov?'

'His friends call him *Anzori*. So do I. We're close enough. He knows me, speaks to me sometimes. Why?'

'Does he trust you enough to tell you his plans?'

'No, not directly. The people he trusts are family: his son, uncles, cousins, advisers from way back…'

'So how do you get *your* information?'

'Second hand mostly, casual talk, gossip over a cigarette, hardly ever directly from Kalmikov. But that's not why you wanted to see me.'

'No. Colonel Meskhi called me to his office this morning. He's under pressure from the politicians. They want the war between Basilia and Kalmikov to stop. And they want us to back-off. They don't like the press the country's been getting and they want things back to how they were.'

'And that's a bad thing?'

'In the long term, yes. If we do back-off now, we might find there's a new balance of power; maybe Kalmikov has gained some territory, or maybe losing his gym has weakened him. It doesn't matter. Once the dust settles, it'll be business as usual. Trafficking will start-up again. And, over time, it'll get more difficult to find the men responsible for the Gali Street killings. Colonel Meskhi understands that but he won't be able to keep the politicians off our backs much longer.'

'That's his problem, isn't it? What's it got to do with me? Or you, come to that?'

'It's our problem as well. If we don't deal with Kalmikov and Basilia now, we'll have to do it next month or next year—and they'll be stronger by then. We'll have to take them on eventually, so we should choose the time which suits us best—and that's now. You see that don't you?'

'*We* choose the time to do it? It sounds like *you've* chosen already.'

'No, that's why I'm here tonight. I want your agreement.'

'To do what?'

'To put a stick in the hornets' nest. Stir things up, bring them to a head.'

'It's a hornets' nest alright. If I do agree, how do we do it?'

'Information and misinformation. You take it to Kalmikov, I take it to Basilia.'

Sandro looked at Donadze closely. 'How would you take your information to Basilia?'

'You don't need to know.'

'I thought we were sharing?'

'We are, but I don't expect you to tell me everything, either.'

'Curiosity killed the cat, I suppose.' Sandro pressed a button on his watch to make the face glow. 'I've been here too long already,' he said. 'So this is coming from Colonel Meskhi? He wants us to stir the hornets' nest, as you put it?'

'Yes, that's our orders,' Donadze lied.

'We'll talk soon,' Sandro said. He turned in his seat, checking there was no one near the car, then quickly got out.

Donadze watched his rear-view mirror as Sandro strode into the shadows, his shoulders hunched and his collar pulled high against the cool breeze, his hands plunged deep into his pockets. He started his engine and drove towards the exit, only now allowing himself to think about Tamuna and the way she'd looked as he'd left their apartment.

ELEVEN

Donadze hesitated before opening the door. It was nine thirty and the apartment was quiet. Tamuna was sitting on an easy chair with her legs curled under her, reading her Kindle by the lamp's dim and shadowed light. She put the Kindle down when Donadze came into the room and lifted her face as he bent to kiss her. 'There's food in the oven,' she said.

'Thanks, I'll get it later. Can we just talk for now?'

'Again?'

'Yes, again.'

'Okay,' she said, uncurling her legs and sitting back in her chair.

'Do you want to sit here, beside me?' Donadze said, indicating the settee.

'I'm okay where I am, Ramaz. Let's talk—if that's what you want to do.'

He sat on the settee, her composure and the distance between them making him feel uneasy. 'I know you're angry with me,' he said.

'You don't know that, Ramaz. I actually think I'm past being angry.'

'What does that mean?'

'I really don't know,' she said, turning to face him. 'I try to be reasonable. I know your job's demanding, that you can't work office hours. I understand why you're so driven and it hurts me to see you suffer that way. I know you love Eka and me. And I love you and want to be with you—but I don't know if that's going to be enough for us.'

'But it *should* be enough. You think I love this job? I don't. I don't know what it is, but it's not love. I've said this before; if it comes to a choice between you and the police, then you win every time.'

'How often have we had this conversation, Ramaz?'

'I know, too often. Tell me what to do and I'll do it. Anything to keep you and Eka. Tell me to quit the police and I will.'

'I'm not telling you to do anything. You do what you have to do and I'll do the same.'

'Let's get married, Tamuna. Things would look different then.'

'That wouldn't work. You'd be giving me a ring, not a ball and chain.'

'You're not my prisoner, Tamuna.'

'We're tired and going round in circles.' She stood, pulled him to his feet and put her arms around his neck. 'Don't look so gloomy,' she said. 'I'm not giving up on us yet.'

'Please, never do that.'

She led him to their bedroom where they made love.

Later, Donadze lay with his head on the pillow, unable to sleep. 'Are you still awake?' he whispered.

'Yes.'

'I meant what I said. Please don't give up on us.'

Donadze's phone buzzed. 'One minute, Father,' he said, stepping onto the balcony and pulling the sliding door behind him. 'Did you see Beso Eristavi?'

His mother mimed exasperation through the glass as she placed his coffee on the breakfast bar. He hadn't put on shoes and his feet were cold on the marble which had chilled under the clear skies.

'Yes, as you suggested. What a despicable man, a pimp, really. Still, not much different from me at that age, I suppose.'

'I doubt that, Father. Tell me what happened.'

'Eristavi was holding court at Shots—the girls seem to like him—but it was easy enough to get his attention. He took a break and we talked. He told me that you and Detective Jaqeli had been to his bar and tried to intimidate him. But cops don't scare him, he said. He's arrogant and a braggart—not good qualities in his line of work, I'm afraid. You'll find him floating face down in the Kura one of these days. Anyway, he seemed to accept my story, the hypocrisy of a priest selling information to gangsters.'

'I know you don't like him but try not to let him see that.'

'Is it that obvious? No, I don't like him but then again, there's none so pure as the purified.'

'What else?'

'I told him that I'd seen Mariam's journal and that the police couldn't use it to bring a case against him. Of course, he said he didn't know what I was talking about, that he'd never even heard of Mariam. But he's no actor. I told him to set up a meeting with Otar Basilia. He wanted to know what I was going to say, but I told him just to set it up, that Basilia wouldn't be happy if he didn't. It's going to happen, I'm sure of that.'

'Good. Have you seen Mr and Mrs Alasania?'

'Yes, they're as good as can be expected.'

'We'll visit today and pass on the information we want to get back to Basilia.'

'Will I see you?'

'No, Basilia may be watching you already. We can't meet.'

'Okay, we can keep in touch by phone.'

'How are you, Father? Any doubts?'

'About helping you? No. But maybe some doubts about myself. All the time I was talking to Eristavi, I just wanted to smash a bottle into his smug, pretty face.'

'But you didn't and that's the difference. Let me know when Basilia has been in touch. And Father?'

'Yes, Lieutenant?'

'Thank you.'

Donadze slid the balcony door open and returned to the warmth of the living room.

'Breakfast, Ramaz,' his mother said, pointing to the breakfast bar.

Tamuna came into the room, carrying Eka. 'Could you

take her while I have a shower?' she said to Donadze's mother.

'Yes, of course, does she need—?'

'Let me take her, *Deda*,' Donadze said. He smiled at Tamuna, 'It's a beautiful morning. After you've had a shower, why don't we take a walk?'

'Do you have time?'

'Yes, of course I do.' he said.

Jaqeli and Arziani were sitting at her desk, drinking coffee.

'Hey, Ramaz,' Arziani said. 'Want to join us?'

'Let's go somewhere we can talk.'

'Interview Room One, then,' he said, picking up his mug and Jaqeli's. Donadze made himself coffee and arrived at the interview room to see her snatch her hand free from Arziani's.

'Irina, Misha, can we get this out of the way?' Donadze said. 'It's obvious that you two are together. And that's great, I'm happy for you, both. But you won't let that interfere with our investigation, will you?'

Jaqeli looked at Arziani who grinned. 'Fair point, Ramaz. No, nothing's going to get in the way of your investigation.'

'Good. What's the latest with your INTERPOL contact?'

'His name's Captain Rezo Murtov.' Arziani looked at his watch. 'I've spoken to him on the phone and we're meeting at one. He thinks he will be able to help—human trafficking is one of INTERPOL's priorities currently and he reckons they'll support us.'

'Great, let's hope that takes us somewhere, then.' He turned to Jaqeli. 'Irina, we're going to Shindisi, leaving in thirty minutes. We'll have lunch with Major Gloveli, check up on Veronika then update Mr and Mrs Alasania.'

'Will we see Father Chanturia?'

'No, we'll keep our distance from the priest for now. Misha, can we get back together—say at five thirty?'

'Okay, see you back here.'

Donadze returned to the detectives' bureau. It was empty, all the detectives were out working their cases. Captain Nakani was in his office. He saw Donadze approaching and reached under his chair to raise it. Donadze caught a glimpse of the screen he had just closed, a Facebook page, he thought.

'*Gamarjoba*, Captain. May I update you on our investigation?' he said.

Nakani looked at his watch, 'Okay, I've got some time. Take a seat.'

Donadze summarised the investigation to date, including Arziani's initiative to contact INTERPOL. After a moment's hesitation he also related being called to Colonel Meskhi's office and the pressure being exerted on Meskhi by his political leaders.

'You seem to have the Colonel's ear,' Nakani said, folding his arms across his chest.

'Possibly, but only for today—tomorrow could be a different story.'

'Where are you with his undercover agent.'

Donadze hesitated. 'We've met, but I doubt he'll be much help. Too low in the pecking order, I think.'

Nakani looked at him closely. 'Well, the Colonel did

say there are aspects of this case you shouldn't divulge. Even to me. Anything else?'

Donadze realised that Nakani was unhappy that he was withholding information but could think of nothing to say in consolation. 'Thank you for your time, sir,' he said, standing to leave.

Jaqeli had returned to her desk.

'Ready, Irina?' he said.

She jumped to her feet. 'Born ready, Lieutenant.'

'Of course you were.'

They took the familiar road to Shindisi and arrived at Gloveli's house with the sun still high in the sky. The table had been brought into the garden and was laden with various food dishes and a jug of wine. Gloveli was sitting on one side of the table, his face in the sun. He stood to kiss Jaqeli and gestured for them both to sit.

'*Gamarjoba*, Major. You didn't tell me you'd organised a *supra*.'

'Hardly a *supra*, Donadze. And it wasn't me who organised it.'

'Veronika?'

'Who else?' he said, shaking his head.

'Well, Irina and I certainly appreciate you taking her in, Major.' He pointed to the laden table. 'We can see how difficult this must be for you.'

'Pour the wine, Donadze. She'll be out in a minute.'

'You're looking well, Major,' Jaqeli said.

'Thanks, Irina. You are too.'

'How do I look, Major?' Donadze said.

Gloveli assessed him coldly. 'You don't want to know.'

'What are you laughing at?' Veronika asked in Russian

as she carried bottles of pear and tarragon flavoured drinks to the table.

'They're laughing at me. How are you, Veronika?' Donadze asked.

'I'm okay. I quite like it here, in the village. Levan has some nice friends—and they're not all sixty, either.'

Donadze glanced at Gloveli and suppressed a smile. 'Well, just be careful who you speak to. Check with Major Gloveli if you're not sure.'

'Yes, thanks, Donadze. I think I might have mentioned that to her already,' Gloveli said, smiling at the girl.

Did you make the *khachapuri* yourself, Veronika?' Jaqeli said putting a slice of the *sulguni* stuffed bread on all their plates.

'Yes, I hope it's alright. A lady in the village gave me the recipe. I can't believe how much cheese it needed.'

'Well, let's see.'

The food was particularly delicious when eaten in the fresh mountain air and with the hazy sun sending precious warmth to—what they all agreed—was this most fortunate part of the world. But the time passed quickly and Jaqeli said, 'We should go, Ramaz.'

The temperature dropped noticeably as a cloud drifted over the sun. Donadze looked at his watch. 'Yes, we should. Veronika, thank you for this delicious meal. I was particularly impressed with your *khachapuri*. Major, thank you for your hospitality. I'll speak to you soon.'

Gloveli eased himself out of his chair and walked with Donadze and Jaqeli to their car. 'The Alasanias? There's nothing you can say or do that can help them, Ramaz. Just pass on your information and then leave them in peace.'

TWELVE

Arziani was waiting in the interview room when Donadze and Jaqeli returned to Mtatsminda Station. He smiled and jumped out of his chair when he saw them.

'Looks like you had a good meeting, Misha,' Jaqeli said.

'Yes, I think we're on to something here. Captain Murtov is great, he said he'll issue a blue notice and request information—'

'Wait. What's a blue notice?'

Arziani took a breath then continued, speaking less excitedly. 'Sorry. As Murtov explained it to me, INTERPOL uses a system of colour-coded notices to communicate across member countries. Blue notices are requests for information. In this case, on Basilia and his trafficking operations, particularly in Ukraine and the EU. Okay?'

'Yes, got it.'

'Good. So the blue notices will hopefully give us insight into what Basilia is doing outside Georgia. But there's more;

Georgia recently joined an INTERPOL information forum which coordinates law enforcement of cybercrime across international borders. Murtov thinks it's likely that Basilia is using an encrypted communication system, probably hosted on the dark web—this forum should help us hack it. If that happens then we'll get huge amounts of intelligence and evidence to help build a winnable case against him.'

'But…' Donadze said.

'But, at this stage Murtov's not sure how easy that will be—it depends on how tight Basilia's security protocols are.'

'Well, it sounds very promising, and certainly worth looking into. When will Murtov get back to you?'

'I said I'd meet him tomorrow, at three.'

'Good,' Donadze said. 'Misha, this is getting too much for Irina and me on our own. We need you to join us full-time—is that going to be a problem?'

'I could see that coming. But no, it shouldn't be a problem. Captain Nakani knows that the Colonel has prioritised your investigation, I think he'll allow it.'

'Do you want me to speak to him?'

'I can do it—we get on okay. We go to the same gym, you know, sometimes work out together.'

'Pumping iron with the boss? Okay, let me know how it goes. But you'll need a briefing if you're joining us on a full-time basis. Has Irina spoken to you about Father Chanturia?'

'What? You think I've been gossiping to Misha about our case?' Jaqeli said.

'It's okay, Irina,' Arziani said. 'Ramaz, I told you this morning, nothing's going to get in the way of our investigation. I know that you've been talking to the Shindisi village priest, but that's all I know. Irina hasn't told me anything that you would consider confidential.'

Donadze held his hands up. 'You're right, I apologise. Let me start again.' He updated Arziani on Father Chanturia's background, his agreement to feed misinformation to Basilia and his initial contact with Basilia's gang through Beso Eristavi.

'Pretty good move, Ramaz,' Arziani said.

Donadze glanced at Jaqeli. She was sitting with her arms crossed, tight-lipped and clearly angry. 'Something on your mind, Irina?' he asked.

She uncrossed her arms. 'Could I ask you a personal question, Lieutenant?'

'I suppose so.'

'If I were a man, would you still be suspicious that I had passed on confidential information to Misha?'

'I've got a suspicious nature, Irina. That's why I joined the police,' he tried to joke.

Jaqeli didn't respond and Donadze finally added. 'No, probably not. I'm sorry, I shouldn't have stereotyped you that way.'

Jaqeli responded with a smile this time. 'Well, I'm glad we got that clear. What's next?'

Donadze looked at his watch. 'Let's wind it up for today. Can we meet back here tomorrow—at seven?'

'You've got somewhere to go?' Arziani said.

'Yes, I'm taking Tamuna to the opera. I managed to get two tickets, it'll be a surprise for her.'

'Opera, Ramaz?' Jaqeli said. 'Who would have thought it?'

Donadze looked at Arziani in mock disbelief. 'Misha, did I imagine it, or did Detective Jaqeli just stereotype me as crusty and uncultured because I'm a man?'

Arziani grinned, 'He's got a point, Irina…'

'Not really. She's right, I hate opera.'

'Are you ready?' Donadze said.

'Ready for what?' Tamuna asked.

Donadze held up two tickets. 'Something called *Pagliacci*. It's about clowns, apparently.'

'You got tickets for the opera!'

'Yes, but we could stay in and watch television if you'd prefer.' He picked up the remote control. 'I'll see what's on…'

'Turn that off, Donadze.' She threw a cushion at him and jumped out of her chair. 'How long have I got?'

He looked at his watch. 'Twenty minutes, I'd say.'

'Such an annoying man,' she said. Donadze's mother was in the cooking area, holding Eka and smiling at the exchange between the two. 'You knew about this, didn't you?'

'Yes, but I was sworn to secrecy. I did say that you'd want time to get ready, but you know what he's like.'

'Yes—annoying,' she said, hurrying to their bedroom.

'That was a nice thing to do, *Ramazi*,' his mother said. 'I used to love the opera, but I've not been since your father died.'

'Take my ticket. You and Tamuna could go together.'

'Tamuna's right, Ramaz. You really are annoying.'

'I know, it's taken years of practice...'

Tamuna came out of their bedroom after only fifteen minutes. She was wearing a short blue dress with pearls, her hair still damp and glistening under the apartment's halogen lights. She stepped up to Donadze, put her arms around his neck and kissed him. 'Thanks, darling. That was really thoughtful of you.' She winced as she put her feet into black heels. 'I'm going to regret this,' she said, standing straight. 'How do I look?'

'Gorgeous,' his mother said.

Both women looked at Donadze. 'You'll do,' he said.

'Annoying,' his mother said.

'Definitely,' Tamuna agreed.

He had booked a car to take them to Tbilisi Opera. They stepped onto Rustaveli Avenue and Tamuna took his arm as they walked up the steps and entered the Moorish styled building. She squeezed his arm and he knew she was excited to be here. Donadze hadn't been honest with Jaqeli and Arziani and had never admitted it to Tamuna, but he loved opera, especially when performed in beautiful and historic settings. He thought that, one day, he would take her to the world's great opera houses: Milan, London, Sydney.

It was a full house but Donadze had managed to buy good seats. The anticipatory buzz from the audience stopped as the house lights dimmed and the orchestra struck up the overture. The opera was a dramatic tale of love, betrayal and murder, performed in its original Italian but with Georgian surtitles helping the audience follow the story. Act One concluded with Canio—knowing that his wife had been unfaithful—wiping away tears as he put on his clown's costume and prepared to make the audience laugh. The lights came up and Donadze turned to Tamuna, smiling as he observed her dabbing her own eyes. 'Let's have a drink,' he said.

They squeezed into the nearest bar and Donadze joined the throng attempting to catch the barman's attention.

'Ramaz Donadze?' a voice said from behind. He turned to see a man of about fifty, smiling and dressed in a dark blue blazer with white, button-down shirt and blue slacks. His greying hair was long enough to be slicked back and was trendily undercut at the sides. One arm was wrapped proprietorially around the waist of a young woman who wore a figure-hugging, sequined dress with bold décolletage, her long blonde hair and dark eyebrows competing for the truth. The man removed his arm from her waist and offered his hand to Donadze. 'I thought it was you,' he said.

Donadze glanced across the bar to Tamuna. She had managed to secure a standing area near the door and was looking at him inquisitively. He ignored the offered hand. 'Mr Kalmikov,' he said. 'This is a coincidence.'

Kalmikov dropped his hand but kept smiling. 'Yes, isn't it? Why don't you join Tata and me? We're having champagne in a private room—French, of course.'

'Of course. But I think we'll stick to Georgian.'

'Are you sure? Your lady friend looks rather uncomfortable over there.' He waved to Tamuna and she, looking uncertain, raised her hand and tentatively waved back. 'Lovely girl—Tamuna isn't it? It's so difficult for young couples to get out on their own, but then I guess having your mum at home helps.'

'Enjoy the opera, *Anzori*,' Donadze said, keeping his

voice low and even.

'Thank you, Ramaz.' He waved at Tamuna again and crossed the bar with his companion, stopping briefly to speak to her. Donadze watched them leave then turned to collect his drinks order.

'What did he say to you?' he asked as he gave Tamuna her wine.

'He said, "Buy something nice for Eka."' She showed him five banknotes. 'A thousand *lari*, Ramaz—who is he?'

'His name's Anzor Kalmikov—a gangster.'

'A gangster—how does he know Eka?'

'He doesn't, he just wanted to rattle me.'

'Well, now *I'm* rattled.'

'I know, that's what he wanted. To get at me through you—don't let it happen.'

'Would he hurt Eka?'

'No, definitely not.'

'How can you be so sure?'

'How? Because he knows I'd kill him if he even thought about hurting my family. And if I couldn't do it, a thousand other cops would. Eka's safe, so are you. Please trust me.'

'How about you, Ramaz? Are you safe?'

'Definitely.' The bells were ringing to warn that Act Two would soon begin. 'Let's go back through,' Donadze said.

'He's crossed a line, Major,' Donadze said. 'Family is out of bounds—he needs to get that message.' He and Tamuna had watched the opera to its dramatic conclusion; Canio stabbing his unfaithful wife and her lover to death before screaming, "The comedy has ended." It was a wonderful performance but they had returned to their apartment in silence, the magic shattered. He had waited until Tamuna had gone to bed then stepped onto the balcony to call Major Gloveli.

There was a long pause and Donadze checked that he was still connected. 'Major?' he said.

'I'm still here. Kalmikov wouldn't hurt your family, Ramaz. It would be suicide and he's not a stupid man.'

'I know, I told Tamuna the same thing and I believe it. But he crossed a line this evening.'

'Yes, you're right. Police have two lives and there must be a line between the two. Professionally, we deal with the worst of humanity, scum, low-lives like Kalmikov and Basilia. Then we go home to our families—the best of humanity. Two lives—and we have to keep the two apart.'

'What about you, Major, how did you do it?'

'Tina would say I never did.' He paused. 'I shouldn't have to tell you this, Ramaz. But, if anything were to happen to you, I hope you know that I'd watch out for your family—that's what being godfather to Eka means. It's something you never have to worry about.'

'I know, and I'm grateful'.

'There's nothing to be grateful for. And, anyway, nothing *is* going to happen to you. But you're right, Kalmikov needs to realise that he made a mistake by involving Tamuna. What's your plan?'

'I don't have one. I haven't been able to think straight—that's why I called you, I suppose.'

'I'm glad you did. You're angry and that's clouding

your judgement. But don't get carried away, keep your response proportionate, let him see that you have his measure, that he hasn't fazed you. It'll be more effective that way.' He paused. 'But you do have to make it personal.'

'Personal—how?'

'Kalmikov has a son—arrest him.'

'Badri? He's in the family business but we've got nothing on him.'

'Does that matter?'

'It should matter, shouldn't it, Major?'

'You want to send a message and make sure it's clear enough for Kalmikov to understand, don't you? Then make it personal—arrest his son.'

'I don't know, Major. It doesn't feel right.'

'Why not? He'll spend a few hours or a night in a police cell and then he'll be released. It's no big deal. You want to keep your two lives separate, Donadze—that's how you do it. It's your choice but, whatever you decide to do, you need to do it soon.'

Donadze ended the call. He shut his eyes and slowed his breathing, the cool night air calming his thoughts. He knew his family wasn't in real danger and he felt uneasy about targeting Kalmikov's son. But then he thought of the two lives he lived and the need to keep the two apart. He took another deep breath then picked up his phone.

Jaqeli answered after two rings. 'Ramaz?'

'We've got work to do. Are you at Misha's?'

She hesitated for a moment. 'Yes.'

'I'll pick you up in thirty minutes.'

'What's going on, Ramaz?'

'We're going to visit Badri Kalmikov.'

THIRTEEN

J aqeli had been angry and alarmed when told that Kalmikov had approached Tamuna at the opera but had argued that retaliating against his son couldn't be justified.

'Don't worry, Irina, you're following my orders—you can't be held accountable,' Donadze said.

'That's not what I'm worried about, Ramaz.'

'Trust me, Irina.'

He stationed his car outside Badri Kalmikov's apartment block and they waited for him to return home. His arrival along the narrow, residential street was heralded by rhythmic, angry rap music blasting from his sports car's sound system. Donadze knew his neighbours wouldn't complain. He caught a glimpse of Kalmikov's passenger nuzzling his neck as he drove recklessly down a ramp leading to private parking. He heard tyres squealing on smooth concrete then the car park became quiet as the car's engine was shut down. He looked up and, after a couple of minutes, saw Kalmikov's apartment lights go on and heard his music resume—loud but muffled by the building's expensive sound-proofing.

They continued to observe the apartment. Twenty minutes passed and Kalmikov, wearing only shorts, stepped onto his balcony and stretched his arms high and wide then leaned forward over the railings, like an entitled lion-king asserting dominion over his subjects, Donadze thought.

They waited for an hour after the lights and music had gone off then approached the security door. Entry codes for access-controlled buildings are routinely supplied to the emergency services and Donadze entered the code he had been given and opened the door. He knew the elevator would be silent but elected to take the stairs, with Jaqeli following behind.

They reached the fourth level and Donadze's stopped at the head of the stairs. 'Okay?' he whispered.

Jaqeli shook her head, tight-lipped and unhappy.

'Don't worry,' Donadze said and led the way to Kalmikov's apartment.

They positioned themselves outside and drew their weapons. Donadze pounded the door and shouted, 'Police. Open up. Do it now, Mr Kalmikov!'

A moment passed and Kalmikov opened the heavy, steel door. 'What's this about?' he demanded. His file said he was twenty two but Donadze thought he looked younger. His hair was dishevelled and his eyes were red and darkly lined. He had pulled on a black silk dressing gown and cinched it tightly around his slim frame, the sheer material accentuating the bony knobs of his rounded shoulders.

'Inside, Badri,' Donadze said.

They followed Kalmikov into a stylish but messy lounge. 'See who's in the bedroom, Irina and bring her through here,' Donadze said. He holstered his pistol and indicated a white-leather settee. 'Take a seat, Badri.'

'I've called my father, this will cost you your job,' Kalmikov hissed, sitting down.

'Maybe, but close your legs would you,' Donadze said. 'There are ladies present.'

'Funny, but you won't be—'

'Shut up, Badri. I'm not in the mood.'

'This is Nico, Lieutenant,' Jaqeli said leading a young man into the room. He was slim with long fair hair and was strikingly good looking. The towel wrapped around his waist did little to cover his toned body.

'Who's this, Badri?' Donadze said.

Kalmikov shook his head. 'Just a friend. Why, what's it got to do with you?'

'A friend? How old are you, Nico?' Donadze asked.

The young man shivered and wrapped his arms across his chest. 'I'm nineteen and I've done nothing wrong.'

Donadze looked at Jaqeli and she nodded—his ID had checked out.

'Does your father know, Badri?'

'Know what, I don't know what you're talking about.'

'So he doesn't know.' Donadze turned to the young man. 'Has he paid you?'

'Yes,' he said after a moment's hesitation.

'Then you're free to go.'

Donadze watched as Nico scurried to retrieve his clothes and quickly leave the apartment. 'Keep an eye on Mr Kalmikov, Irina. I'm going to look around.'

Kalmikov was a known cocaine user and Donadze thought it likely that there would be coke in his apartment—there was. He had attempted to flush at least one baggie down the toilet but a plastic bag containing white powder was floating in the bowl and a bedside unit had been hastily, but carelessly wiped, with white powder left smeared over its glass top and sprinkled like dust on the carpet.

Donadze returned to the lounge holding baggie he had found in a drawer. 'This isn't looking good for you, Badri,' he said. Georgia classed possession of small quantities of drugs for personal use as a misdemeanour that was punishable by a fine. However, Georgian law did not define *small* in terms of volume or weight, leaving the police with wide discretion over the charges they could bring. 'Stand up, turn around and put your hands behind your back.'

Kalmikov stood and turned. 'You have to let me get dressed first,' he said, his voice quivering.

'Hands behind your back,' Donadze commanded.

Kalmikov obeyed and Donadze stepped forward and pushed him onto the settee. He took five banknotes from his pocket and threw them at the young man as he flailed on the white leather, trying to gather his dressing gown around himself. 'Give that to your father,' he said. 'Tell him to buy you something nice.'

'Yes, Father?' Donadze said as he slid his balcony door open and stepped onto the cold marble. He had returned to Badri Kalmikov's apartment in the early hours of the morning and it was still dark outside.

'I met Basilia…'

Donadze's mother had heard him moving around and had also got up. He shook his head impatiently when she offered him a jacket from the other side of the glass door. 'Tell me.'

'It went well, I think. A car pulled up as I was walking to the church. Two of Basilia's thugs were inside. I was—'

'How did you know they worked for Basilia?'

'It was a fair bet. But I know the type, I'm sure you do as well.'

'Yes, I do. Carry on, Father.'

'Well, I was told to get in. No choice of course. They patted me down and took my phone, pen, even my cross. We drove to Tbilisi. I don't mind admitting I was nervous, terrified really. I was put in the front beside the driver. The other guy sat behind me, very close—his breath was rancid. It was like the Godfather, I kept waiting for a rope or wire to be looped around my neck.' Chanturia laughed, 'Well, that didn't happen, obviously.'

'No, what next?'

'Did you know Basilia has an office near the Parliament?'

'Yes, on Rustaveli Avenue. I've been to it. They took you there?'

'We parked on a back street and went up through a fire exit. I didn't see anyone. There's a waiting area outside his office and I was kept there for a while.'

'One minute, Father,' Donadze said as he accepted the jacket his mother had thrust at him. He nodded his thanks and put the jacket on, irritated by the interruption but grateful for the protection from the cool breeze. His mother slid the door closed again. 'You were saying…'

'Basilia brought me into his office—he was very friendly. He was drinking whisky and offered me one. Told me it was very old Scotch—as if that would impress me. It felt like a test so I accepted. I'm glad I did, it soothed my nerves a little and it *was* excellent.' Chanturia paused. 'He must have been waiting for my reaction. "Good, isn't it, Father?" he said and I replied, "Yes, but not on a priest's stipend." That seemed to prompt him and he got down to business. He told me that Beso Eristavi had been in touch. He acted like he had no idea what I wanted to talk about, but I could tell he was interested.'

'Do you think he knew your history.'

'Yes, he would have asked around. We still have mutual acquaintances, I'm ashamed to say.'

'How did you broach the topic if he was acting coy?'

'I just came out with it. Told him I was privy to information which I thought he would find useful and that it was his—for a price.'

'Did he ask why you were making the offer?'

'Yes, but he wasn't surprised. I know the kind of man he is. He's slime but he thinks that, when you strip away self-delusion, we're all the same as him. A few years ago, I might have thought that as well.'

'So you told him you had spoken to the Alasanias.'

'Yes, I passed on what you had told them. That you know he brought Mariam to Gali Street and that Anzor Kalmikov had ordered the killings as a move against him.'

'And he accepted that?'

'I think so. He seemed happy enough. Gave me three thousand *lari*—although I'd asked for five.'

'When will you see him again?'

'He gave me a phone. I've to call when I get new information.'

'You've done well, Father. Thank you, this is going to be extremely helpful.'

'With respect, Lieutenant. I'm not doing it for you.' Chanturia paused, 'The information you gave to Mr and Mrs Alasania? Is it true?'

'It's true enough, Father,' Donadze said.

'Where are you, Lieutenant?' Colonel Meskhi asked.

Donadze looked at his watch. It was nine thirty. 'At home, sir. Detective Jaqeli and I worked late last night and—'

'Yes, I'd heard. Anzor Kalmikov is taking his son's harassment personally.'

'Harassment, sir?'

'That's how he characterises your encounter.'

'Is that how you see it, Colonel?'

'You were following the instructions I give to all my officers—I expect all dealings in narcotics to be investigated and appropriate action taken. In fact, I let Mr Kalmikov know that, in my opinion, you were quite generous in allowing his son a warning.'

'Thank you, sir.'

'I want to discuss something with you, Lieutenant, but not over the phone. Your apartment is in Kandelaki Street?'

'Yes, sir, 7 Kandelaki Street, apartment 19…'

'Stay there. I'll be with you in thirty minutes.'

Donadze stepped into the living room. 'Who were you

speaking to, Ramaz?' Tamuna said.

'Colonel Meskhi.'

'Your boss?' his mother asked.

'My boss's boss.'

'What did he want?'

'I don't know. He's coming here to tell me.'

Donadze observed panic set in his mother's face as she looked around the room which was cluttered with baby equipment and dirty cups and dishes. She retrieved his half-full coffee cup and the plate he was eating from. 'You might have warned me, Ramaz,' she said, dumping his breakfast into the kitchen bin.

He looked at Tamuna in exasperation.

'Well, as you've finished your breakfast, you might want to shave and shower before your boss's boss arrives,' she said, suppressing a smile.

Donadze scrutinised himself in the mirror as he shaved. He wasn't getting enough sleep and it showed in his pale skin and in the shadows under his blood-shot eyes. He knew that police officers often suffered poor health in older age, partly because of lifestyle choices but also through stress and erratic work patterns. He pushed these thoughts aside, showered and had finishing dressing when the doorbell chimed.

Meskhi's tall frame appeared distorted when observed through the door viewer. Donadze let him in and showed him into the living room. His mother had removed her apron and was standing by the breakfast bar, fidgeting. Tamuna was sitting on the settee, the baby asleep in her arms.

'*Gamarjoba*, ladies. I hope I'm not intruding.'

'Not at all, Colonel, you're very welcome,' Donadze's mother said.

'Colonel, my mother. And this is Tamuna.'

'And this is Eka,' Meskhi said, smiling at the baby as she slept. 'She's quite lovely.'

'Thank you. Do you have children, Colonel?' Tamuna asked.

'Four—all girls.'

Donadze was surprised that Meskhi knew Eka's name. He was also surprised that the Colonel had a large family but realised he knew nothing of his personal life. It was clear that he wanted to talk privately and he smiled gratefully when Tamuna said that she and his mother would take Eka for a walk.

'Please don't leave on my account. I only need fifteen minutes. Lieutenant, let's get some air,' Meskhi said, indicating the balcony.

Donadze put his jacket on before being reminded by his mother.

'I would like your opinion, Lieutenant,' Meskhi said after they had stepped onto the balcony. 'On an operational matter.'

'Sir?'

Meskhi took a sip of the coffee Tamuna had given him and grimaced. 'Basilia is expecting a cocaine shipment through Tbilisi Airport cargo terminal,' he said. 'Five hundred kilograms, we think. It'll be on a flight from Istanbul, arriving tomorrow morning at three.'

Donadze didn't reply and Meskhi continued, 'It appears that Anzor Kalmikov has also become aware of that shipment.'

Meskhi paused and waited for Donadze's response.

'Kalmikov knows about the shipment—how did that happen?'

'He has his ways, I assume.'

'So, Basilia has a large quantity of coke arriving and Kalmikov knows where and when he will receive it. That gives him an opportunity.'

'Yes, it seems that Kalmikov will attempt to seize the drugs.'

'At the airport?'

'No, after Customs clearance—at a warehouse Basilia owns. The question is, what do we do about it?'

Donadze took a sip of his rapidly cooling coffee as he considered their options.

'We could intercept the drugs at the airport.'

'We could. What would that do for us?'

'We would take a large quantity of drugs off the streets. It would be a good result for us. The media would report it extensively, we'd get good press and more public support.'

'Yes, and that might reduce political pressure, give us more space to operate. So, you think that's the best option?'

'Will the consignment be accompanied?'

'No.'

'So, we'd seize the drugs but wouldn't make any arrests, the smugglers would remain free.'

'Yes. So probably *not* the best approach, then. What other options do we have?'

'We could send a team to stake-out Basilia's warehouse. Wait for the attempted heist, seize the drugs and arrest Basilia and Kalmikov's men.'

'Yes, we could. Is that your recommendation?'

Donadze thought for a moment. 'No. It's unlikely that either Basilia or Kalmikov will be there and it would be difficult to establish a connection to them if they weren't. We'd make some arrests, but not of anyone who mattered.'

'So, in that case?'

'We could consider a controlled delivery.'

'Defer seizing the drugs? How would that be beneficial?'

'We'd allow Kalmikov to make the heist at Basilia's warehouse and take the cocaine. We'd track its movements, build a case against Kalmikov and his men. Meanwhile, Basilia would be mad and it wouldn't be long before he hit back. We'd keep war going between the families and continue to weaken both sides.'

Meskhi stood. 'Thank you, Lieutenant. I think you've identified the best solution.' He looked closely at Donadze. 'You look awful. I suggest you take the rest of the day off, spend some time with your family.' He slid the door open and stepped into the living room. 'I'm sorry to have disturbed you, ladies,' he said, putting his cup down. He bent over Eka's cot as she slept in her cot. 'Quite lovely,' he said then straightened and crossed to the door.

FOURTEEN

'Are we still good, Irina?' Donadze asked. He had taken Colonel Meskhi's suggestion to stay home as an instruction and had called Jaqeli to tell her where he would be.

'I suppose so. I understand why you did that to Badri Kalmikov, but it didn't feel right, like an abuse of power. It's not the way I want to work.'

'I know, and I wouldn't tell you that what I did was right. But I think it was necessary. And you need to know, I'd do the same again if I had to.' He paused. 'Do you still want to partner with me, Irina? I wouldn't be offended if you don't.'

'No, I like working with you. And I'm not judging you. Maybe I'd see things differently if my family had been threatened.'

'Okay—just don't think of me as your role model.'

He heard her laugh. 'That's hardly likely, Lieutenant.'

'Do you have any plans for this evening?'

'Not really, why?'

'Come over for dinner.' He looked through the balcony door. 'Tamuna and my mother would like to meet you. Bring Misha.'

'Okay, thanks. I'd like to meet them as well. I'll let Misha know.'

'See you about seven then,' he said, sliding the balcony door open. His mother was wiping perpetual Tbilisi dust from the living room surfaces. 'We're having guests for dinner,' he told her.

'That's nice, who are they?' she said.

'Two colleagues, Irina and Misha. You'll like them. And you don't have to worry, I'll cook.'

She smiled, 'I don't think so, Ramaz…' She crossed to the coat stand and selected a warm jacket. 'I'm going to the supermarket. If you have free time, why don't you take Eka out in the buggy, it'd be good for both of you.'

Donadze looked at Tamuna. 'I can't,' she said. 'I didn't know you'd be home and I'm meeting Lela for coffee.' Lela Tabagari was Tamuna's close friend and an obstetrician at the clinic where they both worked.

'How is she?'

'Good, I think. It'll be nice to catch up, I think she has a new man in her life.'

Donadze liked Lela and was grateful to her for the professional advice she had provided during Tamuna's pregnancy. He also thought she was gorgeous. 'Lucky man,' he said under his breath. He crossed to the cot—Eka had woken. 'Looks like it's just the two of us, little girl.'

He changed her nappy and, under Tamuna's direction, selected an outfit warm enough for the cool conditions then strapped her into her buggy with her favourite cuddly toys.

'Have fun with Daddy.' Tamuna kissed the baby and Donadze goodbye. 'Don't look so nervous, Ramaz,' she said, smiling.

He realised it was the first time he had been out with Eka on his own. The elevator took them to ground level and he turned left on Kandelaki Street. Progress was slow as he manoeuvred the buggy around cars which had been parked on the wide pavement. He was stopped repeatedly by older ladies who wanted to admire the baby; helpfully tugging at her socks or straightening her hat, frowning and tutting at the incompetence of men. Donadze didn't mind. It was a beautiful day and his baby girl was gurgling happily with no comprehension of the commentary he was providing as they walked along the busy street.

He stayed out longer than planned and he could see that Eka was becoming sleepy again. He stopped at a coffee shop and took an outside table. The weather had changed and there was a cool breeze blowing across the open terrace. He leaned in and whispered to the little girl as she fought sleep. She gazed at her father for a moment then closed her eyes. Donadze placed his hand gently on her chest and felt it rise and fall with each breath. 'We'll do this again soon, *chemo gogona*,' he said.

Donadze thought that Kalmikov had chosen a good location for the heist. Meore Street was narrow and the truck would have slowed to turn at the junction with Gelovani Street. Both streets were now barriered off and guarded by uniformed officers. Donadze presented his ID and followed Jaqeli under the barrier.

The scorched Range Rover was still smouldering, the stench from its burned plastic components acrid in the cool, still air. The vehicle sat slumped and derelict on tyres which had blown out and melted. Its passenger compartment was severely burned: windows shattered, seats reduced to their metal frames, external bodywork stripped to bare, blackened steel. A fuel container lay in a footwell, testament to the gasoline which had been splashed around the cabin and ignited, making retrieval of useful evidence unlikely.

The executions had been efficient—single shots to the back of the head—and the two men had dropped face-down onto the soil and gravel bordering the narrow road, their lives abruptly ended. Donadze had investigated several execution-style killings during his career and he often wondered why the victims seemed to accept their fates and not put up more of a fight.

The forensic examiner turned from the bodies. 'Hey, handsome.'

Donadze involuntarily touched his nose. It had been broken and badly re-set during national service in the army and he knew that no one, apart from his mother, would consider him to be handsome. 'Hey, Natia,' he said. 'I'm glad you got this one.' Natia Gagua was, by Donadze's estimation, the best examiner in her department. 'How does it look?'

She smiled at Jaqeli. 'I don't think we've met.'

Donadze introduced the two women and they shook hands.

'Watch him, Irina,' Gagua said. 'He thinks he's God's

gift to women—and I should know.'

'How does it look, Natia,' Donadze repeated.

'Only teasing, Ramaz.' Gagua snapped off her disposable gloves. 'Let me show you,' she said. She pointed to a set of tyre tracks which had been left on the dry, gravelly road surface. 'This was the target vehicle. A small truck, double axle, four wheels. Probably a Kamaz.'

'That doesn't narrow it down much,' Jaqeli said. Kamaz was a Russian manufacturer of trucks and engines and their products were sold widely across the former USSR.

'It is what it is, Irina,' Gagua said. 'But, although there are probably hundreds of trucks like this in Georgia, these tracks are useful. They're a bit like fingerprints—no two vehicles leave the same pattern: different tread wear, different damage to individual tyres, different tyre pressures, different tyre types on the same axle, possibly. If you find your suspect vehicle, then we can probably match it to these tracks.'

'What about the Range Rover?' Donadze asked.

'Not much to help us there, I'm afraid. Some footwear prints around the car, but they're scuffed. There won't be anything useful inside. I guess they used the Range Rover to make the truck stop.'

'Yes, but the guys in the truck would have been better trying to force their way through—given what happened to them.'

'Take a look at this.' Gagua walked a few steps and pointed at the ground. 'The truck couldn't go forward but it couldn't go back either because a second car had pulled in behind it.'

'I'm fairly certain we'll find that car as well—probably also burned out.'

'Stolen?'

'Yes, both stolen, I'd bet. Anything else?'

'The prints are useful. We'll photograph them and make casts if we can. They'll be solid evidence if you ever get this to court. Ballistics will look at the bullets when they're recovered. That's probably all we'll get, unfortunately.'

'Thanks, Natia. Let us know if you come up with anything else.'

Gagua left to resume work on the two bodies.

'What's on your mind, Ramaz?' Jaqeli said.

'This wasn't supposed to happen. I discussed it with Colonel Meskhi. We expected the heist to be somewhere else.'

'You expected this?'

'Yes, Basilia's warehouse was staked out. We were going to retrieve the drugs there, make arrests, tie it all back to Basilia and Kalmikov.'

'And now we have two dead, the drugs missing and nothing to show for it.'

'It's worse than nothing. Meskhi was already under political pressure. This is going to go badly for him.'

'And for you?'

'It might,' Donadze said.

'Very unfortunate, Lieutenant,' Colonel Meskhi said. Donadze had been summoned to Meskhi's office and was standing in his doorway waiting for permission to enter.

'Yes, sir.' Donadze hesitated. 'But it was the right thing to do, Colonel.'

'I'm not looking for consolation, Lieutenant—I know it was the right thing to do. Take a seat.'

Donadze crossed to the conference table—no coffee offered this time, he noted.

'What went wrong?' Meskhi said.

Donadze leaned back in his chair, on guard and suspicious that Meskhi seemed to be deflecting blame onto him. 'It's hard to say,' he said. 'How confident are you that Kalmikov had planned to grab the cocaine at the warehouse.'

'Very confident.'

Donadze hesitated, expecting Meskhi to elaborate and feeling more uneasy when he didn't. 'In that case, his plan changed. The question is—why?'

'That's certainly the question. What's your answer?'

Donadze took a moment to gather his thoughts. 'There are only two possibilities. The first is that Kalmikov might have reconsidered and decided that snatching the coke on the road was a better option. The second possibility is that he was tipped off—that he knew we'd be at the warehouse, waiting for him.'

'Do you think the road option was better?'

'No. The heist *did* go well from Kalmikov's perspective. And it was a good location if he had to do it on the road. But he was lucky. The road wasn't as controllable, there were more variables, more to go wrong: the truck driver could have taken a different route, a different driver might not have stopped at the junction, there could have been other cars on the road, witnesses to the heist and the killings. No, the warehouse should have been the better option.'

146

'Yes, that's also my conclusion. So, a tip-off then.'

Donadze paused. 'Sir, do you think I tipped-off Kalmikov?'

Meskhi looked surprised. 'What? No, of course not. What on earth made you think that?'

'I'm sorry, Colonel. Your questions—it felt like you were holding me responsible for the drugs being lost.'

'Ridiculous. Try to keep your paranoia in check, Lieutenant.' Meskhi leaned back in his chair and closed his eyes to think. Donadze was familiar with this habit and waited until he was ready to speak again. 'Who knew about this operation?'

'The officers on the stakeout, Captain Nakani, Detectives Jaqeli and Arziani, you and me.'

'All trustworthy?'

'Absolutely, sir.'

'There's one other person who knew. You may remember, Donadze, I mentioned that I do not enjoy managing the political aspects of this job. That I have concerns one or more of our political leaders may be corrupt. Unfortunately, managing politics involves talking to politicians—even when I consider that to be unwise.' He paused. 'It appears that someone inside the Ministry has betrayed us.'

'Do you know who?'

'Yes, and I know how to trap her.'

'Her?'

'Her,' Meskhi repeated, declining to provide a name.

'Is there something I can help with?'

'I have a disciplinary meeting to attend—my own. It's scheduled for tomorrow morning. I may be suspended pending investigation of this botched operation and our failure, as I'm sure it will be expressed, to restore order to the streets of Tbilisi.'

'That's not fair, Colonel.'

'Fair? Don't be naive, Donadze.'

'What do you need me to do, sir?'

'I have an idea but, if this goes wrong, you will have made a powerful enemy. Even if it goes the way I hope and we do expose this lady, she has friends in power who may take exception to you being involved in her downfall.'

'I'll deal with that if I have to, sir. What do you need me to do?'

FIFTEEN

Donadze pressed the buzzer for Badri Kalmikov's apartment and after a moment observed the security camera's LED illuminate.

'What do you want, Donadze?' Kalmikov said, his voice through the small speaker faint and distorted

'Open the door, Badri. We need to talk.'

'I don't have to talk to you.'

'You don't have to, but I think you should.'

Kalmikov waited a face-saving moment before buzzing the door open. Donadze crossed the lobby and took the stairs to the fourth level. The apartment door had been left cracked open and he pushed it with his foot and went in. The lounge had been tidied since he was last there and he was reminded of how tastefully it had been decorated and furnished.

He must have interrupted Kalmikov's evening meal as there was a half-eaten pizza and a bottle of Mexican beer sitting on a small table in front of the television. The gangster movie he had been watching was paused at an infamous scene; Al Pacino's character, an up-and-coming hoodlum, being forced to watch as a chainsaw is used to dismember his close friend.

'Disney Channel?' Donadze said.

'You've got five minutes.'

'On your own tonight?' Donadze asked. 'Was your friend busy?'

'Tell me what you want or get out.'

Donadze sat on the white-leather settee. 'We're going to do each other a favour. How about getting me one of these,' he said, pointing to the beer bottle.

Kalmikov glared at Donadze then stomped into the kitchen, returning with a bottle which he offered with an outstretched arm.

'*Gaumarjos*,' Donadze said, taking a drink and placing the wet bottle on the polished wooden floor. 'I want you to take a message to your father. It concerns a senior police officer. You may know him—Colonel Gabrieli Meskhi.' Donadze reached into his jacket pocket, took out a sheet of paper and placed it on the settee beside him. 'The TBC Bank—Meskhi has an account there.' He patted the paper. 'The details are there. The account contains money which the Colonel would prefer no one knows about. Payments he would be hard pressed to explain. Your father will know what to do with it.'

'I don't understand, what's this about?'

'You don't have to understand, Badri. Give the paper to your father and pass on what I've just told you.'

'And this is the favour I'm doing you?'

'No, this is the favour I'm doing you and your dad.'

'So what's in it for you?'

Donadze stood. 'You don't have to know that, either. Thanks for the beer, Badri,' he said.

He crossed to the table containing the pizza and beer, picked up the television's remote control and pressed play. He watched as blood sprayed onto Al Pacino's character's face from his friend's chainsaw-inflicted wounds. 'Nasty,' he said, throwing the control onto the nearest chair and crossing to the door.

Donadze took the stairs to ground level, left the apartment block and returned to his car. He watched as the lights in Kalmikov's apartment went off then took his phone from his jacket pocket and listened to the recording he had made. The sound quality was good and had clearly captured his conversation with Kalmikov. He closed the phone's app and called a number.

'Yes?' Meskhi said.

'It's done, sir.'

Donadze was at his desk at Mtatsminda Station the next morning when his phone rang. 'Thank you, Lieutenant, that went quite well,' Colonel Meskhi said.

Donadze took the phone off speaker mode and held it close to his ear. 'You mean your disciplinary hearing went well, sir?' he said.

'Of course. It put the Deputy Minister in an unenviable position and I expect she will resign before the day is out. But that won't be enough, she'll be investigated, I'm sure. Very embarrassing for the Prime Minister but perhaps now he'll exercise better judgement when appointing people into senior roles.'

'Did the Deputy Minister admit to being in Kalmikov's pocket?'

'Hardly, but she didn't have to. She was greedy, took the bait we offered—the outcome was quite satisfactory.'

Donadze thought that Meskhi sounded uncharacteristically smug. 'I wish I'd been in the room, Colonel.'

'Yes, it's not often we come out on top when dealing with our political masters.'

'Can you tell me how it played out?'

'I think you deserve that, Lieutenant.' Meskhi paused as he gathered his thoughts. 'Let's see… We had been into the hearing for about fifteen minutes before the Deputy Minister introduced the bank account issue. She asked if I recognised the account number. I said I did and asked *her*, on record, how she came by it. She told me a source had given it to her but declined to say who that source was. She became quite aggressive, said she had been made aware that I had received large corrupt payments and deposited them in that account. I again asked her how she came by that information and she said from the same, undisclosed, source. She asked if I was prepared to make the account transactions available to the committee. I said, yes, of course, and surprised everyone by distributing copies of the statements I had printed. I explained that I had opened the account for my daughter after she had been given a modest sum of money by her grandfather—five hundred *lari*, to be precise. All my daughters have similar accounts and similar sums of money. The Deputy Minister realised that something had gone terribly wrong and tried to change the conversation to levels of street violence—but the Chairman wouldn't allow it. He asked if I could explain how the details of my daughter's account had come before his committee. I said I could and played them your conversation with Badri Kalmikov. All eyes turned on the Deputy Minister. She bluffed and blustered but the evidence was clear and damning. She's finished.'

Donadze realised he had never heard Meskhi so vocal. 'You must be pleased, Colonel.'

'Pleased? Why would I be pleased? This has been an unnecessary distraction, but at least we can get on with our work now.'

'The disciplinary charges, sir?'

'All charges dropped and an apology received from the Chairman,' he said.

'Even though we lost the drugs?'

'Not lost, Lieutenant—misplaced. And we're going to get them back. When did you last speak to Sandro?'

Donadze calculated how long it had been since he and Sandro had met in the Radisson Hotel's car park. 'Three days, sir.'

There was a pause. 'I expected more from both of you. Tell Sandro I want to know where Anzor Kalmikov has taken the cocaine.'

'Sir,' Donadze said, knowing that finding and disclosing that information would be dangerous for Sandro.

'We hold the moral high ground for the moment, Lieutenant—but we have to make it count. Tell Captain Nakani that I want to see you both this afternoon—let's say at three.'

'Yes, sir. Your office?'

'No, I need to get out of this building. Your station, but find somewhere better than the Captain's office.'

'Yes, sir. Is that all?'

'No. The Deputy Minister isn't the only one whose been embarrassed by our ruse. Anzor Kalmikov—you've harassed his son, made him look foolish, caused him to lose face—a supposed man of honour. I think it's unlikely that he would go after you directly but he may find other ways to hurt you. Stay alert.'

'Yes, Colonel. Thank you,' Donadze said.

'What do you want?' Sandro said on answering Donadze's call.

'It's Dachi. I've been speaking to our friend. We need to talk.'

There was a pause. 'Same place, nine this evening,' he said, then hung up.

Donadze took the phone from his ear and looked at it. 'Have a good day,' he said.

The interview room door opened and Donadze put his phone away. 'Hey, Misha, Irina…'

'So Colonel Meskhi was exonerated?' Jaqeli said.

'Better than that. The disciplinary committee had to apologise. It's worked out well—puts us in a stronger position. Meskhi wants to take advantage of that. He's coming in this afternoon to speak to Captain Nakani and me. I think he wants to take the gloves off.'

'What does that mean?' Jaqeli asked.

'It means we've been too reactive so far—we're going

on the front foot, taking the fight to Basilia and Kalmikov—it's about time.'

'Losing that drug consignment wouldn't have helped,' Arziani said.

'It's not lost—just misplaced.'

'That's a positive interpretation.'

'Not my interpretation—it's Meskhi's. And he's taking the drugs back.'

'Did he say how?' Arziani asked.

'We'll have to find out where they are first—I'll let you know.'

'Can't wait.'

'How did you get on with Captain Murtov and INTERPOL?'

'Murtov's great,' Arziani said. 'That whole area—cybercrime—it's fascinating. And I can't help feeling that we don't put enough resource into it, given the potential results.'

'Potential results for us?'

'Maybe—do you remember EncroChat?'

'Only vaguely.'

'Me too, but Murtov described it to me. EncroChat was a secure communication system which used modified Android phones. It was, supposedly, fool-proof. It encrypted users' messages and had features like auto-delete and a panic code which would completely wipe the phone's data. There were about sixty thousand subscribers in total—that's a lot of people paying to keep their comms secret. But it wasn't as fool-proof as they thought. The Dutch Police cracked the encryption by installing a device on the system's servers. Hundreds of arrests were made—right across

Europe and beyond.'

'But none in Georgia?'

'No, rumours circulated that law-enforcement had found a way-in and users began throwing their phones away. It was too late for some, but others got out in time.'

'Including Basilia?'

'Murtov thinks so. The point is, Ramaz, even though law enforcement has had some success in penetrating the dark web and breaking into message encryption services, criminals still believe in them. It makes them careless. Murtov is convinced there's incriminating evidence to be found. And with modern-day slavery being such a high-profile issue, he's receiving good support from INTERPOL. I think it looks promising.'

'So do I, let's see what Murtov comes up with. You said EncroChat used modified phones?'

'Yes, to make them more secure. Their microphones, cameras and GPS systems were removed and new operating systems and messaging software installed.'

'Basilia gave Father Chanturia a phone. He's to use it when he has information to pass on...'

'That's interesting. EncroChat has been put out of business but—'

'Basilia might be using something similar. We need to go to Shindisi.' He glanced at his watch and frowned. 'I don't have time, Colonel Meskhi will be here soon.'

'Irina and I can go. What do you want us to do?' Arziani said.

'Okay, thanks. I'd like you to find a discreet way to visit Father Chanturia. Remember, it's possible he's being watched. Ask to see the phone Basilia gave him and look for any of the modifications you described. It might be a standard mobile phone—a burner. But if we're lucky, it could be something like the EncroChat phones. If it is, ask Captain Murtov if having access to it would help hack Basilia's comms.'

Arziani grinned. 'Great idea, Ramaz.'

'How about Mr and Mrs Alasania?' Jaqeli asked.

'Yes, it's time they were updated. Remember, whatever you tell them will get back to Basilia via the priest—so, let's send him a message.' Donadze paused to gather his thoughts. 'Tell them that Colonel Meskhi has taken a personal interest in this investigation and has told his officers—Nakani, you and me—that he wants results. Tell him that Basilia can expect to feel the heat soon.'

'Do you think that's okay, using the Alasanias and Chanturia as a conduit to Basilia?' Arziani asked.

'We're not lying to them, Misha.' Jaqeli said. 'Just passing on information that we hope will get back to Basilia. I think that's okay,'

Arziani stood. 'Well, in that case, let's get going,' he said.

SIXTEEN

Nakani led Meskhi into the interview room.
'*Gamarjoba*, Colonel,' Donadze said, standing.
'Lieutenant,' Meskhi said, taking the chair facing him. 'You've contacted my agent as instructed?'

'Yes, sir. We're meeting this evening.'

'Good. We urgently need to know where that cocaine has been taken. I've put a tactical team on stand-by and I want it recovered before Kalmikov has time to move it on.'

'Yes, sir.' Donadze hesitated. 'Who'll be leading the team, Colonel?'

'I will be—why?'

'With your permission, Detective Jaqeli and I will join you.'

'You and Jaqeli are detectives, Donadze. How would your participation help me or this operation?'

'You said Kalmikov might find a way to hurt me. He chose to make matters personal between us and I responded. I know how these people think, their psychology. Neither of us can afford to back down. I have to be there.'

Meskhi looked sceptical. 'Possibly. And Jaqeli?'

'She's my partner, Colonel.'

'Your thoughts, Captain?' Meskhi said.

'I agree with Lieutenant Donadze—I think you should include him and Jaqeli in the recovery operation.'

Meskhi remained silent for a moment. 'Very well, Lieutenant. You may join us. I'll consider where you are best placed to lend support and let you know.'

Donadze caught Nakani's eye and nodded his gratitude.

'Captain,' Meskhi continued, 'as I discussed with Lieutenant Donadze, we have a window to take this fight to Basilia and Kalmikov. I'm sure the politicians will regroup and rein us in again at some point—so let's make the most of this opportunity.' He placed his hands in his lap and closed his eyes. 'I always find it useful to recap—please summarise your investigation to date, Lieutenant.'

Donadze gathered his thoughts. 'If I may start at the beginning. The Gali Street apartment—a staging post for Basilia's trafficking operation. There were three girls being kept there. One, Veronika Boyer, got out and is under police protection in—'

'You mean under Major Gloveli's protection?' Meskhi said, his eyes still closed.

'Yes, Colonel, at his home in Shindisi.'

'Carry on,' Meskhi said.

'The other two girls and one of Basilia's men were killed—on Anzor Kalmikov's orders. One of the girls—'

'Killed for what reason?'

'Because he could. Because Dato Kaldani was dead,

Basilia's gang was weakened and Kalmikov wants to expand his—'

'Yes, I've got that. No need to labour the point.'

'Yes, sir. Well, the war between Kalmikov and Basilia has escalated. The gym bombing at Shroshi Street—two of Kalmikov's men dead. Then the cocaine heist—two of Basilia's men dead.'

'That's interesting isn't it. Two for two—almost a measured response,' Nakani said.

'Or just coincidence. Carry on, Donadze.'

'That's the situation to date, Colonel. Basilia and Kalmikov are fully committed and will keep fighting until there's a winner.'

'Do we favour either as winner, Captain?'

Nakani took a moment to consider. 'I don't see why we should, sir,' he said.

'I don't either. So, Lieutenant, we have a total of seven dead, two of them innocents. What's been your response?'

'I think we're in a good position, sir. We have a witness to the events in Gali Street—Veronika Boyer. She'll be able to testify that Basilia was in the apartment and that he raped Mariam Alasania. She also—'

'Remind me why we haven't charged Basilia with that rape,' Meskhi said.

'Veronika saw and heard enough to know what happened but we wouldn't achieve a successful prosecution without corroboration.'

Meskhi thought for a moment. 'Probably not. Carry on,' he said.

'Veronika also saw the killers on the apartment's stairs as she was leaving—although not well enough to identify them. She believed that they would kill her as well but, for reasons we don't understand yet, they let her get away.'

'Clearly a valuable witness. You're checking on her welfare?'

'Yes, we regularly visit Major Gloveli's home.'

'Good. Go on.'

Donadze took a sip of his coffee and continued. 'We're feeding Basilia misinformation through Father Chanturia. And, of course, your agent has infiltrated Kalmikov's organisation. Hopefully, he can tell us where Basilia's cocaine has been taken.'

'You need to do more than *hope*, Donadze. And the cocaine isn't Basilia's—it's mine. What else?'

'Yes, sir. We've been speaking to INTERPOL through our contact—a Captain Rezo Murtov. He thinks we may be able to find a way into Basilia's encrypted communications and his transactions on the dark web. Murtov thinks there could be evidence there.'

'Interesting.' Meskhi opened his eyes, took a notebook out of his jacket pocket and wrote some text in small, neat handwriting. He finished writing and put the notebook back in his pocket. 'Your assessment, Captain?'

Nakani cleared his throat. 'It's a complex situation. Basilia and Kalmikov clearly know their business but going to war has been a mistake. It's left them both exposed. Let's keep the pressure up and damage them as much as we can.'

Meskhi stood, straightened his suit trousers and jacket and manoeuvred his tie into precise position. 'Thank you, gentlemen,' he said. 'Donadze, contact me when you know where the cocaine is.'

'It sounds like you've got work to do this evening, why don't you spend some time at home before then?' Nakani said.

Colonel Meskhi had left Mtatsminda Station and Jaqeli and Arziani hadn't returned from Shindisi yet. Donadze looked at his watch—four fifteen. 'I've got some paperwork to catch up…'

'It'll keep. Go home, Ramaz.'

Donadze looked at Nakani across the interview room's table, his arms folded in front of him. He thought there was an intensity and brittleness about him which had become more pronounced in the last few days. 'How are things with you, Bagrat?' he said.

'Me? Fine, why do you ask?'

'With respect, you seem a bit tense lately.'

Nakani sat up in his chair. 'Tense? No, it's just pressure of work. But that's nothing new, is it? Don't you ever feel that way?'

'Yes, of course I do. But it's more difficult for you—command can be lonely.'

Nakani stared at Donadze for a moment, his features tight, his eyes bright and piercing. There was a catch in his voice which he covered with a small cough before speaking. 'Listen, Ramaz. I appreciate your concern—but I'm perfectly fine.' He paused and forced a smile. 'Anyway, enough of that, I thought you were going home?'

Donadze stood. 'Thanks, I will. You know, Captain, we've all got issues to deal with, but one thing I've learned— it's always better to talk. Let me know if *you* want to—any time is good.'

Nakani didn't respond and Donadze left the interview room and walked to his car. He was manoeuvring out of the car park when his mobile phone rang on its dash mount. 'Yes, Irina?' he said.

'Just checking in. We're on our way back to Tbilisi. All good—Chanturia was with the Alasanias and they were happy for him to stay while we gave them their update.'

'Good—and his phone?'

'Great hunch on your part, Ramaz,' Arziani said. 'Yes, it's been modified like the EncroChat phones.'

'Chanturia will be using it to get in touch with Basilia?'

'Yes, but I've asked him to hold off until I speak to Captain Murtov.'

'Is that because it's easier to hack the encryption when the phone's in use?'

'I don't know, but Murtov might. I'm calling him next.'

'Did you see Veronika?'

'Yes, she's okay. Major Gloveli was teaching her how to shoot,' Jaqeli said, laughing.

'Really? Well, no harm in that, I suppose.'

'No, we didn't think so either. Something else—it looks like she's seeing someone, a boy from the village.'

'Gloveli told you that?'

'No, Veronika told me—woman to woman. She's happy and it's good to see—considering what she went through.'

'She knows she can't leave Shindisi? No romantic nights out in Tbilisi?'

'She'd have to shoot Major Gloveli first. No, she's sensible. And at least she's not desperate to get back to Ukraine now.'

'How did Colonel Meskhi's visit go?' Arziani asked.

'He's never easy to read but I reckon he's on a high after being exonerated at his disciplinary. And he's determined to recover that cocaine.'

'He knows where it is?'

Arziani hadn't been told about Sandro and Donadze hesitated.

'It's okay, Ramaz. No need to answer that one.'

Donadze chose his words carefully, 'We don't know where the coke is yet, Misha—but we hope to find out soon.'

'What happens when we do find it?'

'There's a tactical team on stand-by to recover it. Meskhi has approved Irina and me joining the team.'

'Sounds like fun,' Jaqeli said.

'Do you need me there, Ramaz,' Arziani asked.

'Sorry, Misha. He's only approved Irina and me.'

Jaqeli said something to Arziani that Donadze couldn't hear. 'I'll let you go,' he said. 'Let's check in first thing tomorrow.'

'Okay, Ramaz,' Jaqeli said and hung up.

The roads were congested but Donadze eventually arrived at his apartment block. He took the elevator to level four, rolling his shoulders to relieve tight muscles. Tamuna gave him a warm, welcoming smile when he walked into their living room. 'Look, Eka,' she said. 'Daddy's home early.'

Contrary to Donadze's expectations, Sandro accepted—

without protest—Meskhi's instructions to locate the cocaine and their meeting in the Radisson Hotel's car park was consequently brief. He returned home at nine forty-five and found Tamuna watching her favourite movie. Richard Gere, at his most handsome, was playing trainee naval pilot, Zack Mayo. Donadze joined her on the settee and they watched the finale together, as Mayo—magnificent in his white officer's uniform, picked up Debra Winger's character and carried her out of the paper mill, her friends cheering as the film's stirring theme music played out. Tamuna dabbed her eyes as she turned the television off.

'I should have joined the Navy instead of the Army,' Donadze said.

She put her arms around his neck to kiss him. 'I really wish you had, Ramaz.'

Donadze kissed her back but after a moment she pushed him away. 'Let's have some wine,' she said. She crossed to the fridge and brought back an open bottle of *Tsinandali* and two glasses. She poured the wine, handed a glass to Donadze and re-joined him on the settee. They clinked their glasses together.

'*Gaumarjos*,' Donadze toasted and took a sip.

'How was your meeting?'

'Perfect.'

'Good.' She paused. 'You remember that I'm going back to work on Monday?'

'Of course,' Donadze said, although he had, in fact, forgotten. 'That's still what you want, isn't it?'

'Yes, it is.'

'Are you nervous?'

'A little, it's been eight months…'

'I know, but you'll get back into the routine soon enough.'

'Probably. It's your mother I'm worried about. We're asking a lot of her, Ramaz. She'll have Eka all day. And some evenings as well if you're working and I'm on call…'

'Yes, but you're only on call one day a week. She knows that and she's looking forward to it, isn't she?'

'She *is* looking forward to it, but it might be too much for her. I don't want her to take on more than she should…'

'We're not planning on doing anything different, Tamuna. Has something changed?'

Donadze watched as tears welled in her eyes and rolled down her face. 'What's wrong,' he said, alarmed.

'She's my baby, Ramaz. I should be here to look after her, to feed her, to keep her safe…'

Donadze drew her close and felt her tears soak through his cotton shirt. 'Of course she's your baby and always will be. Nothing can change that.' He pulled away and wiped her face with his fingers. 'Having children is a life-time sentence, Tamuna,' he joked. 'No time off for good behaviour.'

She sniffed. 'Ignore me. I know what's happening—just that I can't seem to do anything about it. Eka will be fine, I know that.' She wiped her eyes and sniffed again. 'I must look awful.'

'You're beautiful,' Donadze said.

'Thank you. Finish your wine, Zack Mayo.' She stood and held out her hand. 'Don't worry. I won't ask you to carry me.'

Donadze allowed himself to be pulled off the settee. 'Why not? I'm only sorry I don't have the uniform,' he said

166

and bent to scoop her up. She gave a small yelp of surprise and put her hands around his neck to hold on.

He looked down at her, cradled in his arms, and smiled. 'Everything's going to be all right, darling,' he said and crooned, '*Love lift us up where we belong…*' as he carried her to their bedroom.

SEVENTEEN

It was six in the morning and the apartment was still, his mother, Tamuna and Eka all sleeping. Donadze made coffee, put on a warm jacket and stepped onto the balcony. A breeze was blowing through the trees below, rustling the few brown leaves still clinging to their branches. He took a deep breath of cool, clean air. It was going to be a beautiful day.

He sat—the wicker chair chilled under the clear night sky—and took a sip of coffee. He wrapped his hands around the mug, closed his eyes and let the rising steam warm his face. Sleep had come easily and he woke feeling positive and optimistic for the future. Although publicly claiming to have no faith, he secretly thanked God for his family and prayed that He would keep them safe in the days and years ahead. He smiled to himself, acknowledging the hypocrisy. Religion may be the opiate of the masses, but why take a chance?

The persistent chill found its way through his clothing and Donadze knew he would have to go inside soon. He thought about his case, eager to make progress and optimistic about achieving successful, if undefined, outcomes; justice for the girls in the Gali Street apartment, certainly. But something more: punishment and pain for the cruel and the contemptuous, retribution and suffering for the heartless—making Otar Basilia and Anzor Kalmikov pay.

There was a knock on the glass door and Donadze turned to see his mother holding his phone. He had set it to vibrate and left it on the breakfast bar. He slid the door open. 'Sorry,' he said taking it from her and swiping to answer.

'Where were you, Donadze? You're supposed to answer when I call,' Sandro said.

'And *you're* supposed to call me *Dachi*,' Donadze replied. 'But you're right—I'm sorry you had to wait.'

There was a moment's hesitation. 'All right. Meskhi wants to know where the cocaine's been taken. Tell him 6, Samgori Street. It's a chop-shop—Badri Kalmikov runs it for his dad. He normally has a steady stream of hijacked and stolen cars going through it. There's usually only a single guard left overnight—but not tonight. That's when the drugs are being moved.'

'Do you know when?'

'No, but I'd guess early morning.'

'Thanks, I'll pass it on. How are things with Kalmikov?'

'Tense. It's not gone well for him lately. He lost face after you slapped Badri around and then got played for a fool by Meskhi and that bank account. He's not happy and we're all feeling it.'

Donadze refrained from contradicting Sandro's account of how he had dealt with Badri Kalmikov. 'Well, just be careful. If he's—'

'What do you care, Donadze?' Sandro said, ending the call.

He took the phone from his ear and looked at it. 'I think you meant, *What do you care, Dachi,*' he said.

His mother slid the door open. 'Come inside, Ramaz.'

'One minute.' He looked at his watch, slid the door closed again and called Meskhi. '6, Samgori Street, sir. The drugs are being shipped tonight.'

There was a moment's pause. 'Very well. I'll see you and Jaqeli in my office—eight a.m.'

'Yes, sir,' Donadze said.

'I need to pick you up, Irina, we're going to see the Colonel,' Donadze said.

'I'm flattered. What's it about?'

'We're recovering the cocaine that Kalmikov heisted— tonight I think.'

Donadze heard a short, muffled conversation between her and Arziani. 'I'll pick you up at seven fifteen,' he said.

'Okay, I'm at Misha's.'

'Right, seven fifteen.'

He stepped into the living room. Tamuna was up and sitting on the settee, nursing Eka. She looked up to accept his kiss. 'You're up early.'

'Yes, beautiful morning,' he said, then winked, 'and a beautiful night.'

She shot him a warning look and glanced at his mother who was bustling around the cooking area making everyone breakfast.

'When are you leaving,' Tamuna asked.

Donadze looked at his watch. 'Now,' he said, noting her brief frown. He kissed them all and, ignoring the protestations of his mother, collected his ID and pistol and left the apartment.

He arrived ten minutes early and called Jaqeli to say he was there. She left the building with Arziani and both hurried through the cool morning air to his car. She kissed Arziani and got in.

'Be careful—both of you,' Arziani said, standing with his hands in his pockets and watching as they drove off.

'He's worried about you,' Donadze said.

'Will it be dangerous tonight?'

'It's always best to assume so—complacency can get you killed.'

'That's a cheery thought.'

'This *is* serious, Irina.'

'Yes, Lieutenant.'

Donadze glanced at her as he drove. 'Sorry,' he said.

'No problem, Ramaz.'

'Thanks. But it's still serious.'

They arrived at Colonel Meskhi's office early. He was conferring with another officer. 'Lieutenant Donadze, Detective Jaqeli, this is Lieutenant George Losava, tactical commander for tonight's operation,' he said.

Losava was tall and broad shouldered with hair buzzed short and with two-days dark stubble which, surprisingly, Meskhi seemed to tolerate. He was dressed for action: black combat trousers, black T-shirt and black military lace-up boots.

'*Gamarjoba*,' Donadze said.

Losava acknowledged Donadze's greeting with a curt nod.

'We've agreed a plan,' Meskhi said. 'Losava, take them through it.'

'Sir,' Losava said in an unexpectedly high voice. The conference table was strewn with street maps, photographs, hand-drawn sketches and a writing pad containing colour-coded notes and symbols. Losava pointed to one of the photographs. '6, Samgori Street, Kalmikov's chop-shop. We've determined that's where the cocaine's being kept.'

'Good job,' Donadze said, glancing at Meskhi who stared back at him.

'Yes, thanks,' Losava continued. 'Kalmikov would normally be moving cars through these premises, breaking some down for spares, setting others up with duplicate plates and reprogrammed keys then selling them on. As far as we can tell, he's stopped that activity for the moment—probably to protect the cocaine.' He tapped the photo. 'It's a good location from our perspective. Single level, roller-door at the front, two small windows at the back. My team's going in the front. We'll be quick and decisive.' He turned a map around to face Donadze and Jaqeli. 'Park your car here,' he said, pointing to a location about fifty metres from the chop-shop. 'I want you two at the back of the building, just in case.'

'Just in case of what?' Jaqeli asked.

'As I said, Donadze,' Losava said, ignoring Jaqeli, 'this will be quick and decisive. We've done this before and we're good at it. I don't mind you two being there, but I can't let you get in my way.'

'And that's why you want us at the back of the

building?' Donadze said.

'That's where Lieutenant Losava wants you to be positioned, Donadze,' Meskhi said. 'And it's where I want you to be as well. You and Jaqeli are to be there by twenty three hundred. Kalmikov's premises are already under surveillance from the building opposite. I will order Losava's team in as soon as we see indications that the cocaine is about to be moved. I expect immediate containment, arrests and recovery of the drugs. Any questions?'

'Communications, sir?'

Losava reached under the table and passed a radio to Donadze. 'It's charged. Keep it turned off until you're in position. Channel two, but you shouldn't have to use it. Anything else?'

Donadze looked at Jaqeli and she shook her head. 'Nothing else,' he said.

Meskhi dismissed them and Jaqeli followed Donadze to the door.

'*We've done this before and we're good at it,*' she mimicked as they walked to the elevator. 'What's up with Captain Marvel?'

'I don't know, but *my* money's on you, Wonder Woman,' Donadze said.

Donadze and Jaqeli drove from Meskhi's office to Mtatsminda Station. They had to be in position near Kalmikov's premises by eleven—well before the probable time that the cocaine would be moved. He knew it would be a long night and that he should try to rest beforehand, but he also knew that rest was unlikely. Stake-outs, in Donadze's experience, were a combination of extreme tedium and high-adrenaline excitement—an unhealthy mix, he thought.

He wandered into the detectives' bureau and persuaded Arziani to join him for a coffee and a mutual update on their case. Donadze had doubts that INTERPOL, through Captain Murtov, would be able to provide any real help in penetrating Basilia's dark web activities but Arziani's enthusiasm was undiminished. 'Let's give him a chance, Ramaz,' he said. Arziani was worried about Jaqeli's involvement in the stake-out but knew better than to attempt to intervene. Donadze understood his concerns and assured him that Jaqeli could look after herself, but that her safety was his top priority.

It became clear that Arziani wanted to get back to his work and Donadze picked up his coffee and crossed to Soso Chichua's desk. 'Hey, Ramaz,' he said. 'How's my protégé doing?'

'You taught her well, Soso—we'll all be working for *her* soon.'

'Yes, well, time spent with the master is priceless.' He paused. 'It's not like you to be so sociable, Lieutenant. Loose end?'

'Is it that obvious?'

'Yes. I know the feeling. You've got something on tonight, haven't you? Makes it difficult to focus.'

'Well, you're certainly a master detective, Soso. Yes, there is something on tonight—but it's not something I can share, I'm afraid.'

'No problem, Ramaz. But my advice? You're achieving nothing here. Take a long walk, find a dark corner and shut your eyes, go home. Try to relax.'

'You're a wise man, Soso,' Donadze said. He had an idea and stepped away to call Tamuna. 'What are you doing today?'

'Nothing very much, why?'

'I'll be home at eleven. It's a beautiful day for a drive to Shindisi— let's see if we can persuade Levan to give us lunch.'

'That's a lovely idea. Do you mean all of us?'

'Yes, he's desperate to see his goddaughter again and you know how charming he is with my mother.'

'I do, he's such a lovely man.'

'Sometimes. I'll see you at eleven.'

No longer feeling aimless, Donadze returned to his desk to call Major Gloveli. He wouldn't admit it but Donadze knew the old policeman was delighted to host their visit. He spent the remaining time dealing with email and updating his case files. Jaqeli wasn't in the detectives' bureau and he called her to say he would pick her up at ten fifteen that evening.

The drive over the hills to Shindisi was particularly pleasant. His mother sat in the back with Eka, playing and singing to the little girl until the movement of the car's worn suspension lulled her to sleep. Tamuna sat with Donadze, saying little but seemingly enjoying the drive, their time together as a family and the familiar but stunning views of the hills and valleys in their autumn colours.

The sun was still shining but it was noticeably cooler as they got out of the car. Gloveli was in his garden and limped to the gate to greet them. He kissed the women and asked to hold Eka. Tamuna passed the baby to him and he led them all into the garden.

The table had again been brought outside and was covered with cold food, wine and soft drinks. Veronika was waiting by the table, looking young and happy in blue jeans and a crisp white top, her hair gathered into a ponytail. Gloveli made the introductions in Russian, telling his guests that Veronika was visiting him from Ukraine. Donadze caught Tamuna's look and whispered to her, 'No, nothing like that.'

Gloveli and Donadze made a point not to discuss police work and lunch was as enjoyable as he had hoped. Veronika was animated and barely recognisable as the girl who had escaped from the apartment in Gali Street. Gloveli charmed the women and was clearly besotted with Eka.

Several hours passed and Tamuna declared that they should be getting Eka home. Veronika asked if she could carry the baby to the car and Tamuna lent her arm to Donadze's mother—she had allowed Gloveli to top her wine glass more often than was wise. Gloveli laid his hand on Donadze's shoulder, prompting him to drop back.

'Thanks for your hospitality, Major. It was just what we needed.'

'Then don't leave it so long next time, Donadze.'

They walked at Gloveli's stiff pace to the gate. 'Be careful tonight, Ramaz,' he said.

'Careful about what?'

'George Losava—he's a glory hunter, extremely ambitious. He'd put his career above the safety of his men. And that includes you and Irina if you're with him.'

Donadze shook his head. 'How do you come by your information, Major?'

'You don't need to know. Just remember what I said.'

'I will, but it makes sense now. Losava is locating us away from the action—Irina and I will just be spectators. He wants all the credit for himself.'

'Good. Let him have it.' Gloveli squeezed Donadze's arm and he and Veronika kissed their guests goodbye. Donadze waited until Eka was secured in her car seat before driving off, his tyres throwing dust into the air behind them.

'That was perfect,' his mother slurred.

Tamuna smiled at him. 'Yes, it really was,' she said.

EIGHTEEN

Donadze's brain had been too active to allow rest and he was already tired when he arrived at Jaqeli's apartment. He knew from experience that he could function with little sleep when required; fatigue, to some extent, being a state of mind. He flashed his lights and Jaqeli crossed quickly to the car. She was wearing dark trousers, sweatshirt and a baseball cap which kept her hair off her face. Donadze moved the police radio off her seat then handed it to her as she sat down.

'Your weapon?' he asked.

Jaqeli patted her waist. 'Never leave home without one,' she said.

'Turn the radio on—channel two.'

'We were told to leave it off until we're in position.'

'Turn it on anyway—channel two.'

Donadze relayed Gloveli's warning about George Losava's ambitions as he drove.

'Not another one,' Jaqeli said.

They approached Samgori Street from Moscow Avenue and stopped in the lane behind the chop-shop as instructed. It was ten forty.

'Let them know we're here,' Donadze said.

Jaqeli used their call sign to inform Losava that she and Donadze had arrived at their designated location.

'Roger. Maintain your position and observe,' Losava replied, his high-pitched voice sounding strange over the radio.

'Did I say Captain Marvel? More like Mighty Mouse,' Jaqeli said.

Donadze suppressed a smile. 'Let's stay focused, Irina,' he said.

The lane was narrow and littered with smashed glass, empty oil containers and worn tyres, its asphalt surface broken and badly patched. There was no light other than a dim glow through the wired glass of the chop-shop's rear windows.

'It's going to be a long night, isn't it?'

'Yes, it is. Did you bring coffee?'

'No. Why would you assume that I—'

'Just as well I did, then.'

Donadze reached into the back of the car and lifted a bag onto his lap. 'Caffeine—the detectives' friend,' he said. He poured two cups of very sweet coffee.

'Thanks,' Jaqeli said and winced as she took a sip. 'I can feel my teeth melting.'

'You'll need the energy by morning.'

'Do you think there's someone in there?' Jaqeli asked.

'Yes. See the shadows moving on the glass? Someone's keeping an eye on the coke.'

'Okay, so a long night, then. What do you want to talk about?'

'With a psychologist? Nothing.'

'Promise I won't use my super-powers.' She turned in her seat to face him. 'Why haven't you made Tamuna an honest woman?'

'You're a feminist, aren't you? Why hasn't she made me an honest man?'

'Ah, I see…'

'Do you? I wish I did. How about you and Misha?'

'Misha? Well, he's—you know—he's kind of special. But I don't know, it's early days. Anyway, I'm not sure he feels the same way about me.'

'Well, I think he does. More coffee?'

'Brilliant. A classical diversionary tactic designed to avoid uncomfortable dialogue.'

'I'll take that as a *no*, then.'

Jaqeli held out her cup. 'I'm getting to like it.' She paused. 'Do you really think Misha feels the same.'

'What I think doesn't matter, does it. Why don't you ask him?'

She sat back in her seat. 'Thanks, I think I will.'

The passing of time was marked by Losava's team following disciplined radio protocol and confirming their location and status at designated intervals.

At one fifteen Donadze observed lights going on inside the building. 'Something might be happening,' he said.

'Should I call it in?'

'Not yet. It might be nothing.'

A few minutes later Losava's observer reported a small truck turning onto Samgori Street. 'Okay, Irina. Let Losava know that there's activity inside.'

Losava acknowledged Jaqeli's report and ordered his team to stand-by.

A moment later the observer reported that the truck had stopped outside and Losava repeated his stand-by order.

'I think I saw a window opening. Stay in the car, Irina. I'm going to take a look, Donadze said.

'You can't, Ramaz. Losava told us to keep clear.'

'Roller door opening. Stand-by, stand-by,' Losava ordered.

'This is it,' Donadze said.

'Go-go-go,' Losava instructed and Donadze heard Samgori Street come alive with police cars driven at speed, boots running on asphalt and voices identifying themselves as police and ordering compliance.

'Stay in the car,' Donadze said as he turned the courtesy light off and got out.

The turmoil in the front of the premises was subsiding as arrests were made and the building secured. He moved through the darkness to the rear of the chop-shop. A window was open, its hinges creaking as it swung in the light breeze.

'Turn around, Lieutenant,' a familiar voice said.

Donadze hesitated, his gun in its holster.

'Turn around, Donadze.'

Keeping his hands loosely by his side, Donadze turned. Badri Kalmikov was about three metres away, the gun in his outstretched hand pointing at his chest. Kalmikov smiled. 'Want to try pushing me around now?'

'What are you doing, Badri? It's over, the place is swarming with cops. You can't shoot me—even your dad couldn't get you out of that.'

'Maybe not,' he said and smiled again. 'But I think I'll take my chances.'

Donadze looked into Kalmikov's eyes and knew he was going to die. *So this is how it ends*, he thought and watched as Kalmikov took aim.

A shot rang out then another and Kalmikov fell to his knees, his gun clattering to the ground. Jaqeli was in the firing position she had learned at Police Academy, her face frozen in horror. 'Oh, my God,' she whispered.

Donadze raced to her, took the pistol and held her tight. 'You're okay, Irina. You're okay. This is all *my* fault— I was stupid, took a risk, gave you no choice. Thank you— you saved my life.'

He watched as Kalmikov fell from his knees and dropped face down onto the litter strewn lane, a pool of blood spreading around his upper body, dark and wretched in the dim light. Jaqeli was unresponsive in his arms. He lifted her face. 'They'll be here soon, Irina. Remember, none of this is your fault.'

Losava and two of his men appeared, big, black and angry as they appraised the scene.

'What the fuck have you two done?' he screamed.

'Please go to my car, Detective,' Meskhi said. He turned to the officer standing beside Losava. 'Get her a blanket and a hot drink.'

'Thank you, sir, but I'm okay. It's just that, this is the first time—the only time—I've used my gun outside the range,' Jaqeli said.

'Something *I've* never had to do, thankfully. You're in shock, Detective, please go to my car.'

Donadze nodded his reassurance and watched as Jaqeli walked off with the officer. 'Colonel, everything that's happened here is my responsibility.'

'Well someone fucked up, that's for sure,' Losava barked. 'And from where I'm standing, that's you, Donadze.'

'Really? Where were you standing when Kalmikov was climbing out that window, George?'

'Enough,' Meskhi said, barely raising his voice.

'But he's screwed everything up, Colonel.'

'We'll let the investigation team decide that, Losava. But *you* may wish to reflect how Kalmikov would have been detained if Donadze and Jaqeli had stayed where *you* had positioned them,' Meskhi said, pointing to Donadze's car.

Donadze noted Losava's aggression modify into something more conciliatory as he realised that he could be held complicit for a botched operation. 'I'm sorry, sir. I'm just disappointed the take-down wasn't as clean as we'd hoped. But we've got the coke and arrested four. As for Kalmikov getting shot? Better one of them than one of us,' he said, attempting a smile.

'It would have been better if *nobody* had been shot, Lieutenant.' Meskhi held out his hand. 'Is that Jaqeli's weapon? Give it to me.'

Donadze snapped on the safety catch and handed the pistol, butt first, to Meskhi. 'Thank you, sir.'

'Return to your stations and write-up your reports. Keep them factual. Hand them in then go home; you're both suspended pending internal investigation.'

'Sir,' Donadze said.

'Sir,' Losava added a moment later, clearly unhappy.

Meskhi walked off and left the two men facing each other.

Donadze watched as Losava, a bully by his estimation, thought he saw an opportunity. His face tightened and his fists balled by his sides as adrenaline pumped through his blood and he prepared to attack the smaller man.

'Any time you like, George,' Donadze said, smiling at Losava and dropping into a defensive stance, his knees softened for stability, his hands high, ready to defend and to strike.

He watched Losava blink several times, deflating as his adrenaline spiked and his confidence turned to doubt.

Donadze straightened. 'Good choice,' he said, brushing past the big man to return to his car.

Donadze returned to Mtatsminda Station as ordered. The detectives' bureau was empty and he made coffee, sat at his desk and opened a blank template to write-up his report. He didn't think it would take long. He had completed typing the headings when his phone rang—Major Gloveli.

'I've got to be up this early in the morning, Major—what's your excuse?'

'Stopping you from doing something stupid, Donadze.'

'What do you mean?'

'Irina called me, told me what happened. She thinks you're about to throw yourself to the wolves. Don't do it.'

'But I messed up, Major. I had clear orders. I nearly got

myself killed—could have got Irina killed.'

'But you didn't. And who said you messed up? Losava?'

'Meskhi was there, he knows what happened.'

'And how do you think *he* wants this to play out?'

'He told me—keep the report factual.'

'Facts? There's no such thing. Tell me what you think the *facts* are.'

'This isn't going anywhere, Major. I appreciate—'

'Tell me, Ramaz.'

Donadze sighed. 'Okay. Jaqeli and I met Losava and the Colonel in his office. We were given our orders. I was told to park in the lane behind Basilia's shop, fifty metres away.'

'And that's what you did—what happened next.'

'We were in my car observing the back of the shop for over two hours. I saw lights go on and told Irina to call it in.'

'So you alerted the tactical commander that something significant was happening. What next.'

'Well, that's when everything kicked-off. A truck arrived, the roller door opened. Losava ordered his team to stand-by then to go in. That's when I saw a window opening at the back.'

'What significance did you put to that?'

'It's obvious, someone was climbing out of the building.'

'How was the radio chatter at that time?'

'Full on. As I said, that's when everything kicked-off.'

'So the reason you didn't report the window opening was?'

'I know what you want me to say, Major, but the real

reason I didn't call it in was—'

'Irina reports to you, doesn't she, Ramaz?'

'Of course, she's detective rank.'

'What were your instructions to her?'

'No way, Major. Irina saved my life. If you think—'

'You know me better than that, Donadze. The point is: this isn't just about you. Why didn't you call in your suspicion that someone was escaping out that window?'

Donadze put his head back and closed his eyes. 'I didn't call it in as it would have distracted and confused Losava's team at a critical moment,' he said.

'Good, that's what I thought.'

Donadze didn't respond and the Major continued. 'How did Kalmikov manage to get a drop on you.'

'It was dark in the lane, I didn't see him. I thought that, if someone had managed to get out the building, he wouldn't hang around—that he'd get away while he could.'

'Logical. What would have happened if you hadn't seen the window opening and made an informed decision to check it out.'

'Kalmikov would have escaped.'

'Why didn't he just run off? Why did he wait to get you in his sights?'

'It seems that killing me was his priority.'

'Why didn't Jaqeli warn Kalmikov before discharging her weapon?'

'She didn't have time. Any delay and I would have been dead.'

'So, despite being in an extremely stressful situation, she made the right decisions. Quite impressive for an inexperienced officer, wouldn't you say?'

'Yes. Irina saved my life, Major.'

'Okay. And why was she in the right position to do that?'

'She's my partner. She had my back.'

'Yes, and not just at the stake-out. Write it up, Donadze,' Gloveli said and hung up.

NINETEEN

I t was six in the morning. His mother was awake and feeding Eka expressed milk—bliss radiating from both their faces.

'She's got your sister's eyes, Ramaz,' she said.

'You said she had my eyes a few days ago.'

'Babies change. No, she's definitely got Ana's eyes.'

'But not my nose, I hope?'

She glanced at her son. 'There's nothing wrong with your nose, *Ramazi*. It suits your face.'

Donadze turned his back and opened the fridge door so his mother couldn't see him smiling.

'Take her, I'll get you something to eat,' she said.

'Deal.'

He took the baby and cradled her in his arms, tickling her chin and cheek. He wouldn't admit it to his mother, but his memory of how his sister looked was fading. He watched his daughter's eyes grow heavy after the warm milk and thought of Anzor Kalmikov, a father who had lost his son to violence. And he looked at his mother, bustling around the cooking area, her daughter also lost to violence. *What a terrible world*, he thought. But he held his daughter, warm and innocent in his arms and knew that there was also good in the world—if you were lucky and goodness could find you.

'Are you okay, *Ramazi*?' his mother said. 'You look awful. Did something happen last night?'

'I'm just tired, *Deda*. Long night.'

'Do you want this food?'

'No, sorry. I'd better get some sleep.'

His mother took Eka and he went through to his and Tamuna's bedroom. She had taken a shower and was drying her hair in front of the dresser mirror. She turned the dryer off and stood to kiss him. 'It's just been on the news,' she said, looking at the wall-mounted television. 'Your Colonel Meskhi was interviewed; drugs seized by the police, one of the gang members killed. You were there, weren't you?'

'Yes. It was just as Meskhi said. We took a lot of cocaine off the streets.'

She stepped back and looked at him closely. 'So, what's wrong? Wait—it wasn't you who shot that man, was it?'

'No.' Donadze paused. 'It was Irina.'

'Irina! Oh no, how awful. Is she okay?'

'She's upset, understandably. But she did what she had to do. She'll be okay.'

She continued to scrutinise him. 'But you're partners, aren't you? Where were you?'

Donadze sat her on the bed and took her hand. 'Tamuna, please don't be worried. Everything's fine. But Irina shot that man because he was going to shoot me.'

Her eyes widened and she put her hand to her mouth and stared at Donadze for a long moment.

'Everything's fine, Tamuna, I wasn't—'

She slapped him hard on the face, her eyes flashing. 'Were you even going to tell me, Ramaz?'

Donadze rubbed his stinging cheek. 'I didn't deserve that,' he said.

She held his face in both her hands then slid them around his neck and pulled him to her. They sat holding each other tight, the terror of what might have been, a spectre in the room.

After a moment, Tamuna stood and returned to the mirror. 'Yes, you did,' she said and turned the hairdryer back on.

City life was noisy; his neighbours didn't believe in volume control and sound insulation between apartments was poor. Rush hour traffic had begun and was accompanied by the usual cacophony of car horns and instructions barked over police tannoys. Donadze set his phone to alarm at twelve and eventually slept. He woke early and bunched a pillow around his ears, hoping that sleep would return. Inevitably, his thoughts turned to the stake-out and the shooting. He remembered how time had slowed as he turned to see Kalmikov's gun pointing at his chest, knowing that death was certain. He recalled a peaceful resignation and thought he now understood why some of the victims he had encountered hadn't resisted similar fates. He sat up in bed, yawned and stretched then shuffled into the living room.

He was alone in the apartment and he made coffee then called Jaqeli.

'How are you, Irina?'

'Numb, it's so unreal, almost like it didn't happen.'

'Well, it did happen. You saved my life.'

'He *was* going to shoot you, wasn't he?'

'Definitely. He wanted me dead.'

'Is that something you've ever done, Ramaz? Shoot someone, I mean.'

'In the police, no. During the Five Day War, we had skirmishes with the Russians but it was at a distance. Probably didn't hit anyone. Close-up is different, it takes guts to do the right thing. You should be proud of yourself Irina, I know I am.'

'Well, don't get all gushy on me, Lieutenant. Did you file your report?'

'Yes, with some prompting from Gloveli. How did you know?'

'I'm a psychologist remember. I can read you like a book.'

'You're a scary woman.' He paused. 'Irina?'

'Yes?'

'You know you've made an enemy, don't you?'

'You mean Anzor Kalmikov? Yes, that had occurred to me, Ramaz.'

'So, you'll stay close to Misha?'

'Until you get back.'

'Let's hope that's soon. How about when you're off duty?'

'That won't be a problem.'

'You'll stay with Misha?'

'It won't be a problem, Ramaz.'

'Okay. One last thing, Irina.'

'What?'

'Thanks,' he said and hung up.

His mother had left food on a plate. He hadn't eaten for some time and he peeled off the clingfilm and ate the bread and cheese while standing. He put the empty plate in the sink, went to the bedroom and turned the television on loud enough to hear in the shower and in the adjoining apartments. He looked at himself in the mirror: red-eyed with pale, waxy skin—he still looked awful. He reluctantly shaved, spent ten minutes under a hot shower then braved twenty seconds longer under cold water. He towelled himself dry, put on fresh clothes and returned to the living room for more coffee—feeling better but, because of his suspension, unsettled and uncertain what to do next.

He sat on the settee and scanned the television channels, trying to find an updated news report on the drugs seizure. The focus had shifted to the latest political protests and he turned the television off. He was pulling on shoes to take a walk when his phone rang—Father Chanturia.

'How could you let this happen, Lieutenant?'

'What do you mean? Let what happen?'

'Basilia has started trafficking girls again.'

'Through Tbilisi?'

'Yes. Four girls—right under your nose.'

Donadze took a deep breath. 'Tell me exactly what you know.'

'Well, it seems that Basilia is quite pleased that the pressure is off him and on Kalmikov. You—the police—were distracted. It must have seemed like a good opportunity. The girls were already in the pipeline—from Ukraine and Armenia—and he used the opening you provided to bring them into Georgia. He's learned a lesson though—he only kept them in Tbilisi two nights this time.'

'And now they're gone?'

'Yesterday—I heard Istanbul and Dubai.'

'Did you get names?'

'No. These girls are units, commodities as far as Basilia is concerned. They don't need names. They're lost, Lieutenant—why weren't you watching?'

'What do you want me to say, Father? Yes, we should have been watching and yes, we should have intervened. But I can't fix that now.' Donadze paused. 'You said these girls were already in the pipeline. Does he plan to bring in more?'

'I don't know, but I think that's likely.'

'Does Basilia trust you?'

'Let's say he doesn't *mistrust* me. At least for now.'

'How about you, Father? Do you still want to help, to be involved? Basilia might make the connection at some point—you know what that would mean.'

'You remember our conversation, Lieutenant? If something happens to me, you'd make sure my family is looked after. You'd go to the Church and say I didn't die a criminal.'

'Yes, I made you that promise.'

'Then I'm happy to continue—for the sake of these girls.'

'Good. Then try to find out when Basilia plans doing this next.'

'I'll do what I can.'

'Do you still have the phone he gave you?'

'Yes…'

'I'll be in touch,' Donadze said and ended the call. He thought for a moment then called Arziani.

'Are you okay, Ramaz?'

'Yes, thanks to Irina. Have you spoken to her?'

'She called me this morning, told me what had happened.'

'Did she tell you that I messed up?'

'No, she didn't say that at all. Did you?'

'I could have done things differently, we'll see what the investigators say. But that's not why I called; we've taken our eye of the ball, Misha.' Donadze summarised his conversation with Father Chanturia.

'Shit, that's bad…'

'Yes, but we need to get back on the front foot now. What's the latest with Murtov and INTERPOL?'

Arziani hesitated before speaking. 'Is that something you should be thinking about? You're suspended, aren't you?'

'We're just talking, Misha. What's the latest?'

'If we're just talking, then it's going well, But Murtov needs more time.'

'He's run out of time. Can you set up a meeting?'

'So we're *not* just talking. I don't know, Ramaz. I don't think we should pressurise him that way. We've got no authority over him and we need to keep him onside.'

'Keeping him onside has given us nothing concrete so far. We might not have authority, but Colonel Meskhi does—let's get this done, Misha.'

'That sounds like an order to me, Ramaz—and you're not my boss.'

'It's not an order and I know I'm not your boss. If I speak to Meskhi and he agrees to help—will you set up the meeting?'

'What about your suspension?'

'Let's see what Meskhi says.'

There was a long pause before Arziani responded. 'Okay, Ramaz. Speak to Meskhi.'

'Thanks, Misha. I'm sorry if—'

Donadze realised that Arziani had hung up and took the phone from his ear. '…if I was abrupt,' he said to the empty room.

Donadze had a request to make of Colonel Meskhi and he wanted to have the conversation with a clear head. He guessed that Tamuna and his mother had taken Eka for a walk and he scribbled a note for them before leaving the apartment and hurrying to his favourite coffee shop. He sat at an outside table, the cool, fresh breeze ensuring privacy. The waitress pulled on a quilted jacket before venturing out to take his order and he waited until his coffee and pastry had been served before calling.

'One minute,' Meskhi said.

He heard papers being shuffled and chairs being pushed back as Meskhi's office emptied. 'I didn't expect to hear from you today, Lieutenant,' he said.

'No, sir, but there's been a development which I think you'll want to hear about.' He relayed the information he had received from Father Chanturia.

Meskhi took a moment to speak. 'You were right to call

me. This is extremely disappointing. Worse than that—we've failed these young women.' He paused again. 'Basilia must be feeling confident, or else he's exhibiting great arrogance to pull a stunt like that. And, thanks to our lack of focus, he's got away with it. That being the case he'll—'

'Yes, sir, he'll do it again.'

'I'd rather you didn't complete my sentences for me, Donadze. But I agree—he will feel confident about doing this again. You have a proposal?'

'We'll be better prepared next time, Colonel. I've asked Father Chanturia to find out when Basilia is bringing the next girls in.'

'Doesn't that put Chanturia at risk? Basilia isn't stupid, he'll work out where our information came from.'

'Yes, but with your help, we may be able to provide him with cover.'

'I'm listening.'

'Our aim is to deflect suspicion away from Chanturia. Specifically, we want Basilia to believe we obtained our information by other means.'

'Such as?'

'That's where your support would help, sir. As you know, Lieutenant Arziani has been in touch with INTERPOL through Captain Murtov. If we could hack Basilia's comms then he might believe that was the source of our information.'

'And hacking his comms is work in progress, I take it?'

'Arziani tells me that Murtov has been cooperative but we've had nothing firm yet…'

'I'm sure he's a busy man—you would like me to speak to him?'

'I think it would be useful if Murtov appreciates how important this is.'

'Why assume Murtov doesn't already appreciate the importance—don't you think Lieutenant Arziani made that clear?'

'I think he needs to hear it from someone more senior, sir.'

'Am I missing something, Donadze? If I agree to your request and if Murtov can break into Basilia's comms, we surely wouldn't tell him we had done so?'

'No, sir. Basilia would delete everything if he thought that he had been compromised.'

'So, how does that help the priest?'

Donadze felt his brow prickling despite the cool breeze. 'In the short term, it wouldn't, Colonel. But if we can get Basilia into court then it might protect Chanturia from future retaliation.'

'That's feeble, Donadze. The priest's welfare has no real part in this conversation, does it?'

Donadze paused. 'No, sir,' he said, chastened.

'I don't like to be manipulated, Lieutenant. You should have requested my support on its own merits, not by associating it with side issues like this.'

'Yes, sir. In hindsight, I should have—'

'I should deny your request.' Meskhi was silent for a long moment. 'However, I won't let your lack of professionalism impede my own. I *will* speak to Murtov.'

'Thank you, sir,' Donadze said.

'Think very carefully before taking that approach again, Lieutenant,' Meskhi said then hung up.

Donadze remembered the pastry and ate it while

playing back the conversation in his head. He'd achieved his objective but made Meskhi angry. *What's done is done*, he thought.

He had one more call to make.

Arziani was noticeably cool. 'Ramaz,' he said.

'Hey, Misha. Are we good?'

'Good enough, I suppose.'

'Today's not been my best. Sorry.'

'That's okay, we all have them,' Arziani said, his good nature restored.

'Thanks. Well, I did speak to Meskhi and he did— eventually—agree to help.'

'Well, that's good, so long as he doesn't go in heavy-handed.'

'He won't, that's my specialty. I've got a suggestion for you.'

'A *suggestion*, Ramaz?'

'Yes, a suggestion. When you next speak to Murtov, ask Captain Nakani to go with you.'

'Why Nakani? I don't think he'll add anything to the conversation.'

'Have you spoken to him lately? I don't think he's doing well—depression maybe. Getting him involved might give him something else to think about. He's also the same rank as Murtov of course, and that always helps.'

'I don't know, Ramaz. Let me think about it.'

'Of course. You'll let me know if anything comes up?'

'Despite you being suspended?'

'Yes, despite me being suspended.'

'Okay, Ramaz. Try not to upset anyone else today,' he said, then hung up.

Donadze's coffee had chilled and he drank it in a single gulp. He sat for a moment longer, trying to identify what more he could do to progress his investigation while suspended—and concluded that there was nothing. He left a generous tip to compensate the waitress for braving the cold and walked back to his apartment.

TWENTY

I s *that* what you're wearing? Weren't you cold, *Ramazi*?'
his mother said.

'Freezing,' Donadze admitted. He took off his
jacket and dropped it on the settee, contriving not to
acknowledge his reprimand as she picked it up and hung it
on the coat stand.

'You're not working?'

'Not today, *Deda*,' he said.

'Taking a day off?'

'Not really. I was asked to stay home. It's routine
procedure when incidents are under investigation.'

'What kind of incident, Ramaz? Something from last
night?'

'It was nothing, really.'

'Tell her, Ramaz,' Tamuna said.

Donadze looked at her, questioningly.

'She's entitled to know,' she said.

He turned to his mother. 'The police shot a man last

night—a gangster. It was self-defence. When something like that happens, the officers involved are asked to stay off work while the circumstances are investigated.'

'I saw it on television. Did *you* shoot that man, Ramaz?'

'No, *Deda*.'

'And you're not in trouble?'

'Not at all. As I said, it's just procedure. I'll be back at work soon—tomorrow, I hope.'

His mother looked questioningly at Tamuna who smiled and said, 'So, it looks like Ramaz is going be under our feet today. You said something about the kitchen drain?'

'Ah, yes, could you take a look, *Ramazi*. It's blocked—you probably just need to clean the trap.'

Donadze smiled at Tamuna, grateful that she had diverted his mother onto a different topic. She didn't return his smile, probably still angry with him, he thought.

'Okay, I'll see what's wrong. Could you look after Eka this evening, *Deda*?'

'Of course, what's happening?'

'I'm taking Tamuna out for dinner.'

'I can't, Ramaz. I'm back at work tomorrow, remember?' Tamuna said. 'I've got too much to do.'

'We can go early. I'll have you home by eight—promise.'

Tamuna looked at his mother and she nodded encouragement.

'Okay, thanks,' she said, returning his smile this time.

Donadze unblocked the kitchen drain and made other minor repairs around the apartment, grateful to be able to occupy his time. He booked a table for six o'clock at the King David restaurant and they managed to leave the apartment at five forty, Tamuna finding several things to do while he stood, waiting with his jacket on.

He called a taxi and it arrived almost immediately. The roads were congested but the driver, by means of enthusiastic acceleration, heavy braking, a disdain for lane markings and furious gesticulation at other road users, got them to their destination on time. Tamuna took his arm and they walked into the restaurant and were shown to their usual table.

They ordered their favourite dishes and a bottle of *Tsinandali*, Tamuna having said that she would have only one glass. The restaurant was almost empty and their food arrived quickly.

Donadze thought that Tamuna was reserved, their conversation stilted and he eventually asked if she was still angry with him.

'Let's talk about last night,' she said.

He closed his eyes for a moment and leaned back in his chair. 'Okay,' he said.

'You nearly died, Ramaz.'

He considered disputing her interpretation of how close he had come to being killed but knew she would think that to be petty and antagonistic. 'Yes,' he said.

'And then you went to your station to write up your report.'

'Yes, but it's always easier to write when events are fresh in your memory and, anyway, Meskhi had ordered me to do it.'

'And you always follow orders? But, okay, you wrote your report then you came home, chatted to your mother. And then what? You weren't even going to tell me, were you?'

Donadze hesitated. 'No, probably not. It's not that I'm keeping secrets, Tamuna, just that I want to…'

'Protect me?'

'Yes, protect you. Gloveli described it to me. It's like living two lives and I need to keep the two separate. I don't want to bring my work home to you and Eka.'

'What's Levan Gloveli got to do with it? We've discussed this before, Ramaz. I'm not a child. If you're living two lives then I want to be a part of them both. She paused. 'But I know now, you won't change. And I shouldn't try to change you—you are who you are.'

'What does that mean?' Donadze asked, alarmed.

'If you won't change then I have to ask myself: can I be with you the way you are?'

'And can you?' he said, his voice tight.

She paused and reached across the table to take his hand. 'Yes,' she said. 'I have to. Because I love you.'

Donadze realised that he had been holding his breath. 'So, what now?'

She squeezed his hand. 'You asked me something recently. Could you ask me again?'

Donadze stared at her and she nodded. He cleared his throat, took a sip of wine and looked into her eyes to be sure he had not misunderstood. His jacket was hanging on the chair behind him and he reached into a pocket and took out a small box which he opened to reveal a ring, its diamonds sparkling in the soft light. He leaned across the table, took Tamuna's hand and showed it to her.

'Please marry me,' he said.

Tamuna touched the box. 'You've been carrying that around with you?'

Donadze nodded, waiting for her answer.

'Yes, I'll marry you, Ramaz,' she said.

Donadze's mother spotted the engagement ring almost immediately. 'Tamuna?' she said.

'Yes,' Tamuna smiled, holding the ring up for her to admire.

'Well, it's about time, Ramaz,' she scolded before covering them both with kisses. Donadze knew that she was happy for them but also relieved as her religion made it difficult for her to accept parents not being married. She insisted on him going to the supermarket to buy Georgian champagne and they celebrated as Tamuna prepared for her return to work.

Everyone was up early the following morning and it was pandemonium in the apartment as Tamuna insisted on doing everything for Eka whilst getting herself ready for work at the same time. It seemed to Donadze that he was always in the way. Before going on maternity leave, Tamuna usually travelled by *marshrutka* to the Medifirst Clinic where she worked as an orthopaedic surgeon. The Tbilisi minibus fleet was being modernised and was consequently safer than before, but she accepted a lift when Donadze offered. She eventually found the resolve to leave Eka and, giving the baby a final kiss, left the apartment—conflicted and miserable.

They took the elevator to the underground car park and Donadze gave her a hug. 'Don't worry, she'll be there when you get home,' he said.

'I know,' she sniffed.

She sat in the car, twisting her handbag's strap as he drove. Donadze knew that she was nervous and he tried to distract her. 'Have you told anyone yet?' he said, pointing to the engagement ring.

'No, nobody at all,' she said, lifting her hand to look at the ring, twisting it on her finger. 'It still feels a little unreal.'

'Well, you'll see Lela at the clinic, I guess.'

'Yes, I'm meeting her for lunch, we'll catch up then.'

He pulled up in the turning circle outside the clinic and she leaned over to kiss him then hurried out of the car and into the Reception area. He waited a moment in case she turned to wave but, when she didn't, he put the car into gear and drove off. He was almost back at the apartment when his phone rang—Captain Nakani.

'Okay to talk, Ramaz?'

'Yes, go ahead, sir.'

'Good news, your suspension is lifted with immediate effect. You can get back to work.'

'Thanks, Captain. That's great news. Were there any findings?'

'You'll hear formally, but nothing adverse. There was a query about not informing Losava when you noticed the chop-shop's open window but your explanation was accepted. I think Colonel Meskhi's statement helped.'

'Really? That's surprising…'

'Well, it doesn't surprise *me*.'

Donadze waited a moment but Nakani didn't elaborate. 'How about Irina?' he said.

'Fully exonerated. Keep it to yourself for now but Meskhi is giving her a commendation.'

'Good, she deserves it.'

'Yes, I've asked her to come in and see me. We got off to a bad start, I think.'

'I think she'd appreciate that, Captain.'

'Something else. Misha has a meeting organised with Rezo Murtov. He's asked me to go with him.'

'That's great. He'll appreciate your support.'

'I can't help thinking you might have something to do with that, Ramaz.'

'Not me, Captain,' Donadze lied.

'Okay. When can you get in?'

By habit, he had taken his weapon and police ID when leaving the apartment. 'I'm on my way,' he said.

'Welcome back, Ramaz,' Jaqeli said.

'I wanted you to be here before we started, Ramaz,' Captain Nakani said. 'I'm worried about how Kalmikov will react to his son's shooting.'

Arziani glanced at Jaqeli. 'He's not said anything, no threats—not publicly at least,' he said.

'Come on, Misha,' Jaqeli said. 'I killed his son—we all know what that means.'

'Yes, you're right, Irina,' Nakani said. 'But if Kalmikov wants to get to you, he has to get past us first. Nothing's going to happen to you—you have my word on that.' He paused. 'Okay, let's agree some precautions. I don't think leaving the city is a good idea. You'd be on your own if Kalmikov found you.'

'I'm not going to hide, Captain.'

'Good. But until this is over, I want someone with you at all times. Stay close to Ramaz during daylight hours and I'll station a patrol car outside your apartment overnight.'

'I don't need the patrol car, Captain.'

'Yes, you do, Detective. You're too vulnerable on your own.'

'She won't be on her own, Captain,' Arziani said.

Nakani looked between the two. 'I see,' he said. 'Ramaz, what do you think?'

'I think that's the best arrangement we can come up with, sir. You're right of course, Irina should never be left alone and between Misha and me, we'll make sure she's not.'

'Okay. But let me make this clear. Keeping Irina safe is your top priority. Stay focused—don't give Kalmikov any opportunities. Remember, he only has to get lucky once.' He used his fingers to count out his instructions. 'Check your cars before getting in. Don't let anyone get too close. Avoid giving shooters direct line of sight—stay away from windows. Don't open your doors to anyone at night. If you have any concerns, request back-up immediately. And if there are *any* problems with *any* of this, you are to call me immediately. Understood?'

'Just checking, Captain.' Jaqeli said. 'I appreciate your concern, but would you have done the same for Misha or Ramaz in similar circumstances?'

'Yes, Detective—of course I would. Now, have I missed anything?'

'Nothing,' Arziani said.

'We need a deterrent,' Donadze said.

'What?'

'Nothing, Captain. Just thinking out loud.'

'Okay.' He turned to Arziani. 'When are we seeing Murtov?'

'At three.'

'Right. Let's leave here at two fifteen.'

Nakani stood and left the interview room.

'What now, Ramaz?' Irina said.

'You stay with Misha. There's someone I need to see.'

TWENTY-ONE

Anzor Kalmikov had organised his son's wake in his own home, a modern villa on Mefe Street. Donadze drew up at the security gate and stayed in his car until the guard came through a side entrance. 'Who are you?' he said.

Donadze held out his ID but snapped the wallet shut when the guard tried to take it. 'Tell Kalmikov I'm here,' he said.

The guard stepped away from the car and spoke into a radio. Donadze saw a CCTV camera rotate in his direction as the guard returned to his shack to open the gates.

He parked his car in the yard beside a collection of luxury SUVs and sports cars, their low, hard suspension ill-suited to Tbilisi's broken and pot-holed streets. He walked from his car across the terrace to an imposing front entrance. Kalmikov was standing between the two pillars which supported the door canopy. He was wearing joggers, hoody and flip flops, his hair unruly and flopping over his forehead and eyes.

'You've got some nerve, Donadze,' he said. 'What do you want?'

'To pay my respects to your son—if you'll allow me.'

Kalmikov stared at Donadze for a long moment then turned and walked through the double doors. 'Follow me,' he said.

He led the way along a bright hallway, his flip flops slapping the marble floor. He stood by an open door and followed Donadze into a large, bright room. There was more marble flooring to complement a long, curving cream-coloured wall. The floor-to-ceiling glass on the opposite wall was draped in voile to filter bright sunlight and to allow views into the garden and pool area. The ceiling was painted brilliant white and inset with an oval plaster moulding, below which Badri Kalmikov's body rested. He had been dressed in a dark suit, white shirt and tie, a style he would probably never have chosen while alive. The casket and body were illuminated by spotlights which made the young man appear almost saintly. It was a serene setting, Donadze thought, almost like Heaven's waiting room.

Most of the furniture had been removed and replaced by chairs placed around the casket. One was occupied by a woman about Kalmikov's age, Badri's mother, Donadze guessed, the other by a teenage girl—his sister. They sat, gripping hands, their grief real and bitter. There was no sign of Kalmikov's buxom partner from the opera.

Following tradition, Donadze walked around the casket then followed Kalmikov out of the room and back along the marble hallway. They reached the front doors and Kalmikov turned. 'What is it you want, Donadze?'

'I'm sorry you lost your son, Anzor. I mean that.'

Kalmikov blinked rapidly, his eyes misting. He wiped them before tears could form. 'Don't worry, I don't hold you responsible,' he said, his voice tight.

'Who do you hold responsible?'

Kalmikov smiled. 'Well, I think we both know the answer to that one, don't we, Lieutenant.'

'You know Badri had a gun on me, don't you? He could have run-off but killing me was more important to him. Why do you think that was?'

'Because of the way you treated him. Cuffed him so he couldn't fight back then pushed him around in front of his girlfriend.'

Donadze nodded. 'Except, you know that's not the way it happened. What about you—your responsibility? Maybe he thought that was what you expected of him—to be a man.'

'Don't give me that shit, Donadze. You can go now. Tell that bitch I'll see her soon.'

'That wouldn't be a good idea. Badri was your son and you're hurting—but he left Jaqeli no choice.'

'Maybe I don't have a choice either. Get the fuck out of my house.'

'You need to understand this, Anzor. Irina Jaqeli is my partner and my friend. You don't go near her.'

'Or else what?'

'You've lost your son, But you've still got a wife and daughter.'

Kalmikov laughed. 'Is that the best you can do? You wouldn't touch my family and we both know it.'

'You're right. I wouldn't do anything to harm your family. But others might—Basilia for one. Who'd look after them if you weren't here to do it?'

Kalmikov's eyes hardened as he appraised Donadze. 'You haven't got the balls.'

Donadze stepped in close. Kalmikov flinched as he put his hand on his arm. 'I'm sorry you lost your son,' he said. He stared at Kalmikov until the crime boss broke eye contact, then dropped his hand and walked out of the villa.

'Well?' Jaqeli said.

'Well what?' Donadze had joined Arziani and Jaqeli in Interview Room Two.

'Congratulations, Ramaz,' Arziani said, offering his hand.

'You're talking about Tamuna and me?'

'Who else?' Jaqeli held up her phone. 'Facebook, Ramaz. Ever heard of it?'

'Can I have a look?' Donadze said, holding out his hand to take the phone. Tamuna had announced their engagement and had posted images of herself wearing the ring and a close-up of the ring on her finger.

'You're a dark horse, Lieutenant,' Jaqeli said. 'How are we going to celebrate?'

'We?'

'Dinner, this weekend. Misha's treat.'

'Sounds great, thanks. I'll check with Tamuna.'

'Yes, *thanks*, Irina,' Arziani said.

Donadze returned the phone. 'How did you get on with Captain Murtov? Has INTERPOL come up with anything yet?'

'And straight back to business…' Jaqeli said.

Arziani laughed. 'It *was* a good idea to ask Captain Nakani to come along. And Colonel Meskhi has spoken to Murtov as well—so he definitely knows that we need his help.'

'And he doesn't feel he's being pressured, he's still onside?'

'He's fine. And—good news—Murtov's identified the encryption system on Basilia's phones. It's Russian, not as sophisticated as EncroChat and it should be relatively easy to crack. The INTERPOL techs are working on it—two more days he thinks.'

'And then we'll be able to listen in on Basilia's conversations?'

'Yes, it'll be like any other phone once the encryption's broken.'

'How about his messages?'

'We'll get them as well.'

'You thought Basilia might be managing his business on the dark web—buying and selling girls, moving money around. Any progress there?'

'Not yet, but they're still working on it.'

'Okay. Well, this is great, Misha. But it's only going to be useful if Basilia doesn't get to hear about it.'

'I know, we keep it to ourselves for now.'

Donadze looked at his watch. 'I've got to pick up Tamuna. Let's get back to this tomorrow morning.'

'Tell her *congratulations* and that we'll see her at the weekend,' Jaqeli said.

Donadze was late and he hurried from the station and crossed to the car park.

'Lieutenant,' a voice spoke from behind.

He turned to see Father Chanturia. He was dressed in denims and a hooded sweatshirt, the hood pulled over his head and throwing his face into shadow. 'Let's talk in your car,' he said.

Donadze used his remote to unlock the BMW's doors. 'Get in.'

Chanturia opened the passenger door and dropped into the seat, pulling his hood further across his face.

Donadze turned to look at him. 'What are you doing here?'

'Drive.'

'I'm going to the Medifirst Clinic.'

'That's fine.'

Donadze eased the car into the city traffic. 'Are you okay?' he asked.

Chanturia pulled the hood off his head. 'Basilia's suspicious.'

'Why—what happened?'

'I was probably too inquisitive. Or maybe I'm not as good at this kind of thing as I'd thought.'

'You've been asking about the girls?'

'Yes, as you requested.'

Donadze glanced at the priest as he drove.

'Don't worry, Lieutenant—I know you didn't force me to do any of this.' He paused. 'Two Armenian women—tomorrow. He's keeping them at the airport hotel and putting them on the morning flight to Istanbul.' He paused again. 'Or that's what I was told, anyway.'

'What do you mean? You spoke to Basilia?'

'No, his cousin. The thing is—I don't think I believe him.'

214

'I don't understand.'

'I think it's a test. Of me. I don't think Basilia *will* bring girls into Tbilisi tomorrow. I think I've been given false information and if the police turn up then it's obvious that—'

'You're the source. What makes you think you're being tested?'

'It was too easy, almost as if Saba wanted me to know.'

'Saba?'

'Basilia's cousin.'

'But if you're wrong…'

'Yes, two more girls will be lost. You'll have to decide what to do, Lieutenant. But if you *do* think I'm wrong, look after these girls—I'll take my chances.'

'If Basilia's suspicious then you're already at risk. He's unlikely to give you the benefit of the doubt.'

'I know. But he finds me useful for the moment and if this is a test…'

'Then we want you to pass.'

'It's your decision. But tell me what you decide to do so I can be ready.'

'I've decided. We're not going near that hotel.'

'What if I'm wrong?'

'You're not. Your instincts are good. In any event, it's my responsibility, my decision—you've done what you could.'

Chanturia pulled the hood back over his head. 'Better let me out.'

Donadze manoeuvred into the inside lane and stopped. 'I'm going to ask you for a favour soon, Father.'

'What kind of favour?'

Irate drivers were making a show of diverting around the stationary vehicle. 'Not now, but soon.'

Chanturia held Donadze's gaze for a moment then opened the door and got out the car, his head down as he merged with the other pedestrians pushing along the busy pavement.

A line of blocked vehicles was building up behind Donadze's car, their horns blasting their impatience. He held up his hand in feigned apology, put the car into gear and pulled away from the kerb. *Soon, Father*, he thought.

Tamuna was waiting at the clinic's turning circle as Donadze pulled in. She got in the car and leaned across to kiss him. He thought she looked tired. 'How was your first day back?' he asked.

'Funny really, it was like I'd never been away. But good, I was glad to be back. How was your day?'

'Mine was good as well, we're making progress. I can see the end in sight now.'

'That sounds optimistic.'

'Yes, I know, it's—'

'Not like you…' she interrupted then laughed.

They made small talk on the journey home. Donadze noticed her becoming more agitated as they got out of the car and took the elevator to the fourth level. She fidgeted while he opened the apartment door then hurried past him into their living room.

'How was she?' she asked, holding out her hands to take Eka from Donadze's mother.

'No trouble at all. I've not given her a bath yet.'

'That's okay, I'll do that,' Tamuna said as she held the baby close, shutting her eyes to breathe in her smells. 'I missed you so much…'

'It'll get easier.'

'Yes, but I'm not sure that I want it to.'

'How have you been, *Deda*?' Donadze said.

'Me? I've had a lovely day.'

'You look a little tired.'

'Well I am a little tired, *Ramazi*. There's nothing wrong with that.'

'Thanks for looking after her,' Tamuna said. 'You'll let us know if it gets too much for you?'

'Of course, but that's not going to happen. Sit down and we'll eat.'

'Can I help?' Donadze said.

'Please sit down, Ramaz,' his mother instructed.

Salad, bread, cheese and drinks had already been placed on the breakfast bar and she opened the oven to remove the hot dishes.

Tamuna wasn't prepared to put Eka down yet and she ate with one hand, using her fork to spear the *khachapuri* Donadze had cut for her.

'You're quiet, Ramaz,' his mother said.

'Just enjoying the meal, *Deda*.'

In truth, he'd been thinking about his conversation with Father Chanturia and his belief that he was being tested. Donadze had told the priest that he had good instincts and he judged that to be true. He knew that criminals who were able to survive their chosen lifestyles often did so by developing a form of animal cunning and an instinct for recognising when something wasn't right. Chanturia's criminal past had probably honed that instinct and Donadze was almost certain that there would be no women trafficked through Tbilisi. Almost certain.

He considered calling Nakani to request surveillance on the airport hotel but knew there was a strong possibility that Basilia's men, their own instincts on high alert, would spot the police team. Either that, or an officer on Basilia's payroll would tip him off.

Donadze trusted his own instincts and decided not to request surveillance—that he would live with his decision. As would the women if he had got it wrong. Brought from Armenia, they would be taken to Istanbul and Dubai; commoditised, their humanity stripped, sold and sold again, their value as sex slaves diminishing with their youth and their looks until they were finally discarded, dependent on the drugs which kept them compliant, far from home with no way back.

TWENTY-TWO

Donadze was tired. His mother said that Eka had sensed changes at home, that Tamuna not being around the apartment during the day had unsettled the baby. Or she might just be teething, Donadze thought. Regardless, no one in the apartment had slept well. He went to the detectives' bureau and, suppressing a deep yawn, made a mug of strong, sweet coffee. Soso Chichua was with Captain Nakani in his office. Nakani noticed Donadze and waved him over. They were looking at photographs spread across the small desk.

'What do you think, Ramaz?' Nakani said.

Donadze picked up an image and held it to the light. It was a distance shot, known as an overall photograph and composed to show the exact location of the crime scene. 'Is that the Old Town?' he asked.

'Yes—Sioni Street.'

He picked up more images. They showed the body of a young man sprawled on his side, his cheek pressed and distorted by the cobbles he had fallen onto. The forensic photographer had placed his camera on the ground to capture images of the dead man's face. Once handsome, his eyes were now open and milky and his long dark hair was loose and matted with the blood which had pooled around his battered head. His dazzling smile would not be seen again and the corpse, like so many others that Donadze had observed, looked vulnerable and forlorn.

'You know this is Beso Eristavi, don't you, Soso?'

'Yes, we found his ID.'

'Do you know when he died?'

'He was found at around four this morning—killed a couple of hours before then.'

'Do you think this is connected to your case, Ramaz?' Nakani asked.

'It must be. Were any weapons recovered?'

'Not yet. There were several blows to the back of his head and body. Maybe a baseball bat, but we've found nothing that looks like that yet.'

'A lot of anger there, don't you think?'

'Yes, we thought that as well,' Nakani said.

Donadze tossed the photographs back on the desk. 'Let's take a drive, Soso.'

'Where are you going?' Nakani said.

'Shindisi, sir.'

Father Chanturia was working in his garden when Donadze pulled up. He drove his garden fork into the ground and leaned against it as the detectives approached. '*Gamarjoba*, Lieutenant, Detective,' he said. 'You've come to arrest me?'

'Why would we do that, Father?'

'Because I killed Beso Eristavi, of course.'

'Can you tell us why you killed him?'

'You know why. I told you when I first met him, that's what I wanted to do. It's who I am…'

'What did you do with the knife?'

'The knife? It's in the river. But don't worry, you won't need it—you'll have my confession.'

'Eristavi wasn't killed by a knife, Father. And that's *not* who you are.'

Chanturia closed his eyes for a long moment. 'Do you have to take him?'

'You know we do.'

The priest nodded his head in acceptance. 'Would you let me speak to him first?'

Donadze looked at his watch. 'Twenty minutes.'

'Thank you.' Chanturia poured water from a bottle to clean his hands and shook them dry as he walked out of his garden.

'What's going on, Ramaz? Why would you think that priest killed Eristavi? And if *he* didn't do it, who did?'

'Someone with every reason for doing so. Let's sit in the car and I'll bring you up to speed.'

Twenty minutes passed and Donadze drove the short distance to the Alasania's home and parked by the outer wall. He waited until Soso Chichua had extracted himself from the passenger's seat then led the way to the front door. There was no sign of the friendly goat from previous visits and opportunistic weeds had invaded the garden's fruit and vegetable plots. The family home which Donadze had thought dilapidated but charming now looked neglected and sad.

The front door was lying partially open. 'Could you wait here, Soso,' Donadze said.

He pushed the door fully open and stepped into the sitting room. Nodar Alasania and Father Chanturia were facing each other on upright chairs and both turned as Donadze entered. Alasania looked awful; his face pale and gaunt, his eyes blood-shot and bruised, his appearance unkempt beyond caring.

Chanturia placed his hand on the distraught man's shoulder. 'It's time, Nodar,' he said.

Alasania straightened in his chair but didn't reply.

'Your wife and son?' Donadze asked.

There was still no reply and Chanturia said, 'They're with her sister.'

Donadze nodded. 'Why did you do it, Nodar?'

Chanturia shook Alasania's shoulder gently until he blinked and looked around, seemingly surprised to find himself in his own sitting room.

'I want to help you if I can,' Donadze said.

Alasania shook his head then cleared his throat. 'I hadn't meant to harm him,' he said, eventually. 'He was just a boy. I thought I could talk to him, get him to understand what he'd done, the pain he'd inflicted on our family, on me...'

Donadze placed a chair beside the two men and sat down. 'Tell me,' he said.

'Mariam thought that young man loved her—but she had no idea what he really was.' He choked back a mirthless laugh. 'Some boyfriend to choose, don't you think, Lieutenant?'

'How did you find him?'

'Something I let slip, I'm afraid,' Chanturia said.

'It doesn't matter, I would have found him myself, eventually…'

'So you went to see him?'

'He works in a bar called Shots. But you know that already, don't you?'

'Yes. You went to see him?'

'I waited until his shift was over and he was walking home. I stopped him, asked if he knew who I was—he didn't of course. It was cold and he was in a hurry, probably thought I was just a crazy old man.' Alasania laughed again. 'He was right as it turned out…'

'Go on.'

'He tried to push past me and I told him, "Mariam was my daughter, my little girl." He stopped and looked at me, then smiled. He had a beautiful smile—he looked quite kind. I thought I had reached him, that he was going to say he was sorry, that he would show some humanity… But he didn't…'

Donadze nodded encouragement.

'He didn't apologise. He said to me, her father, "Well, old man, she certainly didn't fuck like a little girl." He kept looking at me and smiling and it was then that I realised that young man was evil. He turned to walk away, still smiling and I hit him with the post. He fell and I hit him again and again…'

'Where did you get the post?'

'It was on the road, there was some building work nearby.'

'What did you do with it?'

'Threw it in the river. It was covered with his blood, bone, his brains…'

Donadze watched as Alasania collapsed into his chair. 'Thank you Nodar,' he said. 'But I don't believe you.'

'What do you mean, everything I—'

'Sit up and pay attention.' Donadze waited until Alasania was looking at him. 'Here's what I think happened. You haven't slept since Mariam died and that affected your state of mind. You were frustrated that the police weren't making any progress with their investigations. Then Father Chanturia told you about Beso Eristavi. You decided to speak to Beso to see if he could tell you anything about how Mariam had died. You knew that he was her boyfriend and you didn't believe he could be involved. But you had to be sure—so you tried to speak to him. He told you that tricking her had been easy, that she had meant nothing to him. Yes, you were angry but you were scared as well. You realised that you had put yourself at risk by approaching a dangerous man who was half your age. And then Eristavi laughed and goaded you with that vile comment—which I won't repeat. You couldn't stand to think of your daughter being treated so cruelly and you grabbed a wooden post which was lying on the ground. You remember striking Eristavi with the post and you accept that you killed him, although that was never your intention. You can't remember what you did with the post but you probably dropped it on the ground as you left.'

Alasania was staring at Donadze, open-mouthed. Donadze waited a moment before continuing. 'You were in a state of shock, you couldn't think straight. So you returned to Shindisi and told Father Chanturia everything.

You asked him to contact me as you wished to turn yourself in and confess.'

Donadze watched as Alasania absorbed his words. 'Now, I want you to confirm that I have accurately summarised your version of events,' he said.

Alasania shook his head but didn't reply and Chanturia said, 'That's what I heard, Lieutenant.'

'Good.' Donadze stood and walked to the front door. 'Could you please come in, Soso.'

He returned to the sitting room and placed a small table beside the chairs.

'Mr Alasania, this is Detective Chichua. We're going to take your verbal statement now. Please repeat the account you just gave me of your encounter with Beso Eristavi.' He put the phone on the table, opened its memo app and started recording. 'Start with your state of mind after Mariam had died,' he said.

Father Chanturia walked beside Alasania, his arm around his shoulder, as Donadze led him from his home, perhaps never to return. Major Gloveli was waiting by Donadze's car. 'Could I have a minute, Ramaz?' he said.

Donadze unlocked the car's doors. 'It's cold, Soso, take a seat inside.'

'It'll be okay, Nodar,' Chanturia said. He blessed Alasania then turned to walk in the direction of his own home.

Gloveli limped over to Alasania and placed his hands around the back of his friend's head, his face close, demanding his attention. 'Listen to me, Nodar. You're going to be taken to Donadze's station where you'll charged with murder. Say nothing until your lawyer is with you. Remember this—no matter what they tell you or what they do—the police aren't your friends. They don't care about you—they just want to charge and convict you. When they come to interview you, tell them you'll only speak to Donadze. Do you understand?'

Alasania nodded and said, 'But I did kill that boy, Levan. I should be punished. Why should—'

'Don't you think you're already being punished?' Gloveli put his head against Alasania's. 'You have to trust me, Nodar. Your life doesn't have to be over—but you must do what I tell you.'

Alasania nodded again.

Gloveli released his distressed friend and stepped back. 'Take him away,' he said.

Donadze opened the car's rear door. 'Get in, Nodar.'

'Ramaz,' Gloveli said.

'Yes?'

'Thanks.'

'I didn't do anything, Major.'

'I know, but thanks, anyway.'

'See you soon, Major.'

Donadze started the engine and bumped the car onto the track which would take them through Shindisi and onto the road to Tbilisi. He glanced in his rear-view mirror. Alasania was slumped, head down and jostled as the car's worn suspension failed to deal with unavoidable potholes and broken asphalt. Chichua was looking out the side window, steadying himself against the car's motion.

226

'Everything okay, Soso?' Donadze said.

Chichua looked at him. 'Yes, fine.'

'I'd like you to write this up.'

'That's what I'd assumed.'

They drove for a few more minutes. 'What will your report say?'

Chichua turned to look at Alasania then turned again to face the front window. 'Investigating officers were contacted by the Shindisi village priest and requested to visit suspect at his home. Suspect voluntarily confessed to killing the victim, Beso Eristavi. A verbal statement was taken and found to be consistent with the observations made by investigating officers at the crime scene. Routine stuff, Ramaz.'

'Yes, that's what I thought.' He paused. 'Thanks for having my back, Soso.'

Chichua closed his eyes against the bright sunlight. 'I don't know what you mean, Lieutenant,' he said.

TWENTY-THREE

Arziani was looking smug. 'Guess what?'

'INTERPOL techs have hacked Basilia's phone and we can listen into his comms,' Donadze said.

'Smart ass,' Arziani said, grinning. 'Come and see this.' He led Donadze to his desk where a laptop computer had been placed, its screen displaying control icons and pulsating, coloured graphics. 'We're in,' he said.

'So, tell me what's happening here.'

'Murtov loaned me the laptop.' Arziani sat and adjusted the screen. 'The INTERPOL techs used Father Chanturia's phone to get Basilia's number. This software is configured to his phone and will track and record everything going in or out.' He tapped the laptop. 'All recordings are stored here, backed-up to a secure site and,' he paused, patting his jacket pocket for dramatic effect, 'automatically emailed to my phone in mp3 format.'

'How about live calls?'

'Yes, I can get them on the laptop or on my phone.'

'Impressive,' Donadze said. 'Could you forward the recordings to me?'

'Yes, I'll set it up, you'll get them at the same time as I do.'

'What about the laptop? It's a bit obtrusive—what will these guys make of it?' Donadze said, indicating the empty bureau. 'We can't have this getting back to Basilia.'

'No, you're right, we can't. But I think it's okay.' Arziani closed the lid and pushed the laptop to the back of his desk. 'The software's still running but the screen's locked and password-protected in case anyone decides to look.'

'That should be okay then—hidden in plain sight, I guess. So what now?'

'Basilia's messages—Murtov reckons he'll have them downloaded and sent to me later today.'

'And you'll forward them to me?'

'Of course.'

'Great work, Misha.' He looked at the wall-mounted clock. 'Where's Irina?'

'She'll be in soon, wanted to pick up a few things at the pharmacy.'

'She's on her own?'

Arziani's face fell. 'She's just round the corner, Ramaz. She told me to go ahead…'

'Come on.'

Donadze ran out the detectives' bureau, followed closely by Arziani. They sprinted across the car park and turned onto Mtatsminda Street. The pharmacy was on the junction with Besik Street, about one hundred metres ahead. Donadze was first to see Jaqeli coming out the pharmacy. He also saw a beat-up hatchback parked just beyond it and a young man getting out.

'Police. Stop!' Donadze shouted, unholstering his weapon and running towards him.

Jaqeli was startled and dropped the bag she had been carrying. She pressed herself against the closed pharmacy door, fumbling for the pistol in her belt holster.

The young man had a panicked look and appeared to be considering bolting back to the safety of his car.

'Police! Hands in the air!' Donadze shouted, stopping five metres away and sighting his weapon on the man's chest. Arziani raced ahead, staying out of Donadze's line of fire and pushed him forcibly against the pharmacy's glass window. With his face pressed against the glass, he kicked his feet apart, cuffed his hands behind his back and began to search him.

Donadze holstered his pistol and crossed to Jaqeli. 'Are you okay, Irina?' he said, reaching out to her.

She struck him hard on his shoulders with both hands, pushing him back a step. 'My God, Ramaz! What are you two doing?'

A small number of observers had gathered, some recording the scene on their phones. Arziani completed searching the suspect and turned him around.

He was younger than Donadze had thought. 'What's your name?' he said.

He was trying not to cry. 'Nugzar—what have I done?'

Arziani shook his head—he wasn't carrying a weapon.

'What are you doing here, Nugzar?' Donadze asked.

'Nothing, I just wanted some ointment...'

'Why this pharmacy? Did somebody—'

'Let him go, Misha,' Jaqeli said.

Donadze nodded. 'Yes, let him go…'

Arziani removed the handcuffs and said, 'Do you need a minute?'

Jaqeli put her hand on the young man's arm. 'I'm sorry, Nugzar. That shouldn't have happened—we thought you were someone else.'

He shrugged her hand away. 'Can I go now?'

She stepped to the side and he returned to his car, fumbling to locate his key in the ignition.

'Let's go back to the station,' Donadze said.

'Go on your own,' Jaqeli said, her cheeks burning. 'I don't want to be seen with either of you right now.'

'Irina…' Arziani said.

'I said—go on your own.'

Jaqeli stormed into the interview room, slamming the door shut behind her. 'I can't work like this,' she said with quiet fury.

Arziani glanced at Donadze. 'I'm sorry, I shouldn't have left you on your own.'

She threw her hands in the air. 'You see—that's what I mean. Why are *you* sorry? I had orders, just like you. Captain Nakani told me not to be on my own but I told you to go ahead without me. That makes it *my* fault, doesn't it?'

Arziani shook his head. 'I don't understand, Irina.'

'I know you don't. That's what makes this so—'

'I think I understand,' Donadze interrupted. 'You think Misha and I are being over-protective. That we're showing you consideration we wouldn't show to a man.'

'Well, aren't you?'

'Maybe we are...'

'But that's not what I want, Ramaz. The way we treated that poor boy was awful. And the two of you charging along the road like that? It was *ridiculous*. It made me feel like a little girl being looked after by two doting uncles. But that's not what you are—you're...'

'Colleagues?'

'Yes, of course you're colleagues. And I know we're more than that...'

'Friends?'

'Yes—friends.'

'Is that what I am, Irina—your friend?' Arziani said.

Jaqeli closed her eyes in exasperation. 'This isn't about you, Misha,' she said.

'I know it's not,' Arziani said, his tone flat.

'You're right, Irina,' Donadze said. 'But not entirely right. Misha and I do think and act in a certain way. It's how we've been brought up and it's difficult for us to change. But maybe you could cut *us* some slack. We did overreact—but what if that boy *had* been sent by Anzor Kalmikov? We weren't prepared to lose you.'

'I know...' Jaqeli said.

'Okay—from this point on—you get no special consideration.' Donadze paused. 'You, Detective, acted recklessly by sending Lieutenant Arziani away, despite knowing that Anzor Kalmikov wants revenge for his son's death and despite the clear orders given to you by Captain Nakani. These orders stand and failure to comply with them in future may result in disciplinary proceedings being taken against you. Do you understand this warning, Detective?'

Jaqeli smiled. 'Yes, Lieutenant. Thank you.'

Donadze nodded. 'So we're good?'

Jaqeli sighed. 'Yes.'

'When we go off duty, Irina? I can have a patrol car stationed outside your own apartment—if that's what you want,' Arziani said.

'Why would I want that?'

'Let's get back to work,' Donadze said.

The messages taken from Otar Basilia's phone went back more than a year—the period he had been using the Russian encryption system, Donadze guessed. He printed hard copies of the pdf files Captain Murtov had sent, guarding the networked printer from inquisitive eyes as he transferred ninety-seven sheets from the output tray to a plastic folder.

'See you outside,' he said to Jaqeli as he walked past her desk.

Arziani was waiting by his car. 'Still happy to do this?' Donadze asked.

'No problem. You're bringing Irina?'

'Yes, see you there.'

Donadze had parked his car in an area which had become shaded and cold. He got in and started the engine. It turned over sluggishly and he resolved once again to exchange the car rather than buy a replacement battery. He watched as Jaqeli came out of the station and crossed to the car park. He bleeped his horn to let her know where he was and leaned over to push the passenger door open. She got in and pulled the door shut.

Donadze handed her the folder. 'Take a look.'

They drove in silence as Jaqeli flicked through the printed sheets. She eventually stopped reading, straightened the bundle and held it in her lap. 'There's plenty to work on here.'

'But maybe too obscure to use as evidence?'

'Basilia's certainly not made it easy. If I didn't know better, I'd think *consignment* and *shipment* referred to movements of cars or potatoes—not women and drugs.'

'He was never going to spell it out for us, I suppose.'

'It's so cold, describing people that way. It won't look good for him if we can get it to court.'

'Right. So how *do* we get it to court?'

She lifted the paper bundle and held it in front of her. 'We need a timeline—from the date the messages start to the present day. We'll check our records and place the offences we know he's committed on that timeline. We'll then line up his messages chronologically and connect them to each known offence.'

'What about unknown offences?'

She waved the bundle. 'This'll give us a better idea of *everything* he's done, even the stuff he's managed to keep under the radar until now.'

They parked underground and took the elevator to the fifteenth level. Jaqeli had her own key and let them in.

'Through here,' Arziani shouted. Suspicion that there were corrupt officers at Mtatsminda Station had prompted him to suggest working out of his apartment.

Donadze followed Jaqeli into a bright, spacious lounge. A soft leather sofa with matching armchair and footrest were placed against a wall facing a curved television screen. An exercise area with a static bike and weights had been set up in a corner. There was little else in the room and it felt minimalistic and masculine, in stark contrast with Donadze's own apartment which had baby paraphernalia strewn everywhere.

'Nice,' Donadze said.

'Would you like a drink? No alcohol, I'm afraid.' Arziani had begun tearing sheets from a flip chart and attaching them with adhesive putty to a long wall.

'Let's finish setting-up first.'

They spent several minutes attaching the A1 sized sheets along the full length of the wall and opening the boxes of marker pens, coloured ballpoint pens, packets of post-it notes and notepads they had taken from the station. Jaqeli found a standard timeline template on her laptop and edited it with relevant titles and headings. They stood back to admire their work.

'Our very own incident room,' Jaqeli said.

'Let's get started.' Donadze went to the far end of the wall and wrote the date of Basilia's first message in red. 'This won't do much for your decor, Misha,' he said.

It took more than two hours and an extension of the flip chart sheets onto the adjoining wall before all of Basilia's messages were located on the timeline and matched chronologically with his known activities.

Donadze walked along the wall, reading and re-reading each message, trying to get a feel for the language and terminology used. 'This is good,' he said. He returned to a section he had highlighted with a blue asterisk. 'I'd like to focus here.'

235

Jaqeli joined him at the wall. 'The Gali Street murders.'

'Yes—let's work back a few days.' He drew an asterisk on the adjacent sheet. 'Here's where we'll start. Could you read it out loud, Irina?'

Jaqeli ran her finger down the paper as she read aloud the messages sent and received to Basilia's phone in the five days leading up to the murders.

'Could you read it again, please.'

Jaqeli frowned but re-read the section.

'What do you think?' Donadze asked.

'It's obvious,' Arziani said. 'He's organising the girls going into that apartment and making arrangements to move them to Germany.' He pointed to a section of text. 'Here's where he's told the girls have been killed—and here's where he puts the blame.' Arziani pointed to a single message which read, *K!!!!!* 'And look at this,' he continued, pointing to a message which read, *BOOM!* 'That was the morning Kalmikov's gym was bombed, wasn't it?'

'Yes, it was. The meaning of these messages are obvious to us because we know what happened. Do you think they would convince a jury?' Jaqeli said.

'They might if we can have them corroborated,' Donadze said. He drew a red asterisk and read, *Tell G get shipment ready my inspection.* 'Who do you think G is?'

'The girls' minder, Glonti—David Glonti,' Jaqeli said.

'And the *shipment?*'

'The girls themselves, of course.'

'And *inspection?*'

Jaqeli nodded. 'Veronika told us about that. Basilia paid a visit to the apartment and raped Mariam when he was there.'

'Yes, so Veronika's evidence will corroborate our interpretation of what these messages mean. It'll gives us enough to charge him for rape, trafficking, narcotics and the attack on Kalmikov's gym.'

'So, there's a lot riding on Veronika's evidence.'

'We need to speak to her again.' Donadze looked at his watch. 'It's too late to go to Shindisi. Can I pick you up tomorrow, Irina? Say, at eight?'

'No problem—would you like a glass of wine before you go?'

'So you do have alcohol?'

'Misha doesn't—but I do.'

TWENTY-FOUR

'Take a seat, *Ramazi*, I'm just about to serve,' Donadze's mother said.

He kissed Tamuna. 'How was your day?'

'Fine, fairly busy—but okay. How about you?'

'The same. How are you, *Deda*?'

'Very busy at the moment, Ramaz. Please take a seat.'

'Can I look in on Eka first?'

'If you must,' she tutted, trying and failing to look stern.

Donadze went to their bedroom. Eka was lying in her cot, breathing softly in the darkened room. He placed his hand on her chest and watched as her lips pursed. Probably a dream, he thought, although he preferred to think she sensed him watching over her. He made a promise to himself to return home earlier in future, knowing that his promise wouldn't be kept.

He left the bedroom and took a seat at the breakfast bar. He waited until the food had been distributed to their plates and he and Tamuna had gushed about how tasty it was, then said, 'So, let's talk about the wedding…'

Both women put their cutlery down and looked at him. 'What about it?' Tamuna said.

'We need a date…'

'There's no hurry is there?'

'What if you change your mind?' he joked.

'Then you'll be the first to know,' she said, poker-faced. 'Why the rush suddenly?'

'It's not a rush for me—I've been waiting all my life.'

'Really? Well, waiting a few more months shouldn't be too difficult for you, then.'

'It probably *is* a good idea to at least have a date in the diary,' his mother suggested.

'What about your investigation?'

'There's always going to be investigations.'

Tamuna appeared to think for a moment. 'What date did you have in mind?'

'Two weeks from today.'

She laughed. 'That's *far* too soon, Ramaz.'

'*Far* too soon,' his mother agreed.

'Why? What would stop us?'

'We haven't discussed any of the arrangements yet. We need to choose our gowns, arrange catering, give our guests some notice…'

'Isn't two weeks long enough for that?'

His mother put her hand on Tamuna's. 'It could be— if that's what you both want.'

'Remember, I said I want to be married in church,' Tamuna said. 'We couldn't get that organised in time.'

'Yes, we could and we will—trust me.'

Tamuna and his mother exchanged a look and Tamuna said, 'Two weeks…'

'So, that's settled, then. Two weeks from today—Saturday 20th—we're getting married.'

Arziani and Jaqeli were standing on the pavement outside the apartment block when Donadze pulled up. She kissed Arziani then opened the door and dropped onto the passenger seat.

'One minute,' Donadze said and got out the car.

'What's up, Ramaz?' Arziani asked.

'What are you doing on Saturday 20th?'

'Probably nothing, why?'

Donadze hesitated. 'Tamuna and I are getting married then. And I'm hoping you'll be my best man…'

'Really?' Arziani stepped forward and put his arms around Donadze then let go and slapped him on the arm when he failed to respond. 'Well, that's great and yes, of course. I'm honoured…'

Jaqeli jumped out the car and stepped up to hug him. 'Congratulations, Ramaz—fantastic! I'm so happy for you both. Where are you having the wedding?'

'It needs to be confirmed, hopefully today.'

'You mean you're getting married in two weeks' time—but you don't know where.'

'I do know, it just needs to be confirmed.'

'You're amazing, Ramaz. And I don't mean that in a good way.'

They stood awkwardly for a moment before Donadze

said, 'Right, Shindisi then…'

He and Jaqeli got back in the car and he drove off, watching in his rear-view mirror as Arziani gave them a brief wave before turning away.

Jaqeli turned in her seat. '*Two weeks*?'

'Tamuna insisted—probably worried that I'd change my mind.'

'Yes, I thought that was the reason.' She turned to face forward again. 'So, we're going to speak to Veronika…'

'And Major Gloveli. This case is coming to a head. Veronika's testimony is going to be crucial and I want her to be ready for it.'

Donadze took the familiar, twisting road to Shindisi. Dirty, grey clouds had sidled over the weak sun and a cold, misty drizzle greeted them outside Gloveli's house. He was standing by his open door and they hurried along the garden path and into the house.

Veronika was sitting by the small table. She stood, nodded to Donadze and stepped forward to hug Jaqeli.

'How are you, Veronika?' Donadze said in Russian.

'I'm okay. Has something happened?'

'Let's sit down—coffee's ready,' Gloveli said. He crossed to a battered stove, opened its door to throw wood onto the dancing flames then used a kitchen towel to lift a chipped enamel pot from its top surface. He carried the pot to the table and poured into four mismatched mugs.

'Thanks, Major,' Donadze said, helping himself to four spoons of sugar when offered. 'Something *has* happened, Veronika. We now have enough evidence against the man who brought you and the other girls—Mariam and Anzhela—to Tbilisi. The same man that came to the apartment and raped Mariam. Your description of him matches that of our suspect and supports your allegation that—'

'Allegation? It's not an allegation—he *did* drag Mariam into a bedroom and he *did* rape her.'

'I'm sorry, Veronika. What I meant was that the court will consider it an allegation until it's proved. Our evidence will be corroborated by your testimony and *that* will turn your allegation into a guilty verdict.'

'How tight is the evidence, Ramaz?' Gloveli asked in Georgian.

'With Veronika's testimony—it's tight.'

'So, Basilia only goes down if she's called as a witness.'

He hesitated. 'Probably, yes.'

'I understand what you're saying,' Veronika said. 'This man—he can't afford to let me appear in court. He needs me dead.'

Donadze and Gloveli exchanged a look and Jaqeli said, 'Yes, Veronika. What you tell the court will send Otar Basilia to jail.' She paused. 'But we're not going to let him hurt you...'

'Are you still willing to testify?' Donadze asked.

'Yes, of course—how could I not?'

'Good. You're safe here with Major Gloveli, for now.'

'For now…'

'Finish your coffee, Irina. I've got a call to make,' Donadze said.

The clouds and the drizzle had cleared and he stood in the garden with warm sunshine on his face. '*Gamarjoba*, Father,' he said when Chanturia answered his call.

'*Gamarjoba*, Lieutenant.'

242

'I'm in Shindisi…'

'But you thought it wise not to be seen with me.'

'Yes…'

'What can I do for you?'

'You remember the last time we met—I said I would ask you for a favour?'

'Yes, I remember. What do you have in mind?'

'Saturday 20th, I'm getting married—to Tamuna. I'd like it to be in your church.'

TWENTY-FIVE

Donadze stirred as his phoned buzzed on the bedside table—Sandro. He lifted the phone and stumbled across the darkened room and into the lounge before answering. 'What?'

'I'm in the basement car park—come down.'

He checked the time on his phone—five ten.

'Who is it, Ramaz?' Tamuna had followed him out of the bedroom.

'Sorry. It's just someone I need to speak to about a case I'm working. Go back to bed—I won't be long.'

He pulled on his clothes, tucked his pistol into his waistband and left the apartment. He called the elevator, got in and pressed the buttons for both the top floor and the basement parking. He got out before the doors closed and hurried down the stairway and into the basement. Sandro was standing by the elevator door, waiting for him to arrive.

'I'm here,' Donadze said, watching the other man start.

Sandro turned and said, 'Clever…'

'Just checking that you're on your own.'

'You've got your car keys?'

Donadze unlocked his car, the blip from the horn echoing in the still of the concrete structure. He took his pistol out of his waistband and placed it on the dash as he sat down.

Sandro nodded again. 'Smart.'

'What's this about?'

'Kalmikov, of course. Your warning didn't work—he's going after your partner.'

Donadze leaned back in his seat and closed his eyes. 'How?' he said, eventually

'He's bringing in someone from Kutaisi—the best he has. His name's Merab Shonia.'

'Shonia? Do we know him?'

'He's got a record but nothing recent. Kalmikov keeps him for specialised work like this.'

'Specialised work—is that what you think this is?'

'It doesn't matter what I think.'

'What does Shonia look like?'

'I'll send a picture to your phone, but don't assume he'll look the same when—or if—you see him.'

'He'll be disguised?'

'One of the things he's good at—the classic silent assassin. You won't see him come or go. You only have one advantage: neither Kalmikov nor Shonia know that I've told you about the hit. They don't know that you'll be ready for him.'

'How do we stop him if he's that good?'

'I hope you *can* stop him. But there's only one way—

you need to get to him before he gets to Jaqeli.'

'I told Kalmikov that I'd go after *him* if he harmed Jaqeli.'

'Yes, and he might even have believed you. But he doesn't care. Badri was a weasel—but he was Anzor's only son and he's got to do something about him being killed— he'd lose respect otherwise.'

'How long have we got?'

'Not long—Kalmikov wants this to happen soon.'

Donadze paused, thinking.

Sandro turned in his seat to check his surroundings. 'Well, I've told you what I know, it's up to you—'

'Wait.'

He closed the car door and checked his watch. 'I shouldn't even be here.'

'Does Shonia need a green light, something like the final go-ahead from Kalmikov?'

'You're not serious, are you?' Sandro said, smiling. 'What would you do? Kill Kalmikov to stop him giving Shonia the nod?'

'That's not what I said.'

'I think it was. In any event, it wouldn't help—Shonia has his orders and only Kalmikov can call him off. If he weren't there to do it, the hit would still go ahead.' He grinned at Donadze. 'Maybe it's Kalmikov you need to protect?'

'You think this is funny?'

'No, I don't. Are we done?'

'Let me know if you hear anything new.'

'I'll do what I can,' Sandro said. He checked his surroundings once more then opened the car door and got out, pulling up his jacket collar as he strode towards the stairs.

Donadze closed his eyes, put his head in his hands and rubbed his temples. 'Shit,' he said.

'Is Irina with you?' Donadze spoke into his phone.

'Yes, she is. What's going on, Ramaz?' Arziani said.

'I'm on my way. Make sure your doors are locked and keep away from the windows. Twenty minutes.'

'Kalmikov?'

'Yes. Better if we speak face to face. I'm going to hang up now and call Captain Nakani. Twenty minutes,' he repeated then ended the call. He drove one-handed while looking for Nakani's number.

The phone rang for about thirty seconds. 'Ramaz?' he said.

Donadze glanced at his dash clock. It was five forty but Nakani sounded groggier than the early hour would suggest. 'Yes. Are you okay, Captain?'

Nakani cleared his throat. 'What do you mean? Of course I'm okay. What's this about?'

'Jaqeli, sir—Kalmikov has ordered a hit on her.' Donadze updated him on his conversation with Sandro. 'I think there's only one way to handle this but Jaqeli needs to agree. Can we call you back in about thirty minutes?'

'Okay, I'll wait here.'

'Colonel Meskhi will also want to be informed. Could you please phone him, Captain?'

'Yes, of course. Call me when you're ready.'

Donadze parked a short distance from Arziani's apartment block, turned the courtesy light switch off, then killed the engine. He sat in the dark car for a minute, watching the block, then got out, closed the door and crossed to the entrance. He took the elevator to level eighteen then walked down three flights of stairs. He stopped on the stairwell, looked along the corridor then walked to Arziani's apartment and tapped the door three times. He saw movement through the peephole and Arziani opened the door with the security chain on. He removed the chain and opened the door far enough to allow him to look along the corridor then stepped aside to let Donadze enter.

'How is she?'

Arziani returned his pistol to its belt holster and shrugged. 'See for yourself.' He led the way into the lounge. The papers containing Basilia's phone messages were still attached to the walls. Jaqeli sat on the leather sofa, her legs curled under her, her feet bare. She was dressed in joggers and a sweatshirt and was cradling a large mug of steaming coffee in both hands.

'Hey, Ramaz,' she said, attempting a smile.

'I'm sorry, Irina, I should have stayed in the car…'

'It would have worked out better for me if *I'd* stayed in the car, don't you think?' She uncurled her legs and sat up. 'So, tell us what's happening.'

Donadze looked at his watch. 'We've to call Captain Nakani in about ten minutes, so I'll be quick.' He relayed his conversation with Sandro, stressing that being informed of the planned hit gave them a limited advantage.

Arziani joined Jaqeli on the sofa and sat, hunched with his head in his hands. 'This is terrible,' he said.

'What's your plan, Ramaz?' Jaqeli asked.

'I *do* have a plan…'

'I knew you would. Tell us.'

'We're keeping you safe, Irina.' He paused. 'But we have to be realistic. This man, Shonia—he's Kalmikov's best. Time is on his side and he only needs one opportunity. He probably thinks the odds are stacked in his favour, and maybe they are. So we need to change that. We can't protect you everywhere and all of the time—so we need to change the dynamics. Shonia needs to come to you and you need to be in a place where we can protect you from him.'

'I understand,' Jaqeli said.

'Do you? Well, I don't,' Arziani snapped. 'What are you talking about, Ramaz?'

'You *do* know what he's talking about, Misha. And it makes sense.'

'Okay, yes I do understand—but it's unacceptable.' He stood and pointed his finger at Donadze. 'You want Irina to be the bait which draws Shonia in. No, that's not going to happen—find another way.'

'It's not what I *want*, Misha, but I think—'

'Ramaz is right, Misha.' Jaqeli stood and put her arms around him. 'It's going to work, I know it will.'

Donadze looked at Jaqeli and she nodded.

'I'm calling Nakani now,' he said. He put his phone on speaker. 'I'm with Irina and Misha now, Captain.'

'Good, one minute. I'm patching Colonel Meskhi in.'

Meskhi joined the call a moment later. 'Captain Nakani has briefed me. I'm sorry this has happened, Detective, but—I assure you—your safety is my top priority and the top priority for all the officers under my command.'

'Thank you, sir.'

'Colonel, we've discussed the best approach,' Donadze said. 'Shonia is an accomplished assassin. We can't guarantee Irina's safety if she's moving out and about.'

'I agree—so we set a trap. At Jaqeli's apartment?'

'No, sir. She's staying with Lieutenant Arziani, currently. His apartment will be more easily protected.'

'Good. And do we substitute Jaqeli with a decoy?'

Donadze glanced at Arziani before speaking. 'No, sir. Shonia might realise we've made a substitution. And we'd still have to protect Irina at her new location.'

'Yes, I agree. So, we set up surveillance on Arziani's apartment.'

'Yes, sir.'

'Detective?'

'Yes, sir. Thank you.'

'Lieutenant Arziani?'

'I just want to keep Irina safe, Colonel.'

'We all do—and this is the best way to do it. Where will *you* be?'

'Where? Here of course, with Irina.'

'No, you can't be with Jaqeli—Shonia might stay away. You need to be out of the city. Do you have relatives you could visit? A sick mother, perhaps?'

'No, I can't do that, sir. I need to be here.'

'You don't, Misha,' Jaqeli said. 'Colonel Meskhi knows what he's doing—let's trust him.'

'That's settled, then. Arziani, pack a bag. Jaqeli, you sound a little hoarse, I suggest you take some sick leave.'

'Sir,' Jaqeli said.

'Sir,' Arziani repeated a moment later.

The stakeout was in place by the early afternoon. It had been established efficiently and with discretion but Donadze worried that they had no real idea how long it would have to be maintained as the surveillance team would inevitably lose focus over time.

He thought he recognised the command vehicle from a previous operation that he had been part of, although its external paintwork had been changed to portray a company providing broadband services. It had been located a short distance from the apartment block, its pinhole cameras focused on the main entrance and on Arziani's fifteenth level apartment. Colonel Meskhi was leading the operation and was stationed inside. Donadze sat between him and a technician who operated the communications, audio and video equipment from the vehicle's control console.

Stakeouts were usually tedious but Donadze's mind raced, tormented that the approach he had recommended was reckless, that Jaqeli should have been hidden somewhere safe. He rotated his shoulders and neck to relieve the tension in his upper body.

'Relax, Lieutenant. We may be here for some time,' Meskhi said.

'Yes, sir. I'll try.'

Shonia's photograph had been distributed to the stakeout team with a warning that he could be in disguise. There were three ways in and out of the apartment block: through the main entrance, through the emergency exit at the rear or down the ramp leading to the basement parking. All were under observation and armed officers in plain clothes were also located in an empty apartment on Arziani's level, seconds away from his door if required.

Arziani had left earlier, doing his best to simulate mild concern for Jaqeli's health rather than deep anxiety for her life. She had gone along with the ruse, promising to call if she felt worse and telling him his mother needed him more than she did. 'Keep an eye on her, Ramaz,' Arziani had murmured. 'Call me when you can.'

Jaqeli had been instructed to behave like someone with a real illness. Her sweatshirt had been fitted with a compact, high quality video and audio transmitter, its microwave link beaming her movements as, seemingly bored and listless, she wandered into the kitchen for drinks and snacks, flicked through television channels or read a book, periodically sniffing, coughing and sneezing for good effect. She had called into the station to say she was taking sick leave and had also phoned Donadze to repeat the same message as an apparent courtesy to her partner.

The afternoon wore into evening and residents returned from work, driving their cars down the parking ramp or hurrying through the chilly air into the lobby where elevators were summoned to transport them to their respective levels, their arrival home marked by lights snapping on in lounge and bedroom windows. The surveillance team kept watch, checking in periodically as communication protocols required.

Jaqeli took a couple of calls on her phone. The control van could only hear her side of the conversation but it was clear that the first call was from her mother and the other from Arziani, seemingly checking to see if she felt better.

His call ended and she turned on the television to watch a hospital soap.

As the evening wore on, the volume of traffic passing the command vehicle slowed and business in the few bars and restaurants along the street picked up.

Meskhi took a sip of the strong, sweet coffee supplied by the technician. 'What does your gut tell you, Lieutenant? he said. 'Will Shonia make his move tonight?'

'I really don't know, sir.' He glanced at the technician who was—studiously—not listening in on their conversation. 'We were only told it would be soon. What do you think?'

Meskhi looked at the screen displaying the video feed from Arziani's apartment. 'I think... tonight.'

By midnight, the few remaining customers had disgorged themselves from the bars and restaurants which had closed soon after, the owners and staff locking their doors and hurrying home. Apartment lights eventually went off as weary residents gave up on television and went to bed. The video feed from Arziani's apartment showed Jaqeli slumped on the leather sofa, reading her book.

Meskhi stirred in his seat. 'Can you feel it, Donadze?'

'I'm not sure, maybe...'

Meskhi bent the microphone stalk towards himself. 'All stations report.' He listened as officers confirmed their location and status then said, 'Take a look around, Lieutenant.'

Donadze was grateful to escape the confines of the van. He pulled his black cap low, putting his face into shadow, waited until the technician had killed the internal lights then slipped out the back door, moving clear of the van and into a dark area of the street. He walked around the apartment block, observing the entrance, parking ramp and emergency exit with his peripheral vision then slipped into a wooded area on the other side of the street where he hoped the trees would shield him from view. He spoke into the microphone clipped to his lapel, identifying himself by his call sign and reporting that there was nothing suspicious to be seen.

'Maintain station,' Meskhi ordered.

Donadze leaned against a tree where he could observe both the entrance and Arziani's apartment. Minutes passed and he rubbed his hands together to stop his fingers becoming stiff in the cold, still air. Looking up, he thought he saw movement on the balcony. It appeared to stop and he shielded his eyes to shut out light from the street and looked again. Meskhi's voice came over the radio at the same time, 'Two intruders on subject balcony, go, go, go! Repeat, two intruders on subject balcony, all stations go, go, go!'

Donadze pushed himself off the tree and sprinted for the apartment block, his hand reaching for the holster bouncing on his hip. He was almost at the entrance when he heard a scream followed by the soft, wet thump of flesh and bone falling from a great height onto an unforgiving surface. 'Irina, no!' he howled, a terrible dread gripping his gut.

TWENTY-SIX

Donadze stopped running a few metres from the body. It was undoubtedly male. His immediate relief was short-lived and replaced by fear that Jaqeli could be next to fall. He stepped back and, shielding his eyes against the streetlights, tried to discern further movement on the balcony.

'Location secure, subject safe and well,' a breathless voice spoke over his radio.

Donadze closed his eyes and released a long sigh. *Thank God*, he thought.

Meskhi came on the air a moment later, instructing all exits to be secured with no one allowed in or out.

Two officers from the stakeout team, their semi-automatic carbines held ready, approached the body.

'What's going on, Lieutenant? Who's this?' one asked.

'Let's see if we know him,' Donadze said.

The officer winced then stooped to ease the silk balaclava clear of the corpse's face.

'That's far enough.'

Donadze had not previously witnessed a fall-related death and was surprised by how intact the body appeared to be, broken rather than burst and probably with unseen shattered bones and massive internal damage, he thought. But apart from some bleeding through the mouth and ears, it was largely whole and recognisable from the photograph he and the stakeout team had been given.

'Is that Shonia?' the officer asked.

'Yes, call it in then secure the area.'

He looked at the body once more and the apartment it had fallen from. He tried to estimate the descent time—five seconds, at most, he thought. It really didn't matter, it was long enough for Shonia to feel the terror of free fall and imminent, inevitable death.

The two officers stiffened and Donadze turned to see Meskhi behind him. He gazed at the corpse without comment then said, 'There's one more. Come with me, Lieutenant.'

They took the elevator to the fifteenth level and walked along the corridor, ignoring the residents who peered out of their partially opened doors. Meskhi stopped at the apartment adjacent to Arziani's. He took a pen from his pocket and used it to push the door. It swung open. He unbuttoned his jacket, removed his pistol from its holster and stepped in. Donadze unholstered his own pistol and followed. The apartment was a mirror image of Arziani's and they went room to room, taking it in turn to search while the other provided cover by the door.

They found a woman lying on her side in a bedroom, gagged and with her hands and feet trussed behind her back, her eyes wild and terrified. The apartment's owner, Donadze assumed. Meskhi made a gesture of reassurance and they left to complete their search.

The lounge was empty, its sliding balcony door open, the net curtains hanging above it billowing in the gentle breeze. Meskhi held the curtains back while Donadze stepped onto the balcony.

'Clear,' he said.

He crossed to the clouded perspex screen that separated the two balconies and, with vertigo fluttering in the pit of his stomach, leaned over the railing to look into Arziani's side of the divide.

'Clear,' he said, again.

He returned his pistol to its holster and gazed at the scene in the street below. Police cars had been located to stop traffic moving and to keep members of the public back. Standard crime scene measures would soon be established and the body eventually removed but, for now, Shonia lay where he had fallen, a very long way below.

Meskhi crossed to the balcony railing and gazed at the activity in the street, his face impassive. 'Untie the lady, Lieutenant. Have a doctor look at her.'

Donadze radioed for a medic as he returned to the bedroom. He removed the gag and put his hand on the woman's shoulder. 'Don't be scared—the men who did this can't hurt you now. You're safe,' he told her. Her eyes widened as he took out his knife. 'I'm just going to cut these ropes.'

She had been tightly bound and the skin on her wrists and ankles was broken, the blood making the synthetic rope slippery. He cut carefully and stayed with the woman until the medic arrived.

'Don't worry, you're safe,' Donadze told her again.

Meskhi was in the lounge, speaking into his phone. He hung up and said, 'How is she?'

'The doctor's with her now, sir.'

'Good. I'll speak to her when he's finished.'

'We'll get him, Colonel—he can't get away.'

Meskhi shrugged, 'I believe he already has.'

'But how? Every exit's covered.'

'They're covered now. Who was watching after the body fell? We'll look, make sure he's not hiding somewhere, but I think he's gone.'

'The video footage?'

'Not much to see at that distance and angle. I doubt we'll get an ID from it.'

'He and Shonia must have got here early, found a way in before we had our surveillance established.'

'Yes, I think that's likely.'

'And they came together. So Shonia must have known and trusted him.'

'Right up to the point he helped him over the side.'

'While Shonia was climbing into Arziani's balcony?'

'Yes, we have that much on video.'

'But, why?'

'There are only a limited number of reasons. Either he wanted Jaqeli alive or he wanted Shonia dead. Or maybe he wanted both these things.' Meskhi looked at his watch. 'You'd better check on Jaqeli.'

Donadze turned to leave.

'Lieutenant.'

He stopped walking and turned back to face Meskhi.

'Kalmikov doesn't get to try this again. Do you understand?'

Donadze hesitated. 'Yes, sir.'

'Good, we'll be leaving soon,' Meskhi said.

Donadze knocked on Arziani's door and was let in by one of the responding officers. Jaqeli was sitting on the lounge sofa and rushed to hug him.

'That was a bit close,' she said, trying to keep her voice light.

'It was far too close. Misha was right, we should have found another way.'

'Maybe, but it's done now—tell me what happened.'

They sat on the sofa and Donadze relayed the limited information he had. Shonia and another person, who had not yet been identified, had arrived at the apartment block early, overcome Arziani's neighbour and attempted to climb across the balconies. For reasons unknown, Shonia's companion had turned on him and caused him to fall.

'He couldn't have slipped?'

'No, he only had to climb around a screen. I had a look, it's not difficult if you have a head for heights. Anyway, I think Colonel Meskhi's video will confirm it was deliberate.'

'So, why?'

'Good question—we don't know, yet. Did you see anything?'

'Not really, the balcony lights were off and it was light in here so I didn't have night vision. I didn't even hear much. Someone was hit then some words were said, indistinct but high pitched—he was terrified, I think. It must have been Shonia. And then there was a scream and it all went crazy after that.'

'Do you think Shonia was struck to make him lose his grip?'

'Yes, I guess so.'

'Okay, have you called Misha?'

'I'm going to call him now.'

'Good—he'll want to hear from you.'

She lifted her phone, selected a number, then put the phone down again. 'Ramaz, how does this end? I was lucky—what's going to happen next time?'

'There won't be a next time. It ends tonight.'

'Please tell me you're not planning anything stupid.'

'I'm not planning anything,' Donadze said. He smiled at her, 'Put Misha out of his misery—give him a call.'

Colonel Meskhi called off the search for Shonia's killer after about an hour. He phoned Donadze and told him to go to the building entrance, leaving an officer in Arziani's apartment and a patrol car located outside. Jaqeli was exhausted and Donadze told her to take the day off.

Meskhi was waiting by the entrance, motionless, his breath misting in the cool, early-morning chill. 'The lady couldn't tell me much,' he said, without preamble. 'Shonia was working with his assailant—at least until he turned on him. They forced their way in but were masked. Quite disciplined, didn't speak—so no names or accents picked up. She heard a scuffle and a scream then, a minute or so after that, she heard someone leave her apartment. As I thought, whoever that person was, slipped out during the excitement caused by the fall and our response.'

'Forensics, sir?'

'Doubtful. Shonia was a professional and it's likely his partner was as well. I'll be surprised if he's left any prints or useful DNA. How's Jaqeli?'

'Putting on a brave face, but rattled, I think. Shonia got close.'

'Yes, he did.' He paused. 'Are you ready to do this, Lieutenant?'

'Yes, sir.'

Meskhi gave him an address. 'Take your own car and park a block away—I'll meet you outside,' he said.

Donadze arrived about twenty minutes later. The apartment block was modern, low rise and expensive, as befitted the mistress of a leading crime figure. Meskhi glanced at a slip of paper and tapped the access code into the keypad to unlock the entrance door. The apartment was on the third level and Donadze struggle to keep up as Meskhi climbed the stairs two at a time.

There were four apartments on each level. Meskhi consulted his slip of paper again and took up position in front of the relevant door, filling the peephole's field of vision. He rang the bell several times while Donadze stood, flattened against the wall and out of sight. 'Police, open the door, Tata,' Meskhi instructed, his voice just loud enough to be heard inside the apartment.

The door was thrown open by Anzor Kalmikov. He was wearing checked shorts but was otherwise naked, the hair covering his sagging pectorals flecked white, his face etched from sleep, 'What the fuck do—'

His face dropped as Donadze stepped into view.

'Inside, Mr Kalmikov,' Meskhi said, pushing into the apartment.

Kalmikov's partner from the opera was standing in a bedroom doorway, a printed-silk gown doing little to hide her curvaceous figure.

Meskhi turned to her. 'I would like you to go for a short walk.'

'What this about?' Kalmikov said. 'Tata—stay. This is your apartment, they can't make you go.'

'She does have to go, Mr Kalmikov. You, of all people, must understand how inconvenient witnesses can be.'

'I'm calling my lawyer,' Kalmikov said, his voice breaking.

Meskhi put his hand into his jacket pocket and drew out a small revolver. Its grip and trigger had been taped. He held it up to show Kalmikov. 'I always carry one of these. I've had this one for about a year now. I like it—it's a pity I'll have to leave it here.' He looked at Tata and frowned. 'I asked you to leave.'

She grabbed a raincoat from a stand and ran for the door.

'Tata,' Meskhi said.

She stopped, her hand on the door handle.

'Please don't call anyone.'

'No,' she said and fled, leaving the apartment door open.

Donadze closed the door and took out his phone.

'Listen, tell me what it is you need,' Kalmikov said.

Meskhi transferred the gun to his left hand and used his right to pull a silk balaclava over his head. 'Move,' he said, his voice made deliberately gruff.

'No, this can't be right. Tell me what you need. Is it money?'

Meskhi gestured with the revolver. 'Inside.'

Kalmikov turned around and Meskhi pushed him, stumbling, toward the lounge.

'Is this about Detective Jaqeli? I heard that someone was at her apartment tonight, but I promise it had nothing to do with me.'

'This will do. Get down on your knees.'

'No, please. All right, I admit it, I did send Shonia, but nothing happened, did it? I know, I should have listened to Lieutenant Donadze. Badri wasn't worth it—but he was my son. Jaqeli was just doing her job. I'll do anything you want. Please... you don't have to kill me.'

Meskhi kept his revolver pointed at Kalmikov a moment longer then returned it to his pocket. He took off his balaclava. 'Show Mr Kalmikov your video, Lieutenant.'

Donadze opened an app on his phone and ran the video. He turned the volume to maximum and held the phone in front of the crime boss. He had recorded from the time Tata had fled the apartment and had captured Kalmikov's abject humiliation as he begged for his life.

'Would you like to see it again?' Meskhi asked.

Kalmikov dropped into a chair, his eyes hardening. He didn't answer.

'The video will be stored somewhere safe. No one else need see it—if you cooperate. Who did you send with Shonia?'

Kalmikov shook his head but didn't speak.

'On the other hand, maybe we should make it available. Let your colleagues see the man you really are. How would that affect your standing in the Kutaisi Clan?' His voice hardened. 'Last chance—who did you send with Shonia?'

'Okay! *I* didn't fucking send anyone with him! I sent Shonia, no one else—he always works on his own.'

'I see. Well, given the way things worked out, that sounds like a good policy. I wonder what made this job different?'

'Get out my house.'

'Soon, Mr Kalmikov. One last thing before we go—is your business with Detective Jaqeli over?'

Kalmikov sat back in his chair and crossed his arms.

'Post it, Lieutenant,' Meskhi said.

Donadze began clicking buttons on his phone. He paused and looked at Kalmikov, his finger poised.

'No.'

'Say it, Mr Kalmikov.'

'It's over…'

Meskhi nodded. 'Good. I'm sure we'll talk again soon. Let's go, Lieutenant.'

TWENTY-SEVEN

'Get some sleep, Lieutenant,' Colonel Meskhi said. 'I'll see you this afternoon—Mtatsminda Station, two thirty.'

'Yes, sir. Colonel?'

'What?'

'Thank you.'

Meskhi frowned. 'Two thirty.'

The apartment was in pandemonium when Donadze returned. Eka was crying in his mother's arms while Tamuna fussed between the baby and getting herself ready for work.

She kissed him distractedly. 'Everything okay?' she asked.

'Fine, everything okay here?'

Tamuna grimaced. 'Just about…'

'I'll drive you to the clinic.'

'You're tired. I'll take a *marshrutka*,' she said without conviction.

'Not that tired. I'm ready when you are…'

He took Eka and jostled her in his arms, whispering to her. Her crying stopped and he smiled at his mother. She had also been smiling but contrived a disapproving frown.

'Nothing to it,' he teased.

Tamuna was ready to leave and, kissing Eka goodbye, walked ahead of Donadze to the elevator. He pressed the button for the basement.

She exhaled slowly. 'It doesn't get any easier.'

'That's why I stay out all night.'

'Funny…'

They got in the car and Donadze started the engine, a cloud of blue smoke blowing out the exhaust.

She faked a cough. 'I'm buying you a new car as a wedding present.'

'That's great, do I get to choose it?'

'It depends on what you choose.'

He shook his head. 'It must be me…'

They spent the time on the drive chatting about Eka and their wedding plans. He was exhausted by the time he arrived back at their apartment and glad that it was empty. He set his phone to alarm at one and chewed a piece of bread while he kicked off his shoes, undressed and crawled under the duvet.

He woke before his alarm and rummaged in the fridge for something to eat, shaved and showered then drove to Mtatsminda Station.

Captain Nakani was in his office. 'You had an eventful night, Ramaz,' he said.

'Yes. We got lucky with Shonia.'

'Not so lucky for him, though. Very strange. No clues

on the killer's identity?'

Donadze shook his head. 'Nothing at the moment.'

'What about Irina? Kalmikov is likely to try again.'

'I don't think so, sir.'

Nakani sat back in his chair and appraised Donadze. 'Are you going to tell me?'

'I can't, Captain. I'm sorry. Perhaps if you spoke to Colonel Meskhi…'

'I see, more secrets between you and the Colonel.'

'Not secrets, Captain…'

Nakani sighed and pulled his keyboard towards himself. 'Don't worry.' He looked at his watch. 'We're meeting in the incident room at two thirty—he'll be here soon. I'll see you there.'

Donadze stood and looked down on Nakani as he hunched over the keyboard. 'Sorry, Captain,' he said and left his office.

'As you were,' Colonel Meskhi said as he entered the incident room and took up position in front of his four officers: Donadze, Nakani, Arziani and Jaqeli. 'How are you, Detective?' he asked.

'Relieved, sir. Thank you,' Jaqeli said. Donadze had told her, without providing details, that Meskhi had extracted a reliable commitment from Anzor Kalmikov that he had no further interest in harming her.

'That was an unfortunate interlude but, as I told you, the safety of my officers is always my top priority.' He took the nearest seat. 'Let's begin. I called you here because I feel that now *may* be the time to arrest Otar Basilia. We will, however, get only one shot at bringing a successful conviction so we must be confident that our case is as tight as we can reasonably make it. Captain Nakani—your thoughts, please.'

Nakani had been doodling on a notepad. He put his pen down, cleared his throat and said, 'Sir, we have enough evidence against Basilia to bring charges of people trafficking and rape. That evidence comes largely from intercepted messages and is only credible when corroborated by one of the victims—Veronika Boyko. The question must be—do we go with what we have or do we spend more time building a stronger case with more compelling evidence?'

'What we have isn't compelling?'

'Yes, it is, but corroboration is vital. We would be relying on a young Ukrainian girl's testimony.'

'She's eighteen and, respectfully, sir, I believe Veronika is credible and will make a reliable witness,' Jaqeli said.

Meskhi tapped a finger on the desk while he took a few seconds to think. 'Let's explore our options,' he said, at last. 'If we *were* to spend more time building this case, where would our new evidence come from?'

'Why don't you update us on the latest from INTERPOL, Lieutenant?' Nakani said.

Arziani started to get to his feet but was waved back down by Meskhi. 'Yes, Captain. I think it's fair to say that we wouldn't even have a case against Basilia without INTERPOL. They gave us access to his phone and the messages Captain Nakani mentioned. My contact, Captain Murtov, thinks it's likely there's even more evidence hidden on the dark web and that INTERPOL will find it—given time.'

'Time and the belief that Basilia won't destroy it first?'

'Well, yes, sir. There's always that risk, I suppose.'

'You suppose? Try not to be so sensitive, Lieutenant. I'm not criticising you or the support you received from INTERPOL.'

Donadze noted Jaqeli winking at Arziani as he was about to respond. 'Yes, sir. Of course, there's no guarantee. And time is certainly a factor…' he said.

Meskhi nodded his approval. 'Your thoughts, Donadze?'

'It occurs to me, sir, that with Kalmikov on the back foot, now would also be a good time to take Basilia down. Both organisations will be weakened simultaneously and that should make a step reduction in crime across the city— it's the right thing to do. As for securing a conviction, Captain Nakani is correct when he says that corroborating testimony will be required. But I also agree with Detective Jaqeli—Veronika Boyko will make a compelling and reliable witness. We have a tight case—let's get that man into a courtroom.'

Meskhi looked around the room, checking for dissent, then nodded. 'Good. I agree—bring him in.'

Donadze parked by the casino's main entrance. He walked to the patrol car which had pulled up behind him, its lights strobing blue and red against the gilded pillars and porch. The driver wound down his window. 'Shall we come with you, Lieutenant?'

'Stay here. We'll be out soon. Let's go Irina,' he said.

He led the way through the ornate doors and paused to observe the banks of slot machines and the gaming tables; his eyes and ears adjusting to the glare of the lights and the rhythmic clunk of winnings being paid and change and tokens being dispensed.

'Lieutenant Donadze, isn't it? Welcome back, sir. Is Mr Basilia expecting you?'

Donadze ignored the security manager. 'After you, Irina,' he said.

Jaqeli led the way to the central stairway, climbed the carpeted stairs and turned left at the top. They stopped outside Basilia's office. She looked at Donadze and he nodded. She banged the door and shouted, 'Police, open the door, Mr Basilia.' She attempted to turn the handle and found it locked. 'Open the door, sir.'

'One minute, for God's sake,' they heard. The door opened and a young woman ducked out, her stiletto-heel shoes in one hand, her free arm supporting her impressive breasts as she fled along the corridor.

They stepped into Basilia's office. He was sitting behind his desk. 'What do you two want, now?'

'I hope we're not interrupting,' Jaqeli said.

Donadze showed him his handcuffs. 'Stand up, Otar. You're under arrest.'

'Fuck you,' he said, reaching for his desk phone.

Donadze slammed his fist onto Basilia's hand, crushing it against the phone's handset. 'I said, stand up.'

Basilia stood, flexing his injured fingers. 'Big mistake, Donadze.'

'Turn around, hands behind your back.'

The gang boss turned, his shirt straining against his

muscular shoulders, arms and his bulging belly as he put his hands behind his back.

'Read the charges and make sure Mr Basilia knows his rights, Detective.'

Basilia ignored Jaqeli as she intoned the charges against him and informed him of his right to remain silent. He turned to face Donadze and smiled. 'How are your friends in Shindisi, Ramaz?'

'Let's go, Otar,' Donadze said and walked Basilia through his office door.

They continued along the corridor. 'I like it there, lovely scenery, fresh air. Maybe I should pay a visit—drop in on Major Gloveli.'

'Down the stairs—be careful.'

Basilia took several steps down the stairway. 'On the other hand, I wouldn't want to impose—maybe I should wait until young Veronika has returned to Ukraine. Her mother and sister must be missing her.'

The security manager was waiting at the foot of the stairway. 'What's happening, sir?'

'I believe Lieutenant Donadze is taking me to Mtatsminda Station—call the lawyer and tell him to get there now.'

They continued walking through the casino's gambling hall where only a few of Basilia's customers were interested enough to look up from the spinning reels, cards, dice and roulette wheels to watch him being led out.

'Take a good look, Otar—you might not be coming back.'

'Oh, I think I will. And sooner than you realise.'

The uniformed cops got out of their car when they saw

Basilia being led from the casino.

'Take him,' Donadze said.

Basilia turned to face Donadze. 'Tell me, Ramaz. You're like me—no oil painting. How did you persuade a girl like Tamuna to marry you?'

'I said take him.'

One of the officers laid his hand on Basilia's shoulder. 'Let's go, sir,' he said.

Basilia shrugged the hand off. He smiled at Donadze and winked. 'Give her my love. Maybe we'll see each other soon,' he said.

TWENTY-EIGHT

Donadze's hands shook as he stood in front of the bedroom mirror and clipped the bow tie around his neck. An introvert by nature, he dreaded being the centre of attention.

'How are you getting on?' Arziani shouted from the living room.

'Okay, I suppose.'

He was polishing his shoes as Donadze walked through. 'Looking sharp, Ramaz,' he said.

'Thanks.' Donadze wished the day could be over. He would have preferred a small civil ceremony but had inevitably gone along with Tamuna and his mother's wishes for a traditional wedding. His acquiescence had not however extended to wearing a *chokha*. The hired dinner suit he wore in its place was the best he could find in the time he was prepared to spend looking, but the trousers were loose on his waist and the jacket tight on his shoulders.

The *nishnoba* had been a chore. They had driven to

Tamuna's family home in west Georgia a few days earlier to allow both families to formally meet. Donadze had been introduced to Tamuna's brother, Erekle. With their father dead, Erekle was head of the household and Donadze had bitten his tongue as he'd issued perfunctory instructions to Tamuna and her mother. He evidently judged Donadze to be an unworthy match for his sister and, slurring his words after several glasses of wine, had made what he believed to be humorous remarks about the police and Donadze's home region of Abkhazia. Donadze hadn't risen to his jibes but Tamuna had eventually lost patience and crossed the room to whisper in her brother's ear, her hand gripping the back of his neck to focus his attention and restore his manners.

Arziani finished tying his shoes and stood. 'Let's go,' he said.

They took the elevator to the basement parking where he had left his Mercedes. Tamuna had insisted on following the custom requiring the groom and best man to attend a reception in the bride's home and to take the bride and bridesmaid from the reception to the church. It was impractical to travel to west Georgia and Lela, Tamuna's friend and bridesmaid, had offered to host the gathering in her apartment.

Arziani drove the large car casually, one hand on the wheel, the other beating time to the rock music booming through its sound system. Donadze envied his even temperament; the traffic was, as always, dense and ill-disciplined but he made steady progress without being drawn into feuds with other road users.

They arrived at Lela's apartment and Arziani bumped onto the pavement to park illegally, seeing no contradiction with his role as a police officer. He turned to look at Donadze. 'Ready?' he asked.

'Let's get it over with,' Donadze said.

Arziani laughed and jabbed him on the shoulder. 'Relax, it's going to be fine.'

They took the elevator to Lela's apartment. Her door was open and Donadze fixed what he hoped was a pleasant expression on his face and followed Arziani in. There were more people than he expected and most turned their attention on him, slapping his shoulder and beaming good-naturedly. Erekle was lording over the proceedings and made a point of hugging and symbolically offering him a glass of his best wine. Donadze went round the room, greeting friends and Tamuna's family members—relieved that he remembered most of their names.

His mother was sitting in an easy chair with Eka sleeping in her arms. They were his only relatives at the reception, his remaining extended family living in Abkhazia and unable to travel to Tbilisi. He knelt to kiss them.

'You're looking very handsome, *Ramazi*,' his mother said, then tutted, 'Stand up, you're going to ruin your trousers.'

'Thanks, *Deda*. Is everything okay?' he said, getting to his feet.

'Everything's perfect. I'm so happy for you.'

'I know you are. I'd better go and talk to some of these people.'

'These people?'

'You know what I mean.'

He took a sip of wine and looked around. Jaqeli was standing on her own, looking spectacular in a knee-length sleeveless dress, her hair curled and falling loosely to her shoulders. He crossed the room and said, 'Has Misha abandoned you?'

'He'll be back.'

'I'd be amazed if he isn't.'

'Thank you. Are you having fun?'

'Would you believe me if I said I was?'

'No—psychology can be such a curse.'

'Thanks for coming, Irina. It's good to see a friendly face.'

'You've more friends here than you might think, Ramaz.'

Donadze made a non-committal noise. 'I'm expected to circulate,' he said.

'Yes—you are. See you at the church.'

Nakani and several officers from Mtatsminda station had been invited to the reception, but Donadze was trapped by Tamuna's many relatives who were keen to demonstrate their willingness to welcome him to their family and to assess the man she had agreed to marry. He half listened to their incoherent toasts and sipped, without swallowing, the wine they pressed on him.

He was caught by a man with bad breath, whose name he didn't remember, when the room stirred as Tamuna and Lela walked in, their preparations complete and both looking heart-stoppingly gorgeous. The ladies rushed to surround and admire the bride and bridesmaid, touching their satin dresses and clutching their hands to their hearts to express their love and good wishes. The men held back, beaming and holding up their wine glasses in salute.

Being alone with Tamuna during the reception was out

of the question, but eventually Misha declared that it was time to leave. It took an additional thirty minutes to escape the apartment and get into his car for the fast and dangerous drive through the city with a convoy of *makrioni*—close friends and relatives—who blew horns, waved and leaned out their windows as they sped through crowded streets, jumping lanes and ignoring red lights as they invited pedestrians and other drivers to share their joy.

After a few kilometres Arziani dropped his speed, wound up his window and joined the twisting road which would take them to Shindisi. 'Everyone okay?' he asked.

'There should be a law against it,' Donadze said.

'Actually, I think there is.' He glanced in his mirror. 'Okay, girls?'

'Fine,' Lela said.

Donadze turned in his chair to look at Tamuna. 'We'll be there in half an hour,' he said. 'How are you feeling—nervous?'

'Not at the moment. How about you?'

'Never,' he lied.

Weak sunlight was shining on the old church as Donadze and Arziani helped Tamuna and Lela out of the car. They walked up the mound and positioned themselves at the foot of the worn stone steps which led to the wooden doors, where Father Chanturia stood, awaiting their arrival. He smiled and said, 'When you're ready,' then turned and went back into his church.

Tamuna took Donadze's arm. 'Ask me if I'm nervous now,' she said.

'Are you?'

'Very. How about you?'

He squeezed her arm and brushed a loose strand of hair from her face. 'Not anymore,' he said.

They climbed the steps and entered the church. Chanturia stood before them, his hands outstretched in welcome. The light was dim, the air perfumed with incense and alive with whispered prayer. Donadze looked at the witnesses positioned around the frescoed walls: Tamuna's relatives and friends, his mother and Eka, Major Gloveli and Veronika, Jaqeli, officers from his station and Colonel Meskhi with his family. He squeezed Tamuna's arm again. She turned to look at him and he smiled at her.

The ceremony began. Chanturia blessed them and gave them each a lit candle. He then blessed their wedding rings and placed them on their right hands, nodding encouragement as they were exchanged three times. Then, with Arziani and Lela following, he led Donadze and Tamuna to a carpet located in the middle of the church. He joined and tied their hands with ribbon then placed wedding crowns on their heads. Litanies were chanted and prayers recited and the crowns exchanged three times. Chanturia blessed a glass of wine and invited the couple to drink from it. He then untied and removed the ribbon from their hands and lifted the crowns from their heads. The ceremony over, he blessed the newlyweds—Ramaz and Tamuna, joined as husband and wife, united in the eyes of God and His Church.

Donadze lifted Tamuna's head and kissed her. He held her as the witnesses rushed to offer their congratulations. 'Better let me go, Ramaz,' she whispered.

He kissed her once more. 'Never,' he said.

TWENTY-NINE

'Can you come to the village, Ramaz?' Major Gloveli said. 'I'm sorry, I know you're still on leave, but it's important.'

'One minute, Major.' He put his phone on mute and looked across the living room to Tamuna. With his murder investigation ongoing, they had decided to postpone their honeymoon but had taken three days leave to drive to Kakheti to buy their favourite *Tsinandali*, *Mukuzani* and *Kindzmarauli* wines direct from the vineyards.

'We can't go to Kakheti,' she guessed.

'No, we're going. I'll ask Irina to speak to Gloveli.'

'And you'd fret every minute you're away. No, tell Levan it's okay, we can go another time.'

He looked at her to gauge if she was upset or angry.

'I told you it's okay,' she said.

'Thanks. I'm sorry.' He took his phone off mute. 'On my way, Major.'

He called Jaqeli while changing his clothes. She was at

Mtatsminda Station and he told her that he would pick her up in thirty minutes.

She was waiting outside the station entrance. She got in the car and turned to look at him. 'Has Tamuna filed for divorce yet?'

'Don't give her ideas.'

'What's this about, Ramaz?'

'I don't know. It's not something Major Gloveli wanted to discuss on the phone. We'll find out soon enough, I guess.'

They left the city and picked up the road to Shindisi. Snow was falling on the higher ground but the ploughs were operating and keeping the main routes open. 'Early this year,' Jaqeli said. 'Could be a hard winter.'

Gloveli's garden was dusted white. A thin plume of grey smoke spluttered from the chimney stack, dispersed and diluted by the swirling breeze, with only a faint aroma of burning wood drifting down into the garden. Donadze sniffed the air and, with a sharp pang, was taken back to his family home in Abkhazia and the stove his father had tended—his role as head of the household to keep the family safe and warm. The mob which had broken into their home had killed his daughter, displaced his family and broken him as the man he thought he needed to be.

'What is it?' Jaqeli asked.

Donadze shook his head to clear the memory. 'Nothing,' he said. 'Just something from my past.'

The door was opened by Veronika and they stepped into the warmth. Gloveli was sitting at the wooden table with his leg outstretched to ease the pain in his joints.

Father Chanturia was sitting opposite and stood as they

entered the room. 'I'm sorry to drag you away from your wife, Lieutenant,' he said.

'That's okay, Father, she understands. What's this about?'

'Sit down,' Gloveli said, struggling to his feet and pulling a chair out for Jaqeli.

Veronika picked the coffee pot off the stove, poured black, oily liquid into two mugs and placed them in front of Donadze and Jaqeli with a brief smile.

'*Madloba*,' Jaqeli said.

'*Arapris.*'

'Your accent is so much better now,' Jaqeli said, translating to Russian when she received a blank look.

Donadze held the mug to his lips then put it down again when he realised the coffee was too hot to drink. 'What's this about, Father?' he repeated.

'It's about Otar Basilia.'

'Basilia has been charged and will be tried in court. Has something happened?'

'You remember I told you his cousin had spoken to me? Told me about the girls Basilia was supposedly trafficking through Tbilisi?'

'He was testing you. There were no girls. The cousin's name was… Saba?'

Chanturia nodded. 'Saba Khodeli. He was here.'

'In the village?'

'Right here, outside this house—talking to Veronika. And then talking to me—in my church.'

'What did he say to you, Veronika?' Donadze asked.

She hugged herself. 'It was a nice day. I was outside with Lasha. We were—'

'Wait—who's Lasha?'

'A boy in the village. We're friends, maybe a bit more than that…'

'I know Lasha,' Gloveli said. 'He's a good boy. There's no problem with Veronika seeing him.'

'Okay. What happened next, Veronika?'

'We were sitting in the garden when a car with two men pulled up. One was driving, the other one was obviously his boss. I knew *what* they were right away. The boss got out, said hello, told me his name was Saba and that Otar Basilia sent his regards. He knew who I was, of course—even knew who Lasha was. He asked me if I was bored living in the village. He even made a joke—asked if I wouldn't prefer to be back in the apartment in Gali Street. He didn't get a chance to say much more because Levan came out with his shotgun.'

'You would have shot Khodeli in broad daylight—in front of witnesses?' Donadze said.

Gloveli seemed to ponder the question. 'I'm not sure. In any event, I didn't have to. Khodeli's typical of his kind, a coward—he's only brave when intimidating young girls.'

'And priests, apparently,' Chanturia added. 'After Levan scared them off, they came to my church. Saba came in to see me.'

'To do what?'

'He asked for my blessing.'

'And you gave it to him?'

'Of course. I offered to hear his confession as well—although I knew he wouldn't accept that offer.'

'What else.'

'He asked how Keti and Sergo were—by name. Wished

me good luck with Keti's pregnancy.'

Donadze's coffee had cooled sufficiently and he took a sip. 'There's no doubt what this is about is there, Major?'

'Of course not. Basilia sent his cousin to scare Veronika. He also knows Father Chanturia was working for you, Ramaz.'

'Yes, that's clear,' Chanturia said. 'And I suppose it was always likely that he would find out. But he must be worried to send his people here. How do you think the trial will go?'

'We have a strong case. He'll be an old man if he ever gets out of jail,' Donadze said.

'When does it start?'

'In two months. He's out on bail until then.'

'He didn't have a problem posting bail? Wasn't seen as a flight risk?'

'He definitely is a flight risk, but the judge gave him bail, anyway.'

'Do you know this judge—what's his reputation?'

Donadze shook his head. 'I don't know him…'

'I do,' Gloveli said. 'He's corrupt, always has been.'

'I see. That won't make bringing a conviction any easier,' Chanturia said.

'It's a jury trial. There's a limit to how much a corrupt judge can influence their verdict.'

'Maybe…'

There was silence for a moment. 'So what do we do now?' Jaqeli asked.

Gloveli picked up his mug then put it down again when he saw that it was empty. 'None of this make any difference. Veronika is safe, here with me, until the trial starts.'

'What do you think, Veronika? Do you still want to stay here with the Major?'

'Yes. I feel safe with Levan.'

'I can protect *you* as well, Father,' Gloveli said.

Chanturia smiled and stood, straightening his cassock. 'No, Levan. I don't believe you can,' he said.

Donadze answered his phone, '*Gamarjoba*, Colonel.'

'Where are you, Lieutenant?' Colonel Meskhi said.

'Jaqeli and I have been to Shindisi, sir. Basilia sent his cousin to—'

'To intimidate your witnesses—yes, I'd heard. I asked where you are.'

'In my car, sir. On my way home.'

'Cutting your leave short wasn't a good idea, Donadze. But since you've done it, I'd like to see you in my office.'

'Yes, sir. Is this about my investigation?'

'We'll discuss that when you get here,' Meskhi said, then hung up.

Donadze wondered if he was in trouble. He arrived at the Ministry of Internal Affairs' HQ and made his way to Meskhi's office, knocked on the door and pushed it open.

Meskhi and Sandro were sitting at the conference table.

'Come in, Lieutenant, help yourself to coffee,' Meskhi said, pointing to the tray containing the vacuum flask and mugs.

Donadze stood with his back to the other men, stirring sugar into his mug purposefully while trying to guess why he had been summoned.

'You can stop playing for time now, Lieutenant.'

'Sir.' He carried his mug to the conference table and sat beside Sandro.

Meskhi looked between the two men, appearing to appraise them. 'Lieutenant Ramaz Donadze,' he said at last. 'This is Sergeant Nic Brachuli.'

Donadze glanced at Brachuli. His physical presence was as menacing as the first time they had met and he had been told to call him *Sandro*; a big man, dressed in leather and denim, his stubble somehow accentuating the scar which ran—red and ugly— from his ear to his mouth.

'Sergeant,' he said.

Brachuli shook his head but didn't reply.

'Sergeant Brachuli is unhappy that I am withdrawing him from his current role.'

'I'm not unhappy, Colonel—I just think it's crazy that you're doing it now.'

'You've just demonstrated one of the reasons I *am* doing this, Sergeant. Kindly watch your tone when speaking to me.'

Brachuli straightened in his chair. 'Yes, sir. Sorry.'

'And to be clear—I'm not doing anything *now*.' Meskhi turned to Donadze. 'Sergeant Brachuli has been working undercover for almost two years. I'm happy with his performance but it's almost time for him to reintegrate.'

'You want Brachuli to join my investigation, Colonel?'

'No, he is to maintain his current role for now. But your investigation is coming to an end. We have a strong case against Basilia and he'll probably die in jail. Kalmikov and his organisation have also been weakened.' Meskhi paused to choose his words. 'But there will be others—there always are. The question we face, the question *I* face, is this: are there better, more effective ways of dealing with these criminals? Well, I think there are. But I need officers with certain qualities to help me achieve that.' Meskhi looked at the two other men, inviting their questions.

'You think Brachuli and I have these qualities, Colonel?'

'You two don't know each other well but you're more alike than you realise. You're both driven to get results and you're prepared to take risks—personal risks—to do so.' He paused. 'You're also, *unconventional* in your approach.'

'Unconventional, sir?'

'Don't act coy, Donadze. You know what I'm referring to. We work within the law, but there are sometimes grey areas to explore, weaknesses to identify, personalities and frailties to exploit.'

'Yes, sir,' Donadze said. 'We'd be working outside the normal command structure?'

'You would report directly to me.'

'And I'd report to Donadze?' Brachuli asked.

'Yes, Sergeant, you would report to *Lieutenant* Donadze.'

'You said I *would* report to you, sir?'

'Yes, Lieutenant. You both have a choice—there will be no repercussions if either or both of you decline this offer.'

Donadze looked at Brachuli. He shrugged and said, 'Okay.'

'When do we start, Colonel?'

'I'll let you know. You've still got work to do: find the men who killed these girls in Gali Street, find whoever pushed Merab Shonia off that balcony and find who is responsible for the gym bombing and the killings at the drug heist. Then we'll talk. Any further questions?'

Brachuli shook his head.

'No, sir,' Donadze said.

'Good, you're dismissed.'

Donadze stood to leave but Brachuli grabbed his jacket and pulled him back onto his seat. 'Give me ten minutes, I'm still undercover, remember?' he said, standing.

Donadze watched the big man cross the office floor. 'I'll be in touch, Nic.'

Brachuli turned at the door. 'My name's *Sandro*,' he said.

Donadze left Colonel Meskhi's office and returned to his car. Driving home, he thought about his offer and wondered if he had agreed too readily. Meskhi had provided no details but Donadze was not naive; he knew that his precarious work-life balance could only deteriorate and that he should have consulted Tamuna first.

He thought about Nic Brachuli, or *Sandro* as he reminded himself he should be called. Sandro seemed to be unnecessarily antagonistic. Meskhi said that they were alike but Donadze wondered if they were too alike and if that would create problems when working together.

He opened his apartment door and paused for a moment to savour the sounds and smells of family life. He stepped into the living room, kissed his mother and Tamuna then lifted Eka from her baby bouncer.

'We kept her up for you,' Tamuna said. 'Do you want to give her a bottle and put her down?'

'Do you want Daddy to give you your milk, *chemo gogona*?' he cooed.

'Well, Ramaz, the sooner you give the child her bottle, the sooner we can all eat,' his mother said, not quite managing to stifle her smile. She bustled away to warm the milk and hand the bottle to her son, pausing to kiss her granddaughter goodnight before turning her attention to finishing preparation of their evening meal.

Donadze carried Eka into their bedroom and sat in the easy chair which Tamuna had located beside the cot. He needlessly checked the temperature of the milk then settled the baby in the crook of his arm to give her the bottle. 'Is that good, *chemo tkbilo*?' he said as the little girl stared back at him, her eyes growing heavy. He spoke to her in monotone, telling her how wonderful she was and how much she was loved. She stopped drinking and seemed to have fallen asleep but stirred when Donadze tried to take the teat out of her mouth. 'Still hungry?' he murmured, letting her finish the milk. A minute or two later, he watched as the baby's mouth fell open, releasing the teat. He held her a moment longer then stood and laid her on the cot. Donadze looked down on his daughter as she slept. 'I wish you could have met your Aunt Ana,' he said. 'One day, when you're a big girl, I'll tell you all about her.' He gazed at his baby a moment longer, then composing himself, returned to the living room.

Tamuna smiled at him. 'Aren't you glad you got home in time?'

'Yes. I am.'

'Good. Eka likes it when her daddy's here.'

'Well, we're all glad that Ramaz is here—that means we can eat at a civilised time for a change,' his mother said as she opened the oven door to remove the food.

Donadze was hungry and the meal was delicious. His mother ate little and insisted on tidying up afterwards. They left her to wash and dry the dishes by hand—her preferred method—and sat together on the settee watching television while he had a second glass of *Mukuzani* and Tamuna sipped tea. His mother finished wiping down the work surfaces and joined them for a few minutes before declaring herself to be very tired and taking herself to bed.

There was little of interest on the television and Donadze turned it off. 'Sorry,' he said. 'This isn't the honeymoon you dreamed of.'

'Maybe not.' Tamuna put her cup down and snuggled into him. 'But it's what I signed up for so I'm not complaining.'

'You'll tell me when I get it wrong?'

'You can be sure of that, Donadze,' she said.

THIRTY

Donadze reached to his dash to answer his phone, '*Gamarjoba*, Major.' There was no response. 'Major?' he said again.

He barely recognised Gloveli's tight, strangulated voice, 'The bastards…'

'Tell me what's happened, Major,' he demanded.

Gloveli took a moment to answer, 'It's Father Chanturia…'

'Chanturia! What—'

'Dead. They got to him Ramaz. He was right, we couldn't keep him safe…'

'We're on our way. Where should we go?'

Gloveli let out a long sigh before answering, his voice flat, 'On the road, this side of Kojori. I'll see you there.'

Donadze used his lights and siren to force his way through the tight city traffic then took the road to Shindisi, swinging round corners on worn suspension and bullying other vehicles out of his way.

Jaqeli braced herself with one hand on the door rest, the other on the dash. 'Careful, Ramaz,' she said.

He raced through the village and continued on the same road for about ten minutes until he saw the police barriers ahead. An ambulance and two marked cars blocked off the road in both directions.

He drew up behind the first of the cars and he and Jaqeli got out. He showed his identification to the uniformed officer who opened the barrier to let them through. A small hatchback car was parked by the side of the road, empty, with both of its front doors open. Donadze remembered seeing it outside the Chanturia family home.

Gloveli was standing beside a uniformed officer, both of them smoking. He looked at Donadze, shook his head and took a long, deep drag of his cigarette, its tip glowing red as soothing nicotine was drawn deep into his lungs. Donadze hadn't seen him smoke in more than a year.

The officer took a last draw of his own cigarette then threw it down and ground it into the asphalt. 'This way, Lieutenant,' he said and led Donadze and Jaqeli down the slope which fell away from the side of the road.

Chanturia was lying on his side near a patch of thorny scrub. He was wearing denims, a white shirt, padded jacket and trainers. The blood that had emptied from the bullet holes in his chest had soaked through his clothes and blackened the surrounding soil.

'Oh, my God,' Jaqeli's said, her face draining of colour.

'Do you want to wait in the car, Irina?' Donadze asked.

'No, I'm okay…'

Donadze turned to the officer. 'Has the forensic examiner been called?'

'Yes, Natia Gagua, I think—she should be here soon.'

Donadze nodded then spoke to Jaqeli. 'I don't want to move the body or touch anything until Natia gets here. But let's try to figure out what happened.'

Jaqeli nodded then forced her stare away from Chanturia's body to look over the surrounding area. 'That's his car up there.' She turned to the officer. 'Was he on his own?'

'No, his wife put the call in. She was here with her son when we arrived. She's at home now.'

'So, he was driving with his family but stopped here for some reason.' She looked at the soft earth. 'There's two sets of footprints, someone was with him—so he was probably forced down here.'

'What else?'

'You don't have to distract me, Ramaz—I'm okay now.'

'I'm not trying to distract you—I need your help to figure this out. What else can you see?'

'That looks like a trail of blood going back up the slope. It can't have come from Father Chanturia so it must be from whoever shot him.'

'Yes. I think there's been a struggle. Maybe Chanturia tried to take the gun and it went off. Or maybe he had his own weapon, a knife possibly, and was able to use it before being shot.'

'Why do you think he was brought down here and not just killed on the road?'

'I don't know. Maybe to spare his wife and son, some kind of warped sense of decency, possibly. But I don't think this was the spot the killer would have chosen.' Donadze pointed to a wooded area a short distance downhill. 'I think they were probably heading for these trees. I also doubt he had planned shooting Chanturia in the chest—head shots are usually more reliable. Maybe he stumbled and Chanturia saw an opportunity.'

'Chanturia must have realised what was going to happen. Why did he stop his car?'

'To save his family, of course. You're too young to remember the carjackings we used to have in Georgia. A fast car would pull alongside the target vehicle and the driver would be shown an AK-47. He had a choice: stop or be stopped by the Kalashnikov. Back then, of course, it was usually just the car that was stolen.'

'So, another vehicle and an accomplice were involved.'

'I think so, Keti can confirm it.' He turned to the officer. 'Thanks. Cover the body until Gagua arrives but be careful not to contaminate the evidence.'

The officer bristled. 'This isn't my first crime scene, Lieutenant.'

Prima donna, Donadze thought but said, 'Okay, I understand—but please do as I ask.'

They walked back up the slope. Gloveli was standing by the roadside, his head down and smoking another cigarette.

'Please take the Major to my car, Irina,' he said.

Gloveli looked up, seemed to consider taking a last draw from his cigarette but dropped it instead. She stepped forward and took his arm. 'Please come with me, Major.'

Donadze took a last look down the slope and around the area within the barriers then walked to his car.

Gloveli was sitting in the front passenger seat, staring

out the window. Jaqeli sat in the back, pale and oblivious to the tears welling in her eyes.

'Professional hit,' Donadze stated.

Gloveli startled. 'Obviously,' he said.

'Otar Basilia?'

'Yes, of course.'

'Because of me?'

'No, not because of you, Donadze. Because Father Chanturia wanted to do the right thing. He knew—better than you—the risk he was taking.' He sighed. 'Don't beat yourself up, Ramaz. You were doing your job.'

'Thanks, Major.' He paused. 'Any witnesses?'

Gloveli frowned. 'Just Keti, as far as I know.'

'Why do you think Chanturia was out here?'

'Why wouldn't he be? Maybe he was taking his family for a day out. Maybe they were just shopping. He probably thought he was safe staying away from Tbilisi. Ask Keti if you think it's important.'

'Yes, I'll do that.'

Gloveli's eyes blazed. 'You're a cold one, Donadze. Aren't you angry? Don't you want to find these bastards and make them pay?'

Donadze blinked, Gloveli's ferocious words stinging. 'Yes, I'm angry. This was the man who helped me bring a case against Basilia. The man who, only a few days ago, married Tamuna and me. The man I should have kept safe. But being angry won't help me find his killers. And you should understand that, Major—because it was you who taught me.'

Gloveli reached over and patted Donadze's knee. 'You're right. I'm sorry, Ramaz. Very sorry. I'm old, seen too much death, the misery it brings.' He shook his head. 'Keti, little Sergo—what will this do to them?'

Donadze started his engine. He glanced in his mirror. 'Are you okay, Irina?'

She nodded, 'Yes, I'm okay.'

'Good. I've got an idea.'

'Welcome back, Lieutenant, Detective. I'm afraid Mr Basilia's not in the Casino at this moment. Did you make an appointment?'

Donadze hadn't remembered the security manager's name and he glanced at the tag pinned to his jacket—Tengo Sakhokia. 'It's you we want to speak to, Tengo. Your office—let's go.'

'Now? We're terribly busy. Could you come back, say in about two hours?'

'Why don't we make it less busy, shut you down for the night?' Donadze turned to Jaqeli. 'What do you think might be going on here, Detective? Drugs, counterfeit booze, prostitution?'

'All that and more, Lieutenant,' she said.

'And it looks to me like Mr Sakhokia is in charge—so that makes him responsible, doesn't it?'

'Definitely, Lieutenant. In fact—'

'All right!' He took a deep breath. 'All right, I'll make time—please follow me.'

They climbed the central stairway and turned right at the top, walking away from Otar Basilia's office. Sakhokia stopped and used a key attached to a chain to unlock his door. Donadze and Jaqeli followed him in. His office was just big enough to hold a small desk with a single chair behind it.

Sakhokia sat on the edge of the desk. 'All right, tell me what this is about,' he said, attempting to establish his authority.

Donadze stepped in close, forcing him to lean back over his desk. 'This is very important to me, Tengo. I want an answer to one question and I want it to be truthful. I'll know from your face if it isn't and I won't be happy. Do you understand?'

He watched Sakhokia's mouth tighten in resolve. 'I know what you're thinking, Tengo. That anything we could do to you would be nothing compared to what Basilia will do if you talk. And normally, you'd be right. But I told you already—this is very important to me.' He looked closely at the security manager's face and could tell he wasn't convinced yet. 'Detective, stand outside, no one gets in.'

'Are you sure, Lieutenant?' Jaqeli said, picking up on her role.

'Outside!' Donadze snapped.

He waited until the office door was closed then leaned closer to Sakhokia. 'It's just you and me now, Tengo. I could make this difficult for you—but let's try something else first. Answer my question and you won't see me again. Don't answer or lie and Basilia will get to hear that you *did* talk to me. He might believe your version of events—but do you want to take that risk?'

Sakhokia coloured and sweat prickled his forehead. 'I might not even know what it is you're looking for…'

'Let's see, then. My question is: if one of Basilia's men

296

needed medical treatment but couldn't go to hospital, where *would* he go?'

Donadze could see recognition flicker on the security manager's face. 'See, you do know,' he said.

Sakhokia hesitated. 'There's a doctor Mr Basilia uses. I don't know if he still has a licence, but he does have a surgery. He's good with wounds, setting bones, abortions for the girls…'

Donadze smiled. 'That's great, Tengo, I knew you'd want to help.' He dropped his smile. 'Give me his name and address.'

Donadze thought that Father Chanturia's killer was losing blood and required immediate medical care. He hoped that he and his accomplice had gone to the location the security manager had provided and that they were still there. If so, he knew that they would be armed and likely to resist arrest. He told Jaqeli to call for tactical support and raced his car across the city using his lights and siren, shutting them down when he was two blocks away and coasting the remaining distance at legal speeds.

The address he had been given was a low level apartment block on Fridoni Street. There was nothing on the outside to indicate that it contained a doctor's surgery. Cars were parked along the street, including a black Audi saloon which had been left on the pavement.

'We're in the right place,' Jaqeli said, pointing to a trail of brown-red spots leading from the car to the entrance.

The tactical unit hadn't arrived yet. Donadze checked

his watch. 'Wait here,' he said.

He unholstered his pistol and held it loosely by his side as he entered the apartment block. The building was neglected: large sections of plasterwork had crumbled, the stairs were worn and handrails hung off the walls, most of the lights were out and the air was dank. He waited until his eyes had adjusted to the dim light then confirmed that the front entrance was the only way in or out. The first level properties appeared to be unoccupied but the blood trail led to a door on the second level. He saw light shining through its peephole and, stepping close, heard people talking inside. The distinctive tang of disinfectant oozing past the badly-fitted door confirmed he had the right location and he turned and walked back down the stairs and out into the street.

The tactical unit had arrived, ten menacing men—black, booted, masked and armed with carbines, pistols and knives. They stood in a tight line close to the apartment building to avoid detection from the windows above.

'You can stand down now, Donadze,' one said in a high-pitched voice.

Donadze realised he was still holding his pistol and returned it to its holster. 'Why would we do that, George?'

Losava pulled off his mask and stepped closer, emboldened by the men at his back. '*You* requested *my* help,' he hissed, his mouth tight. 'Stand down and let me get this done.'

Jaqeli touched his arm. 'Let them do their job, Ramaz.'

'Give her a radio,' Losava snapped, his eyes fixed on Donadze.

An officer stepped forward and handed Jaqeli a radio,

positioning himself so that his commander couldn't see his conspiratorial wink.

'Thanks,' she said with a straight face.

Losava turned to look at his men, a smirk playing on his lips, satisfied that he had established himself as the alpha male. He turned back to Donadze. 'I'll let you know when it's safe to come up.' He stepped to the edge of the pavement and looked up at the apartment windows. 'What do we have here?'

Donadze shrugged. 'Second level, first door on the left—you'll see the blood trail going in. Not sure how many there are inside: a doctor of sorts, maybe a nurse. I'm hoping there'll be two more that we want to take into custody. One's injured—seriously, I think. They'll be armed, possibly with automatic weapons.' He paused. 'Be careful—they killed a priest—they've got nothing to lose.'

Losava smiled. 'Sit in your car, keep low with your lights turned off. I'll let you know when it's safe to come up,' he repeated then turned his back to issue orders to his men.

Donadze and Jaqeli returned to the car. '*I'll let you know when it's safe to come up…*' she mimicked.

'Captain Marvel?'

'No, definitely Mighty Mouse.'

They sat low in their seats, observing the apartment windows and the tactical unit going into action. Radio communications were minimal. Losava sent two officers into the building. A minute later they reported that they were in position and deploying their devices to see and hear into the apartment: a fibre optic camera and a wall-contact microphone. Losava allowed them a few minutes to gather information on the apartment's occupants before sending two more officers in. Several minutes later, they reported that a charge had been set on the door. Losava pulled on his mask and led the rest of his team through the entrance.

'Should be soon,' Donadze said.

Another minute passed before the street was shaken by a muffled explosion followed by the clamour of men running into the apartment, bawling orders. An intensely loud bang sounded soon after and a blinding flash simultaneously lit up the apartment windows.

The uproar was soon over. Donadze realised that he had been holding his breath and slowly let it out.

'That was impressive,' Jaqeli said.

'Yes,' he admitted. 'Did you hear gunfire?'

'No, there wasn't any.'

Losava came on the radio a moment later. 'Location secure, four arrests, all personnel stand-down, stand-down.'

'Come on,' Donadze said, opening his door.

'Shouldn't we wait until Losava tells us it's safe.'

'He's not going to do that, it's part of the game he likes to play.'

They got out the car and walked back to the building. One of Losava's men had taken up position at the entrance.

'How did it go?' Jaqeli asked.

'Nothing to it,' he said, his eyes crinkling above his mask. 'There's an ambulance on its way for one of your men though—his ID says Khodeli. Is that who you're looking for?'

'Saba Khodeli, yes.'

'Well, he looks pretty bad to me—a bullet in the gut— and it's not one of ours either.'

Donadze and Jaqeli took the stairs to the second level.

The apartment's steel door was hanging by a single hinge, its paint blistered and blackened by the explosive charge which had blown it open. They made way for the six officers trooping out then stepped into the apartment. It was small: a kitchen, bedroom and a lounge which doubled as a surgery. Two men and a woman were sitting on the floor, their hands and feet secured with cable-ties. A third man was lying on a grubby surgical cot, stripped to his underpants, semi-conscious and deathly-pale, a gauze-sponge dressing failing to staunch the flow of blood from his abdomen.

Losava was in a corner of the room talking into his phone while two of his men watched over the prisoners. He ended his call. 'Just updating Colonel Meskhi,' he said.

'Why am I not surprised?'

'Teamwork, you should try it sometime, Donadze,' he said, grinning at his officers and inviting them to join the fun.

Jaqeli put her hand on Donadze's back as he was about to retort. 'Thanks for your help, Lieutenant,' she said.

'No problem, Detective. Let me know if there's anything else I can do for you,' he said, grinning at his men again. He made a show of consulting his military-style wristwatch. 'I think you should be able to handle things now, Donadze.' He snapped his fingers at his men and followed them out of the apartment.

'Watch you don't trip over that ego, George,' Donadze muttered to his back.

Donadze parked outside the Chanturia family's home. He

hesitated before getting out of the car, unsure of how he would be received by the murdered priest's wife.

'It'll be alright, Ramaz,' Jaqeli said.

They walked through the small garden and Jaqeli knocked on the door.

'Come in,' they heard Keti call out.

Sergo shifted and hid his face in his mother's arms when he saw them enter.

'I'm sorry, he won't let me put him down,' Keti said, looking down on her son.

Jaqeli crossed the room and stroked the little boy's hair then bent and kissed the top of his head. He burrowed deeper into his mother's arms.

'How is he?' Donadze asked.

'He's two, he doesn't understand. But he senses something sad has happened to his daddy.'

Donadze didn't answer. He had spoken with bereaved families many times and had seen how young children were often affected by emotions they couldn't comprehend.

'I've given my statement,' Keti said.

'That's not why we're here. We wanted to see you, check if you have any questions for us, ask if there's anything you need.'

'Thank you—there's nothing I need.'

'How are you, Keti?' Jaqeli asked.

She gave them a sad smile. 'I'll be okay. I have to be— for his sake. And for his sister's when she arrives.'

'Do you know what you're going to do?' Jaqeli asked.

'I haven't really thought about it, yet. I'd like to stay here, in Shindisi, but that might not be possible.'

'Keti,' Donadze said. 'I hope you know—I never

wanted this to happen. I knew that there would be risks but I wouldn't have gone ahead with any of it if I'd known that Zurab would be hurt.'

'*Zurab* would be hurt? That's the first time I've heard you call him by his first name. It's always been *Father Chanturia* up to now. You never really liked him did you, Lieutenant? He said you were always reserved, something from your own past, he thought.'

Donadze paused before speaking, 'I'm sorry I gave that impression. It wasn't to do with not liking Zurab. I did come to like him and to respect him—greatly. But, yes, there is something in my past and it involved a priest—it's something I need to come to terms with…'

'Well, don't worry. He knew what he was doing. I knew as well. I went along with it because it was important to him. It's strange but, somehow, I've always known that I wouldn't keep him forever. He was always reckless, didn't care enough about himself, I think. No, Lieutenant, he chose his path—you needn't hold yourself responsible.'

'It's probably no consolation, Keti,' Jaqeli said. 'But the men responsible for Zurab's death—and for much more—they'll spend the rest of their lives in jail. These men—parasites, predators—they brought misery to countless people: young girls taken from their homes and sold as slaves, drugs, prostitution, blackmail, corruption—all backed up with violence and murder. The world is going to be a better place—thanks to your husband.'

'Good for the world…' Keti said, stroking her son's face and head.

Donadze thought that Jaqeli was subdued as they returned to Mtatsminda Station. 'Are you okay, Irina?' he asked.

She shook her head. 'I'm not sure that I am. What happened to the Chanturia family—it's so sad, so depressing. I know I'll get over it, but what about the next time and the time after that?'

Donadze didn't answer immediately, knowing that her question was largely rhetorical. They drove in silence for a few minutes. 'You know, Irina, this life doesn't suit everyone,' he said. 'Some cope better than others, but it can be destructive and there are other ways to make a difference.'

'Who says I want to make a difference?'

'I do. When we started working together, you told me you joined the police to help smash their glass ceiling. But you want more than that. I've seen how you work, how you relate to people, how you get them to open up. You *do* want to help and you *do* want to make a difference. That makes you a good detective—better than I'll ever be.'

Jaqeli turned to look at him, smiled, then laughed. 'God, you're good,' she said. 'I almost believed you.'

Donadze didn't return her smile. 'You should believe me—because it's true.'

She sat back in her seat. 'Maybe. But thanks anyway, Ramaz—it helped.'

'Anytime.'

The station desk officer seemed keen to greet them. 'This has been a bit of a surprise, Lieutenant,' he said.

'What is?'

'You don't know? I'm sorry if I spoke out of turn,' he said, looking sly.

They walked to the detectives' bureau. Captain Nakani was in his office with Arziani, packing personal items into a plastic box.

'Ramaz, Irina…' Arziani said, his smile hesitant.

Nakani looked up but didn't speak.

'What's happening, Captain.'

Nakani still didn't speak and Donadze looked at Arziani. 'Captain Nakani is taking on a new assignment, Ramaz,' he said.

'I'm sorry, Captain. I didn't know.'

'Strategic Communications Lead,' Nakani said at last. 'Colonel Meskhi insisted.'

'Head Office? That sounds like he needs someone good to handle our messaging.'

Nakani dropped into his chair. 'No, it means he thinks I'm not up to a command role. Not right now, anyway.'

'Did the Colonel say that?'

'He didn't have to. I've been a bit down lately, you saw that yourself, Ramaz. But I was coping, or at least *I* thought so. But Meskhi made me report to the doctor—I'm clinically depressed, apparently.'

'But that's treatable, isn't it?' Donadze said.

Nakani shrugged. 'So the doctor says. He's organising counselling and behavioural therapy—no pills yet. Oh, and I've got to swim three times a week.'

'That sounds positive. You'll get over this, Captain.'

'Of course I will. But look on the bright side, eh, Ramaz? This means you'll be getting your command sooner than you expected.'

'Actually, no,' Arziani said. 'Colonel Meskhi spoke to me earlier today. He's putting me in temporary command.'

Nakani laughed and shook his head. 'So, I'm not the only one getting bad news.' He stood and shook hands with the other three, wished them good luck then picked up his box and left.

'Sorry, Ramaz,' Arziani said. 'I don't know why Colonel Meskhi did that.'

'I do—you're the best person for the job and he knows it.' He paused. 'We've still got a case to solve. Any changes you want to make, Misha?'

'No.'

'Good, then let's get back to work.'

THIRTY-ONE

The murder of a priest was both rare and shocking and, as the police had not yet released information on probable motive, media speculation had created unwelcome interest in the funeral. Chanturia was to be buried in Shindisi and Tamuna had offered to accompany Donadze to the service, leaving Eka with her grandmother. Donadze slowed his car at the police check point outside the village but was recognised by the uniformed officer and waved on. The check point had been established to turn away the grief tourists who had not known Chanturia in life but who nevertheless felt compelled to attend his funeral and demonstrate the depth of their loss to the world.

Donadze continued driving to Gloveli's house and parked by his garden gate. It was a good day to bury the dead; the sky was clear, the air dry and crisp and the sun offered warm solace to the grieving. Veronika opened the door, kissed Donadze on his cheek and hugged Tamuna. The small house felt crowded. Gloveli was stretching his arthritic leg by the stove and struggled to stand as they entered, Arziani and Jaqeli had already arrived and a young man, who Donadze didn't recognise, was standing in the middle of the room, holding two bottles of wine and looking awkward.

'Put them on the table, Lasha,' Gloveli said.

Veronika crossed the room to take Lasha's arm and, speaking in faltering Georgian, introduced him to Donadze and Tamuna.

'Ah, so *this* is Lasha,' Donadze said, watching colour rise in the young man's face.

'We've got about an hour,' Gloveli said. 'We'll have some food and something to drink. Lasha, pour the wine please.'

'Have you seen Keti today?' Donadze asked.

Gloveli shook his head. 'Veronika and I went over but we didn't stay long. Her sister's here for a few days. She'll be okay.'

'How does she feel, you know—about how her husband died?'

'How he died helping you, you mean? Don't worry, she doesn't hold you responsible.'

'That's what she told me, but it's not that easy.'

'I didn't *say* it's easy.' He waited until everyone had been given wine then held up his glass to the light and sniffed its contents. 'Father Zurab Chanturia,' he toasted, then tipped the wine into his mouth.

'Father Chanturia,' the others repeated.

Lasha helped Veronika to carry food from the cooking area and lay it on the table.

'How's my goddaughter?' Gloveli asked Tamuna.

'She's wonderful—told me she can't wait to see you again, Levan,' she joked.

'Well, I want to see her as well so get that husband of yours to bring her up here.'

Tamuna laughed and said, 'What will you do after the trial, Veronika?'

She glanced at Lasha. 'It depends…'

Gloveli frowned. 'You could do much worse than marry a Georgian man. We're famous for our good looks and virility.'

'Really?' Tamuna and Jaqeli said together then suppressed their laughter as they remembered the solemnity of the occasion.

The time passed pleasantly and Gloveli said, 'We should go.'

Keti had not wanted an extended wake and her husband's body had been taken from his home to his church. A priest, sent from Tbilisi for temporary cover, had conducted the funeral service. Outside, a group of mourners crowded around the hearse, its rear door open, ready to receive the casket. A pickup truck had been positioned in front of the hearse, its occupants' role to spread flowers in the path of the deceased as the procession made its way to the graveyard.

The mourners fell silent as the open casket was carried from the church. Chanturia had been dressed in his priest's cassock, his arms across his chest, a silver crucifix placed in his hands, his dark hair and beard stark against the white cushion his head rested upon.

Keti walked a few paces behind the casket. She looked beautiful but fragile, dressed in black and noticeably pregnant, her young son—worryingly silent—clinging to her neck. A slightly older woman, her sister, walked beside her. The casket was carried down the church steps and manoeuvred into the hearse. A moment passed then the cars' engines were started and the procession departed for the graveyard, the hearse spluttering fumes into the path of the mourners who walked behind it on the rough, broken ground.

The graveyard was less than a kilometre away but Donadze dropped back alongside Gloveli in case the old man needed help on the walk. They passed through rusted gates and joined the press of people tightly positioned around the fresh excavation, a scar on a scrappy piece of ground. There was no family burial plot but Chanturia's grave would, in time, be demarcated by a low, polished marble wall and a headstone, laser-etched with his image. Space would be allowed for his family to gather on Easter Sundays; to leave offerings, splash wine onto the soil in which he rested and to eat a meal in his presence, thereby ensuring that Zurab Chanturia—the man they had loved— would never be forgotten.

The internment was brief, the gravediggers maintaining a respectful distance while the casket was closed and lowered into the rich, dark soil. The priest completed the service and Keti knelt to help her son drop a small bunch of blue flowers into the grave. She closed her eyes to pray then picked Sergo up and carried him away, his arms tight around her neck.

The mourners slowly drifted away, allowing the gravediggers to lift their shovels and fill the excavation with the soil they had removed the day before.

The Chanturia family's garden was too small to hold the funeral *supra* and long folding tables and benches had been set up in the grounds of one of the village's wealthier residents. Places had been set for around three hundred, with cold drinks, jugs of wine, cheese, bread, salad and cold meats already on the tables when the mourners arrived.

Donadze sat with Tamuna, Gloveli and Veronika and made polite conversation with the strangers who sat with them.

'Lieutenant,' he heard a voice from behind and turned to see Mrs Alasania and her son, Luca, behind him.

He extracted himself from the bench and lent his arm to support Gloveli as he also got to his feet. He stood, feeling awkward, while Gloveli hugged the woman and patted Luca's face.

'How are you Mrs Alasania?' Donadze asked.

'We're okay, thanks.'

'And your husband?'

'He'll be okay as well. He knows what he did was wrong— but he also knows that we'll always be here for him.'

'He didn't *do* anything wrong...' Luca mumbled, kicking the soil at his feet, his head down.

She pulled her son to him and held him for a moment, her eyes closed. 'He did, Luca, but your father is still a good man.' She smiled at Gloveli. 'Levan told me that you'd helped Nodar as much as you were able, Lieutenant—thank you.'

'It wasn't enough...'

He watched while Mrs Alasania took her son away then sat back down. 'You'll keep an eye on them, Major?'

'Yes, of course I will.' He patted his friend's knee. 'It was more than enough…'

The speeches and toasts began, the men standing while the few women not serving remained seated on the benches. Donadze was restless and keen to leave. He glanced at his watch and wondered how much longer he would have to stay.

'You can go now, Donadze,' Gloveli said.

He looked at his watch again. 'Are you sure, I don't want to appear rude.'

'No, that's okay. Keti will be glad that you and Tamuna came.' He smiled at Veronika. 'Are you meeting Lasha this evening?'

'No, it's alright, I'll wait and go home with you.'

'Do me a favour, Ramaz—take Veronika to Lasha's house, she'll show you the way. It's not far and Tamuna can look after me while you're gone.'

'Thanks, Major.' He and Veronika stood to leave then sat down again as another toast was proposed. It eventually concluded and he made a pretence of swallowing his wine then stood and stepped over the bench.

The sun was setting and throwing long shadows as Donadze followed Veronika along a dusty path.

'So, tell me about Lasha,' he said, in Russian. 'Do you think you might be staying in Georgia a bit longer than planned?'

Veronika smiled, 'We'll see.'

As they walked, Donadze sensed that someone was following behind. He unbuttoned his jacket but continued making small talk as the path they were taking led onto the main village street. They rounded the corner of a closed store and Donadze took Veronika by the arm and moved her into the shadows of the doorway.

'What are—'

He held a finger to his mouth, waited until she nodded her understanding, then released her arm and positioned himself at the corner they had just turned. Controlling his breathing, he eased his pistol from its holster and waited.

A tall, dark figure turned the corner. 'Stop! Get your hands in the air!' Donadze ordered, his pistol held outstretched in front of him.

The man stopped walking. 'God, Donadze. What do you think you're doing?'

'Sandro? Why are you here?'

'Why? To see you of course. I knew you'd be at the funeral and I followed you from that *supra*. I need to talk to you.'

Donadze returned his pistol to its holster. 'Couldn't you have called?'

'I don't think so.'

'It's okay, Veronika. I know this man,' Donadze called to her in Russian.

She stepped out from the shadows.

'Where does Lasha live?' he asked.

'Just along the road, one hundred metres.'

'Okay. Go straight there. I'll watch you from here.'

'Are you sure?' she said, sounding worried.

'Lieutenant Donadze and I have important business to discuss,' Sandro snapped. 'Do as he said. Go home now.'

Veronika didn't reply and Donadze turned to see her holding her hands to her mouth. 'It's him...' she said, her voice small and tight.

'What's she talking about, Donadze? We don't have time for this.'

'It's him, the man from the apartment—the man who let me leave. That's what he said to me before…'

Donadze sensed movement and turned quickly. Sandro was nearly on him. He instinctively drove his straight fingers into the bigger man's throat then stepped close and used right and left elbow strikes to drive him back. A cut had opened on Sandro's forehead and blood was streaming into his right eye. He roughly wiped the blood away and staggered forward. Donadze twisted and threw a low kick, slamming his shin into Sandro's thigh, numbing his muscle and almost making him collapse. He allowed Sandro to stumble forward again then, bending his knees for greatest force, brought his elbow up fast to connect with his protruding chin, knocking him out. Sandro fell badly and blood flowed from his burst nose and split forehead. Breathing heavily, Donadze searched the prone figure for weapons then took his phone from his pocket and dialled Mtatsminda Station. He looked at Sandro, sprawled and bloody on the ground, then turned to Veronika as he waited for the call to connect. 'Let's hope we got that one right,' he said.

THIRTY-TWO

Donadze observed Nic Brachuli, or *Sandro*, as he still thought of him, through the interview room's one-way glass panel. He was sitting upright on one of the four chairs which were bolted to the floor around a small metal table, his stare fixed, disconcertingly, on the panel, seemingly aware that he was being watched. A doctor had sutured his lacerated forehead and given him anti-inflammatory pain killers for his broken nose, but his face was still swollen, with deep, dark bruising under his eyes.

Brachuli squirmed on his chair and seemed to consider rising when Colonel Meskhi and Jaqeli entered the room. She took a chair facing him but Meskhi remained standing by the door for a moment, staring at the disgraced officer. He shook his head slightly then sat beside Jaqeli, trying and failing to push the chair back to allow more space for his long legs.

'Is there anything you need, Sergeant?' Meskhi said.

Brachuli hesitated then shook his head.

'Let's get started, then.'

Jaqeli activated the recording equipment and everyone in the room identified themselves.

Meskhi let the silence build, then said, 'Was it my fault, Sergeant? Did I leave you in too long?'

Brachuli sat back in his chair and smiled but said nothing.

'Character, possibly. Or lack of it. You're not the first officer I've sent undercover. What was it that turned *you*— was it money?'

Donadze watched as Brachuli sat with his hands on the table, clenching and unclenching his fists.

'So, not money. Lifestyle then—girls, gambling, drugs?'

Brachuli's mouth tightened and he sat straight in his chair, his stare fixed on Meskhi.

'Is this uncomfortable for you, Sergeant? You're not used to people speaking to you like this? Was it about power, then? You're a big man, quite strong I assume. You like to scare people, don't you, have them under your control, hurt them when they don't do as you say.'

Brachuli spoke for the first time, 'No,' he said, his voice tight.

'No? Then what was it?'

'I know what you're doing, Meskhi.'

'You're still a police officer, Sergeant,' Meskhi snapped. 'You will address me as *sir* or *Colonel*.' He waited a moment then spoke more gently, 'You should have come to me. I could have helped.'

Brachuli shook his head, 'You couldn't help. I got in too deep, too soon. Once you start, it's impossible to stop.'

Meskhi paused a moment then said, 'Tell me about Gali Street.'

'I can't go to jail…'

'You have to know that you *will* go to jail. But your cooperation may sit well with the Prosecutor. That's all I can promise you.'

'No.' He pointed at Donadze through the glass panel. 'Get him to leave something in my cell: a rope, a belt. It'll be better for you, better for me. I'm not going to jail.'

'Don't judge others by your own standards, Brachuli. That's not going to happen. Tell me about Gali Street.'

Brachuli put his elbows on the table and rubbed his temples, thinking. After a moment, he seemed to come to a decision and nodded.

'Gali Street; you were acting under orders from Anzor Kalmikov?' Meskhi asked.

'Yes.'

'Direct orders?'

'No, his son told me what to do.'

'Did he tell you that the orders came from his father.'

'Of course he did. Badri was a weasel—I wouldn't have done anything on his authority.'

'Was that the first time you'd killed for Kalmikov?'

'I didn't kill anyone—not then anyway.'

'It wasn't you who shot the girls?'

'It was one of Kalmikov's thugs—Dima Tugushi.'

Meskhi looked at Jaqeli and she nodded—Tugushi was known to her.

'Why were you at Gali Street if Tugushi was to do the killings?'

Brachuli snorted. 'Kalmikov wanted it to be clean…'

'Clean? Two innocent girls killed?'

'That's what he wanted.'

Meskhi took a sip of water. 'Tell me about the girl on the stairs.'

'Veronika Boyko…'

'You let her go—why?'

Brachuli shrugged. 'Why? I don't know. There wasn't any need to kill her, I suppose.'

'But then there was a need. Is that why you went to Shindisi—to get rid of a witness?'

'Yes. But I'd given her a chance—she should have gone back to Ukraine when I told her to. She didn't have to go to the police.'

'Was it your decision to kill her or were you acting under orders?'

'Kalmikov told me to do it, he was mad that I'd let her get away the first time. Told me to clean up my fucking mess.'

Meskhi turned to Jaqeli. 'Tell us about Merab Shonia,' she said.

Brachuli laughed. 'Is she the best you've got, *Colonel*. Is it a quota thing? Got to let the little girls have their turn?'

'Maybe it is, Nic,' Jaqeli said. 'But this *little girl* is asking the questions and it's you who's going to answer them. Tell me about Merab Shonia.'

'Let's cut this short, *darling*. Yes, I threw Shonia off your balcony.'

'Why did you do that, Nic?'

'Why not just say *thanks*, Detective?'

'Shonia was going to kill me and you intervened—why?'

Brachuli paused before answering. 'Because you're police—and so am I. Or part of me still is, I suppose.'

'But Shonia worked on his own, didn't he? Why did he let you come with him?'

'I told him Kalmikov wanted me along because of what you are—a detective. Shonia believed that—he didn't have any reason to be suspicious.'

'And did you—'

'We've got enough for now, Detective,' Meskhi interrupted. 'Take the Sergeant's written statement and charge him.' He stood and looked down on Brachuli. 'I don't want to spend any more time in this man's company.' He shook his head once more and left the interview room.

There was a knock on the door of the observation room. Donadze stood and opened it. 'Bring in Anzor Kalmikov and Dima Tugushi,' Meskhi said. 'Charge them with the Gali Street murders.'

Donadze was surprised when the liaison officer told him that his request for an audience had been granted. He had been summoned to the Ministry of Internal Affairs HO and had met with Captain Nakani in his new role as Communications Lead.

'Thanks for setting this up, Bagrat,' he said.

'I'd like to take the credit, but His Holiness seems intrigued, he didn't take much persuading, apparently.'

Nakani had sat, smiling as the liaison officer had

coached Donadze on the protocol he should follow when meeting His Holiness and Beatitude, Ilia II—the Catholicos-Patriarch of All Georgia and Archbishop of Tbilisi.

'I'm sure Lieutenant Donadze won't let us down,' Nakani said.

Donadze had been instructed to wear dress uniform for the audience. He put his on, looked at himself in the bedroom mirror, then changed into a suit with white shirt and tie.

'You're looking very handsome, *Ramazi*,' his mother said as he entered the living room. 'Are you doing something nice today?'

'I'm meeting the Patriarch,' he said.

'Well, you don't have to tell me if you'd rather not,' she huffed.

'No, I really am meeting—'

'I'll explain later,' Tamuna interrupted. She stood to kiss him, 'You'd better get going—good luck, Ramaz.'

'I'll give His Holiness your regards,' he said to his mother, a staunch believer, who gaped as she realised her son truly was to meet the head of her Church.

Donadze drove to the Avlabari district and parked close to the gated entrance of Sameba Cathedral. Erected on Elia Hill and one of the largest religious buildings in the world, the cathedral dominated the city, the faithful only having to look up to its golden dome and cross to be reminded of the power and the glory of God. It was inaugurated in 2004 and a source of pride for most, but Donadze was ambivalent, believing that the money required for its construction could have been put to better use. *And it's not like Georgia needed another church*, he thought. He walked past stalls selling over-priced fruit to tourists, stooping to give coins to the old women begging outside the gates and nodding his thanks as he received their blessings in return.

Donadze was nervous. He thought about the man he was about to meet. Elected as Patriarch in 1977 and now in his late-eighties, Ilia had led the Georgian Orthodox Church during the collapse of the Soviet Union and during all of Georgia's subsequent, traumatic history. Despite dated and inflammatory pronouncements on homosexuality and his poorly-received call to restore the monarchy, he continued to be the most trusted and revered figure in the country. Donadze knew that he was privileged to have been granted an audience.

He walked into the cathedral's grounds and paused to orientate himself. He knew from earlier sight-seeing visits that the complex which faced him across the flower-lined plaza and imposing stairway included numerous chapels, a monastery and a stand-alone bell tower. He had, however, been instructed to report to the Patriarch's residence and, glancing at his watch, made his way to its entrance.

A tough looking security guard stood beside a podium and rope barrier. Donadze identified himself and told the guard that he had been granted an audience with His Holiness. The guard checked a clipboard then reached behind the podium to retrieve his radio. He spoke into it and listened to the reply. 'Wait there,' he said.

A few minutes later a priest came to the barrier. 'Please come with me, Lieutenant,' he said.

The guard lifted the rope and Donadze followed the priest along a dim corridor, their feet ringing on the tiled floor. The walls were hung with painted, wooden icons depicting Christ, Mary, the saints, angels and miscellaneous religious scenes—reminding visitors, if that were necessary, that they were indeed in a holy place. They reached the end of the corridor and the priest opened a simple wooden door and stood aside to let Donadze enter.

'Please take a seat, Lieutenant. His Holiness will join you shortly.'

After the gloom of the corridor, the room was surprisingly well lit. It was dominated by a huge fresco depicting Mary holding the baby Jesus while surrounded by angels and other haloed figures. Two throne-like chairs were located in front of the fresco: one for the Patriarch and one for the prominent individuals he occasionally met. Donadze did not fall into that category and he took one of the chairs which had been set out in a semi-circle around a white, marble-topped table.

Ten minutes passed before a different door opened. Donadze stood as the Patriarch entered, taking small, careful steps and clutching the arm of the same priest. Ilia was stooped and shrunken with age. He wore a black cassock with no headwear, his white hair tied in a bun behind his head, his beard full and long.

Donadze hadn't considered how he would greet the Patriarch but instinctively held out his crossed hands and requested a blessing. Ilia made the sign of the cross then placed his hand in Donadze's to allow him to kiss the hand that had touched the Body and Blood of our Lord. He blessed Donadze with a prayer then said in a thin voice, 'Please sit down.'

He waited until Ilia had been helped into his chair then

sat beside him.

'His Holiness will allow you fifteen minutes,' the priest said before taking up his position behind the Patriarch.

Ilia looked at Donadze inquisitively.

'Your Holiness,' Donadze said. 'I asked to see you today to keep a promise I made to one of your priests. I want you to know who that priest—who that man—truly was.' He looked up to see the Patriarch nodding encouragement. 'Your Holiness,' he continued, 'Father Zurab Chanturia was a criminal who turned from crime and found redemption in helping others, in helping me. He was a good man, a man our Church and our people can be proud of.'

The Patriarch appraised Donadze for a moment. 'Please continue, Lieutenant,' he said.

'Your Holiness, I want to tell you how Father Chanturia lived and how he died—as a true Christian warrior. For him, there was no way back.'

End

ACKNOWLEDGMENTS

I'm deeply grateful to the following people for their kind and generous support in helping me write this book:

My wife, *Jacqui Liddle*, my greatest supporter and most persistent critic, who read and re-read every scene and advised what worked and what didn't. She was usually right.

My beta reviewers for their informed and immensely valuable feedback: *Annette Rose, Fiona Macdonald, Tom Stewart, Mary Puttock, Douglas King, Brian McKinstry*, and my daughter, *Kirsty McMillan*.

I am again indebted to *G.R. Halliday,* author of the DI Monica Kennedy series and to *Marion Todd*, author of the DI Clare Mackay series. Both took time from their busy writing schedules to offer me advice and encouragement.

My Georgian friends, *Sandro Chitadze* and *Nino Meladze* warrant special mention. Both reviewed my draft manuscript and offered invaluable feedback as well as keeping me right on aspects of Georgian life and culture, thereby ensuring, I hope, a high level of authenticity. The fact that they were able to do that in their third language, English, is amazing.

Ruth Sherpa was an incredible proofreader, scanning all my writing to track down and eliminate fugitive typos and other annoying mistakes.

Lastly, I would like to thank *Bob McDevitt*, Director of the Bloody Scotland Festival for running what is probably Scotland's most prestigious crime writing festival and his organisation's shortlisting of my previous novel, *No Harm Done* for the best debut novel of 2021. Receiving external validation of my writing was extremely motivating and helped me complete this book.

ABOUT THE AUTHOR

Alistair Liddle is a former ships' captain, business advisor and operations manager in the oil and gas industry. No Way Back is the second novel in his series featuring Lieutenant Ramaz Donadze.

Alistair is married with two grown children and a granddaughter. His interests, when not writing, include travel, walking, cooking, playing guitar badly with The Grumps and—most recently—swimming in Scotland's beautiful lochs.

After a lifetime of travel, Alistair has settled in Stirling, Scotland.

ajliddlebooks.com

AUTHOR'S NOTE

Georgia's geographical location and long history have shaped its unique culture and I hope I've described that accurately in this book. There are, however, a few deliberate inconsistencies introduced to make the story more understandable for non-Georgian readers e.g. it is usual to address a man as *Batono Ramaz* (Mr Ramaz) rather than *Mr Donadze*.

I was privileged to have lived and worked in the Republic of Georgia for more than fifteen years. This country has given me so much and I'm genuinely happy to be able to raise its profile, however limited, in my writing. It's a wonderful country and you should visit if you can— I'll see you there!

Printed in Great Britain
by Amazon